Right Royal Friend

One of Scotland's best-loved authors, Nigel Tranter
wrote more than ninety novels on Scottish history. He
died at the age of ninety in January 2000.

'Fishing and hawking, porridge and game, the smell of
peat and bitter cold Highland nights: a page from any
of Nigel Tranter's Scottish historical novels evokes the
lie of the land better than a library of history books'
The Times

'Through his imaginative dialogue, he provides a voice
for Scotland's heroes' *Scotland on Sunday*

'He has a burning respect for the spirit of history and
deploys his characters with mastery' *Observer*

'A magnificent teller of tales' *Glasgow Herald*

'Tranter's popularity lies in his knack of making
historical events immediate and exciting'
Historical Novels Review

NIGEL TRANTER

Right Royal Friend

CORONET BOOKS
Hodder & Stoughton

First published in Great Britain in 2003 by Hodder and Stoughton
A division of Hodder Headline
This paperback edition first published in 2004
by Hodder and Stoughton
A Coronet paperback

A CIP catalogue record for this title is
available from the British Library

ISBN 0 340 82357 7

Typeset in Monotype Sabon by Palimpsest Book Production Limited,
Polmont, Stirlingshire

Printed and bound by
Mackays of Chatham Ltd, Chatham, Kent

Hodder and Stoughton
A division of Hodder Headline
338 Euston Road
London NW1 3BH

Principal Characters in order of appearance

David Murray: Second son of Sir Andrew Murray of Arngask.

James the Sixth, King of Scots: Son of Mary Queen of Scots.

Esmé Stewart, Duke of Lennox: Cousin of the monarch.

John Erskine, Master of Mar: Foster brother of the monarch.

William, Lord Ruthven: High Treasurer. Later Earl of Gowrie.

Francis Stewart, Earl of Bothwell: Son of a bastard of James the Fifth.

Master George Buchanan: Great Protestant Reformer. Tutor to the monarch.

Patrick, Master of Gray: Heir to the sixth Lord Gray. Courtier.

Elizabeth Beaton: Daughter of David Beaton of Creich.

Sir William Murray of Tulllibardine: Powerful laird, kinsman of David.

John, 6th Earl of Mar: Former guardian of the king.

James Hamilton, Earl of Arran: Chancellor of the realm.

Colin Campbell, Earl of Argyll: High Justiciar.

Master Andrew Melville: Principal of St Andrews University. Presbyterian divine.

Sir Thomas Randolph: English envoy at the Scottish court.

Sir John Maitland: Vice-Chancellor and Keeper of the Great Seal.

Princess Anne of Denmark: Sister of King Christian.

King Christian: King of Denmark.

Alexander, 6th Lord Home: Great Borders noble.

George Gordon, 6th Earl of Huntly: Great northern Catholic noble.

James Stewart, 6th Earl of Moray: The "Bonnie Earl". Protestant.

Henry, Duke of Rothesay: Infant son of King James. Heir to the throne.

George Heriot: Edinburgh goldsmith and money-lender.

John Graham, 3rd Earl of Montrose: The new Chancellor.

Master David Black: Prominent Presbyterian divine.

Charles Stewart: Second son of the king, later King Charles the First.

Sir Robert Cecil: English Secretary of State, later Lord Burghley

Elizabeth Tudor: Queen of England.

Part One

I

David Murray looked glum. Why was his brother always so pleased with himself, so superior, knowing it all, ever correcting him? He was barely two years older than himself, after all. Heir to their father, yes; but that did not make him a genius, any sort of hero and marvel to be looked up to. Why must he preach to him about the deer, as over so much else? Andrew might choose to ride, chasing the creatures on horseback, with the servants. But he preferred to stalk the stags alone, afoot, even on his belly, up on the heathery heights, creep up to them, using every inch of cover to get within range of his crossbow, keeping the wind in his favour. Admittedly the chances were usually in the deer's favour, with more often than not the creatures drifting off unharmed. But this of contest was good, and great the satisfaction when he won. Even though somehow he had to get the carcase back down to the castle, taking a garron part of the way beforehand, to drag it. All part of the challenge.

But Dand declared that it was not playing the laird, unsuitable. Who did he think he was? Playing the laird! They might be lairds in some fashion, although their father was the real laird, Sir Andrew Murray of Arngask and Kippo and Conland. He did not need to play the laird – he was one, as all recognised, a baron indeed. Dand and himself could be termed that he supposed, if they so desired, Andrew of this Balvaird, he of Gospertie, however small a lairdship that might be, really only a large farm. But who were they seeking to impress? Everybody knew who and what they were. Dand was daft in all this, as in much else.

David Murray, as he grumbled thus to himself, was sitting in a stable within the forecourt of Balvaird Castle, feathering his crossbow arrows preparatory to having an attempt at stags on the Binn Hills. Balvaird was the main seat of the barony of Arngask in Glen Farg, none so far south-east of Perth, on the southern edge of great Strathearn, a good place in which to live, with the fishing in the Farg and the Earn, the stalking and hunting in its hills and woodlands, the fertile ground around between them and the village of Abernethy, and Scone, with its abbey and coronation-place just to the north of St John's Town of Perth. None the less Dand envied their Tullibardine Murray kin's territory a dozen miles or so to the west, never failing to remind friends and neighbours of that illustrious connection, although it was four generations back since their line sprang from that lofty family, a younger son wedding the Barclay heiress of Arngask and winning this barony and lands. Moreover, their own mother, Lady Janet, was the daughter of the Graham Earl of Montrose, which was surely every bit as notable as was Tullibardine.

David, it was to be feared, had a concern about his brother Dand, however well he got on with his two younger brothers Robert and Patrick.

His feathering, like his musings, was interrupted by the noisy arrival of the said Rob and Pat, aged seventeen and fifteen respectively, who had managed to net four brown trout down where the Binn Burn joined the River Farg, which they deemed a feat indeed, netting trout no easy matter. David was much appreciative, even though he preferred angling with line and hook. They discussed the pros and cons of this fishing sport. It was in fact rather similar to the question of stalking as distinct from hunting and driving deer, a matter of challenge

4

rather than of quantity of gain and catch obtained, angling more of a test.

They were still arguing when a servitor came to inform them that the midday meal was ready, and they trooped up to the lesser hall of the castle.

Sir Andrew was away visiting his property of Conland. The Lady Janet, a handsome woman, shook her fair head over her sons and their arguments, anxious not to seem to take sides but, David imagined, favouring *his* attitude rather than Dand's.

The elder brother was heavily built, taller than David and of a confident carriage symbolising his assured view of life, aged twenty-three years. As they sat down to eat, he began to declaim against the folly of creeping about on hands and knees in the heather after single deer. But his mother halted him with her quiet authority. They had more vital matters to talk on than the killing of deer, she said.

"Your father is much concerned. There is dispute in the governance of the realm, with our young King James only in his fourteenth year. And much of the trouble is centred near enough to Balvaird to be all but on our doorstep, with Esmé, Duke of Lennox, the king's cousin and closest minister, at odds with William, Lord Ruthven, the High Treasurer. And the duke lives at Methven Castle, only six miles from Perth on the west, and Ruthven Castle is still nearer, just over two. They mislike each other. It was Lord Ruthven who all but forced our poor Queen Mary, while imprisoned by his Lords of the Congregation in Lochleven Castle, also none so far from here, to sign a declaration of her abdication of the throne, and the succession of her infant son James, so that he became monarch at the age of one year. And now she is a prisoner in England, where she went seeking Elizabeth Tudor's aid—"

"We know all this, Mother," Dand interrupted. "At least, *I* do. What is new?"

"It is this of money. Siller. The treasury of the realm is empty. Has been for long, with this of warfare between the Protestant lords and the Catholic queen. And Ruthven is the treasurer. To gain influence over King Jamie he has been putting his own money into the coffers, for he is very rich. And now he accuses the Duke of Lennox of using it for his own advantage. Your father does not believe this. Lennox is using the money to pay for men and arms, to be in a position to threaten England at the border, this to gain the release of poor Queen Mary, a worthy cause your father holds. Lennox, made High Chamberlain, was a Catholic when he came from France, but has declared himself Protestant now, while Ruthven is fiercely Presbyterian. It is a grievous situation."

"Need it greatly concern us?" Dand demanded.

"Could it result in war?" David wondered. "I mean, not war with England necessarily, but warfare nearer home? Between these two, Lennox and Ruthven?"

"Perhaps not outright war. But fighting, yes. The Protestant Lords of the Congregation are very ready to draw sword. My own father, your grandsire, has discovered that! He and *your* father fear something of the sort. Control of the young king is, of course, the vital matter. Lennox holds the youth's affections. But Ruthven holds the purse-strings."

The two younger brothers were bored with all this talk of power and influence, and were eager to recount their success with the netting of the trout. Their mother, patient, heeded them, although Dand scoffed.

The meal over, David was anxious to be off on his deer-stalking. It was mid-October, and the sun was beginning to set early. So although he had no great distance to go, time was important. He left the others, and hurried off to the stable for his crossbow and arrows, and out through the gatehouse arch for the paddock where the horses grazed, to collect his garron.

The Binn Hill and its subsidiary, Castle Law, lay just a mile north of Balvaird. Mounting, he rode over the gently rising ground to reach the hillfoots, crossing the Binn Burn. It was open woodland here, birches and occasional gnarled pine. There was an empty herd's cottage at Cattochill, where he left the garron, tethered, and climbed to a slight knoll nearby where he could scan the heights ahead.

The Binn Hill was no great mountain, rising to under a thousand feet, but it was quite a favoured haunt of the red deer, especially the stags, the females, the hinds, usually preferring the lower ground and woodlands with their calves at this season. The hills, heather-clad, rose in the shape of a rough crescent, the Binn Hill itself at the southern end, overlooking Glen Farg, with the escarpment curving round to the Castle Law, somewhat lower at the north, so called because of an ancient Pictish fort's ramparts sited on it. Between, there was a great corrie, or hollow, divided by a slight rocky ridge; and it was in these two dips that the deer were apt to be found.

Gazing up, David could see no sign of life, other than a buzzard hovering – but from here he could survey only one flank of the nearest corrie, and not at all into the further one. So there was no call for disappointment yet.

He was testing the breeze. It was light and from almost due west. That was fairly satisfactory, and important, for the deer had the keenest of nostrils, and could scent a man, downwind, at half a mile. So he must keep well to the east, which meant the lower ground, and use every possible scrap of cover, bluff, fold in the surface, burn channel and outcrop to hide his ascent. He was seeking to reach that rocky ridge between the two corries, from which he ought to be able to spy out the prospects.

But he spotted a group of three stags up near the top of the southernmost corrie before ever he reached his ridge, half a mile up. No doubt they could see him; but it was their noses that the creatures relied upon more than their eyes, and his movement down on the lower ground would not necessarily distract them. At any rate, they were still there when he gained the rocks of the dividing broken bank where the cover became ample.

Now he was in a position to survey the other northern corrie. And there, higher, a single stag grazed.

Panting a little with his crouching climbing, David calculated and assessed. Best, almost certainly, to go for the one rather than the trio, for three noses and six eyes were probably more effective at warning. His route, then, to that lone creature? It was fully four hundred yards away. And sure range for a crossbow arrow, to kill not just to wound, was no more than seventy yards. So, much manoeuvring, crawling and dodging.

As far as he could, from this position, he worked out his route. He decided that, by continuing on up this ridge for quite some way, he could reach a point where another, lesser rising in the corrie side would give him quite a lot of cover for some one hundred and fifty yards. After that, it would just be hands and knees, or even belly progress. He would have to watch, however, that climbing this ridge, out of sight of the lone stag, he did not alarm the three in the other corrie. These might flee in a northerly direction and give his quarry warning.

It demanded a very careful ascent further. Fortunately there was much outcropping rock to hide behind and among; but he had to ensure that all this covered his progress from both sides.

When he got as far as he reckoned to be advantageous, he started the really taxing part of his endeavour. Although it was only some one hundred and fifty yards further to the animal, to get within range unseen would demand fully three times that amount of ground to keep out of sight, by using any and every hollow and dip and obstacle of the intervening area. Fastening his arrows securely to his person and holding his bow carefully so that its taut string did not catch on protuberances, even heather stems, he took a deep breath and started off on his zigzag approach. At this stage he could see only the antlers of his quarry, and was pleased to note that they were very fine ones. There was great pride in winning the best stag's antlers, twelve points or tines being the very height of achievement. These seemed to be scarcely that, but he thought ten points, which was sufficiently notable. He must win this one.

The last crawl took much time, and David was worried that the stag might well move off meantime, even though not alarmed by his approach. But when, at length, he got to an outcrop from which he had thought he might be within range, it was to find that the beast had actually moved somewhat nearer. Clearly it was totally unaware of his presence.

Hiding behind his rock, he fitted an arrow to his bow and, flat on his stomach, wriggled half round. He had to raise himself on his elbows to take aim. Fortunately there was heather high enough to hide him. But even so the stag sensed movement, lifted its head high from its grazing, to gaze. That stance, momentary as it was, provided the marksman with just what he needed. A hand's-breadth behind the shoulder he aimed. His finger released the bowstring catch. The arrow flew and struck, plunging deep.

The deer reared, snorting, staggered and its hindquarters collapsed. It rolled over and lay twitching, shot through the heart.

David rose, much gratified that his eye had not failed him. A hand's-breadth behind the shoulder usually reached the heart. Merely to wound a beast was to be deplored, for the creature could possibly still run for miles, and ought to be pursued and finished off, if at all possible. But there was no question of that here. This animal was dead. And, yes, it had ten white-tipped points projecting from its antlers.

David drew his dirk and, kneeling, proceeded to slit open the stag's belly, to perform the necessary if unpleasant task of disembowelling, and pulling out the steaming and bubbling entrails, all part of the ritual. A great heap they made, still moving. But their weight had to be got rid of, for he was eventually going to have to lift that carcase on to his garron's back, no easy accomplishment for a single man. But David was a practised hand at it, and knew the routine. He extracted that arrow.

Now, down for the garron. He would wash his hands and wrists at the first burn he came to.

It was none so far to the tethered horse, however lengthy had seemed his so cautious ascent. He loosed it, and led it back up the hill, no need for cover now.

Hoisting that stag up on to the garron's back demanded not only muscular strength but care and indeed knowledge; for a beast of this size could weigh as much as twelve stone. David had a rope hitched to the horse's saddle, and taking this, he tied the stag's hind legs together at the hooves, then threw the other end up over the garron's back, to go round and pull mightily, this to raise the hindquarters of the carcase up so far, the horse sidling and tossing its head. He tied that rope taut to the saddle.

Now for the really difficult part. He had to go and hoist the heavy forequarters and the dangling antlered head of his kill up, to get it all on to the horse, so that the forelegs could be placed beside the hind, and there tied together, leaving the head and horns hanging over on the other side. It took all David's strength to achieve this; but he had done it frequently before, and despite the side-stepping of the garron he managed it. That animal had been through all this before also, to be sure.

Panting but thankful, he began to lead the laden beast downhill. This all was why brother Dand scoffed at stalking deer as suitable only for peasants and servitors.

Down David went, with his ten-pointer, well pleased with himself.

With that burden to carry, which must not fall off the garron and have to be lifted on again, he chose a different route for his homeward journey, one somewhat longer but offering easier ground to cover, heading further eastwards and into the Abernethy Glen, where there was a track for herding cattle down to the Earn and the Perth markets. A couple of miles of this and he would swing off for Balvaird.

He was halfway along this, and in open woodland, when he heard the noises, shoutings and calls and the jingle of harness. And rounding a bend of the track, he came on the cause of it, quite a large company of horsemen and led pack-horses, these last laden with the carcases of many deer, headed by more sportsmen but of a different sort, his brother Dand's sort.

Or not quite that, for these were very differently clad from the laird of Arngask's sons, clearly high and mighty folk, with many followers. David eyed them wonderingly. He had never seen the like, and on Balvaird land. These were going in the opposite direction from his own, and they had to pass each other.

It was only when they came near that he realised that, at the head of this column, riding beside a handsome man of middle years on a fine horse was a mere youth, little more than a boy indeed – and if the man was good-looking the youth was not, however richly if untidily he was clad. And this youngster was staring and pointing, not at David but at the stag on the garron's back, with its dangling head and antlers.

"See!" he cried thickly. "See yon heid! The tines o' it! Is it ten? Aye, ten, Esmé."

"So it is, Sire," the older man agreed. "A fine beast. Where from, I wonder?"

"A deal finer than ocht *we* hae!" the youth declared, pressing forward for a closer look, quite ignoring David. "Johnnie! Johnnie Mar – see it. We've no' seen the like this whilie."

"Aye, and gralloched," another youth, slightly older than the first, pointed out. "Gralloched a'ready. And just the yin, Sire. Some hunter's done richt weel."

It was that double use of the word sire that had David blinking and the more alert. Only monarchs, so far as he knew, were entitled to be so styled. Could it be so? Could this gangling youth with his slobbery speech be really James Stewart, King of Scots? David knew that he was young, yes, but . . .

The said youth now dismounted, to come up and inspect the stag's head, actually touching the points projecting from the main horns. He seemed to be knock-kneed and dribbled as he spoke, but his eyes were keen enough. He turned these on David now.

"Whae's kill is this?" he demanded.

"Mine," he was told simply.

"Hech – yours? How, where?"

David turned to point. "Up there. On the Binn Hill. On the north corrie."

"You? Alone?"

"Alone, yes. One can only stalk deer alone or in small numbers."

"Stalk? You mean creep and crawl? Like some brute-beast?"

That certainly reminded David of Dand's remarks, almost identical. But he was not going to accept it, even from a monarch, if so this one was. "Like a man who sets out to win stags on the high tops!" he amended.

"Eh? And who are you?"

"I am David Murray." And shrugging, he added, "Of Gospertie." That last a little doubtfully. He did not often use the style.

The handsome man and the other youth had dismounted now also. "Are you related to Murray of Arngask?" the former asked. "I know him. We are near his land here, Sire."

"You are *on* it," David told them. "He is my father."

"Ah. So that is it. And you hunt thus, afoot?"

"If you can call it hunting, sir. I name it otherwise. Stalking."

"We hae only won beasts wi' but puir heids this day," the youth declared. "In Pitmedden Forest."

"Only the younger and lesser stags go down to the low ground, with the hinds and calves. The older and better ones stay on the high ground, see you."

"Address His Grace as Sire, Murray," the older man instructed, but not haughtily. "I am Lennox. And this is the Master of Mar. We have come from the hunting palace of Falkland. And go to my house of Methven."

James Stewart was still admiring the stag's head. "I havena done the like," he said. "Sought the beasts afoot. And high. It's no' the way it's done by us."

"Perhaps not, Sire. But if you seek fine heads . . ." David wondered at the way the young monarch spoke, in the broad Scots tongue.

"Aye. Stalk, you name it? Creeping? Hae you heard o' this stalking, Johnnie?"

"No. Not o' deer. Stalk is to step oot right stiffly, is it no'?"

The Master of Mar spoke in the same fashion as the young monarch.

"Could you teach us the way o' it?"

Swallowing, David eyed them all. "If, if so you wished, Sire. But . . ."

"No' the noo. Murray, is it? No' the noo. We're for Methven the noo. But, come you to Falkland. I'm aye at Falkland when I'm no' at Stirling. Come you there and teach us, Murray man."

"If so you wish, Sire." David, astonished at it all as he was, could not bring himself to refer to the youth as Your Grace. Anything less graceful than James Stewart would be hard to imagine.

"Aye. You can teach us on yon Lomond Hills. There'll be beasts there? On the tops?"

"I would think so, Sire." A thought struck him. "Would you wish to have *this* head, Sire? I could give you it, if so you wished."

"You'd dae that? Gie it to me? It's a bonny heid."

"I shall bring it to Falkland, Sire."

"I'll be at Methven for twa nichts, mind. After that . . ."

The king mounted his fine horse, the duke and the Master of Mar nodded, and the cavalcade moved off northwards, leaving David to go in the other direction.

His father was back from Conland when he reached Balvaird with his booty, and his exciting tale to tell, Dand frowning and seeking to play it all down as of no account. But Sir Andrew was quite impressed, seeing it as a notable introduction to their young monarch, especially this of going to Falkland and teaching the king to stalk deer. Who knew whither this might lead? Lady Janet was equally complimentary.

Falkland, with its royal hunting-seat, lay to the east some seven miles, in Fothriff, the western section of Fife, beneath the twin Lomond Hills known as the Paps of Fife. Their Balvaird was in fact placed all but on the border of the shires of Fife, Perth and not far from that of Stirling, a quite useful situation in the centre of Lowland Scotland, and quite close to the Highland Line. But it did mean that the Murrays could be pulled in various directions in their allegiances and alliances.

Before skinning and handing over the stag as venison for the pot, David cut off the head. He would boil this in a cauldron of water to get the flesh off the bone, and then saw the skull with the antlers into a shield-shaped trophy to present to the king.

2

David waited a week before he set off for Falkland. Presumably the king would still be there. If not, it was only an hour's ride each way. Whether, of course, the royal youth would remember the incident in Abernethy Glen and still wanted to be taught to stalk remained to be seen.

He went by the low hills of Kincraigie over into Fife, to reach the community of Strathmiglo and Cash, and so south by east, with the green Lomond Hills, much higher, rising before him, two rounded breast-shaped summits a full mile apart. Falkland lay at the foot of the eastern hill, among woodland.

When he arrived, it was to be told by the keeper of the establishment that the king was out hunting, this his favourite pastime. Whether, when he returned, he would be too tired to do any stalking training was questionable.

As he waited, David inspected the lower slopes of that East Lomond Hill, climbing as far up as the first of the heather, the bracken lower not being apt for stalking, and not the haunt of stags. He kept his eye on the approaches to Falkland and, after an hour or so, he saw the hunting-party coming riding out of the woodland. He turned back.

He found King James watching the dead deer being unloaded from the garrons' backs, and shaking his head over the short and unspiked antlers of the one staggie they seemed to have slain, however many hinds and calves they had. There was no sign of the Duke of Lennox today, but young Johnnie of Mar was with the monarch.

When James saw David, he grinned and pointed. "Hey, Murray man – nae proud heid to hang on the wa', this!" he gabbled. "Nary a single tine! Och, the deer here are no' what they were."

"The good beasts will be up on the high ground, Sire, I am sure." David went over to his own garron nearby and untied the antlered shield of skull, to bring it to the monarch. "Yours, Sire."

"Hech! Hech!" James exclaimed, taking it admiringly. "You've scoured it. Bonny! But it's no' mine. I canna claim it. Yours it is. What's your name, man?"

"David, Sire. David Murray of Gospertie, second son of Arngask."

"Ooh, aye – Arngask. Sir Andrew they tell me. Davie Murray. Whaur's Gos . . . ? What you ca' it?"

"Gospertie, Sire. It's a small property east of Balvaird. No great place."

The king was fondling the white-tipped tines of his new possession. "I'll hae to hang this separate frae mine," he said. "Come you within, Davie. I'll show you. And we'll hae a drink to celebrate. This, no' these we've gotten this day. We hadna great sport. Johnnie, Johnnie Mar – see this that Davie Murray's gien me."

They went into the hunting-lodge, although it was more than that, but scarcely a palace, however favourite a royal residence. Its corridor walls were hung with the heads of both stags and roe-buck, but only one caught David's eye, an eight-pointer, and not a particularly widespread one, another standard of excellence, the wider the better. David's antlers measured fully twenty-eight inches apart. He did not comment.

"We'll hae to win one to match this, eh Johnnie?"

"No' sae easy, Jamie." The other youth shook his head, then remembered that he was not alone with the monarch, and added a Sire. Obviously they were close friends these two. Of course the Earl of Mar was hereditary keeper of the royal castle of Stirling, James's home.

In a lesser hall a table was laid with food and drink, already being sampled by some of the sportsmen.

"I can dae wi' this, I can so!" the king declared, and he reached out for a flagon, to pour no little of its contents into a tankard. David recognised, by the colour of the liquor, that it was whisky, not wine. Similar quantities were handed over to Johnnie Mar and himself.

Surprised indeed that a thirteen-year-old should drink whisky at all, moreover in this quantity, David merely sipped a little and laid his tankard down; but the other two quaffed deeply, appreciatively.

James reached for a bannock spread with honey, and bit into it. "Noo – this o' the stalking," he said. "What's to dae? And when? And whaur?" At least that is what he probably said, the royal mouth full.

"You will try it now, Sire? Good. Then we will go up the hill some way, to where the heather grows, beyond the bracken. And I will show you."

"How far?"

"Half a mile, no more."

The king looked doubtful, finished the whisky in his tankard, shrugged, and led the way out, shouting to the grooms for his horse. Apparently half a mile was further than he was prepared to walk, with those knock-kneed legs.

So it was riding up the East Lomond for the three of them.

When they reached heather they dismounted, and David led the two fine mounts and his rougher garron some way ahead to a slight mound, where he tethered them loosely, and came back.

"We will think of them as stags," he said. "And we now

have to approach them unseen. And, what is important, with the wind from them to us." He had tested the breeze. "So, from here will not serve. We must work round yonder, to begin."

He took the pair a good two hundred yards downwind, James making but a poor, stumbling progress over the heather and broken ground, mumbling objections.

David halted them behind a rise. "This will do. Now we move as silently as may be, up to where this levels off. But before that, we get down on our hands and knees to approach the summit, for there we will be in sight of the horses." He led the way.

Well before the crest, if that it could be called, he sank to the ground among the purple heather stems, and signed to the others to do likewise.

"Now, pick your way on, using everything that will hide you as you reach the top, hollows and dips even though they are damp on your knees. Work this way and that. Part the heather carefully, not to make any rustling sound. Stags have good ears. Slowly, like this." He crept up a little way, but not in any straight line.

He heard his liege-lord muttering behind, and called for silence. This was no occasion for respectful speech, siring and the like.

Near the levelling-off of the little ridge, David sank down flat on his stomach, and told the pair behind to do the same. Now their persons were over-topped by the heather stems. These had to be parted most heedfully for passage through them, without making any obvious disturbance, a very deliberate process, and devious, to deal with the inequalities of the ground. More grumblings from the rear. At one stage, looking back, he saw the king raised on hands and knees again, and promptly ordered him belly-down.

On that minor summit they could see the horses, but

believed that they would remain invisible to the beasts. David waited for the others to come alongside.

"Now is the main pass," he whispered. "We are by no means within range for the crossbows. We must get almost one hundred yards closer. And without being seen. So we pick our route, this way and that. Even if we have to backtrack here and there. We peer, without raising head and shoulders overmuch, to plan the best routes. You have it? Belly-down work, almost all of it."

"It's a right trauchle, this," James objected.

"You would not grouse if those were antlered stags," he was told, with a belated Sire to soften the rebuke. "And deer have much better noses and ears than have horses."

They crept on, by three differing courses, more than once David, watching the others' advances, calling out that they were insufficiently hidden. He emphasised that there was but little straight advancing in stalking, cover being the essential requirement. He pointed to another slight rise, half right, and said that he judged that would be within fair range of the horses.

They were all panting now with this unaccustomed crawling motion on stomachs.

At last they were all on the eminence, and saw their mounts only some fifty or sixty yards away, and duly upwind. David now went through the motions of levelling a crossbow, fitting an arrow, aiming and shooting, this without raising himself sufficiently to be evident to the quarry. He told the others to go through the motions of doing likewise.

Deep-breathing, they did.

Then they could all rise, first lesson taught, however haltingly it had been learned.

"Och, man Davie – yon's a fair scunner!" James declared. "And I'm a' wet! It would hae to be a right fine beast to be worth yon draggle."

"That is stalking, Sire. And rewarding enough if you want fine antlered stags. You will not get them otherwise, I fear."

"It's nane sae bad, Jamie," Johnnie Mar said.

"There is, to be sure, still the gralloching to be done and getting the carcase down to the low ground and a garron," David added.

"Och, we could send men up to dae that," the monarch asserted.

They went over to the horses, to mount and ride off.

"Is that enough of stalking for you, Sire?" David wondered.

"Na, na, I'll gie it a go," he was told. "If there's nae other way to win the guid heids. When will we hae a try at it?"

"That is for you to say, Sire. But where? I am none so sure that there will be good stags up on these Lomond Hills. There is scarce enough heather, I think. There may be, but I would suggest that for your first try we go somewhere that I know will give you sport. For your first attempt, I say."

"Aye, maybe. Where?"

"Well, there are usually beasts on our own Binn Hill at Balvaird. Where I got that ten-pointer. Or we could go further. Across Earn and into the higher hills."

"Och, where yon one came frae will do fine."

"Very well. Do you wish to have another lesson at the learning of it, first?"

"Na, na, I hae the meat o' it, Davie. The morn's morn we'll come to you at Balvaird. If the weather's no' bad. Yon would be ill work with the rain! And I hae to go back to Stirling soon. The man Ruthven, the High Treasurer, is at me to go and sign papers. Aye he's at that."

"Very well, Sire."

They parted, after an offer of more liquor, the visitor recognising that the previous imbibing had not seemed to have any observable effect on the young monarch.

Back at Balvaird they were not a little intrigued to learn that they were to have a visit from the King of Scots, even Dand being uncritical although he did suggest that this stalking was demeaning for a monarch.

Later, David went off to spy out the situation on the Binn Hill and Castle Law. He was glad to see three stags still on the high ground, whether the same three or otherwise, these in the northern corrie. It looked as though there was likely to be sport for them on the morrow.

James and Johnnie Mar duly arrived next noon-day at Balvaird, and there was some delay in setting off for the Binn Hill, for the Lady Janet felt bound to offer the royal visitor and friend hospitality, only the wine of which the king accepted. They had brought with them a number of horsed attendants and garrons, which seemed unduly optimistic. Indeed, David recommended that all but two men and two garrons were left behind at the castle, for a fairly large party would be conspicuous from the high ground, and might well alarm any deer that saw them.

David pointed out that the breeze today was almost due westerly, with little of south in it, which was all to the good in the circumstances; that is, if the stags still grazed the corrie as they had been doing the day before.

James was volubly if wetly animated, and was clearly assuming success, which had David warning was by no means to be taken for granted, and that deer-stalking was very often uproductive of aught but challenge. There might well be no beasts on the hill this day although there had been yesterday. With a west wind, a due easterly approach was called for, which meant that they would have to approach the higher ground by the corrie floor itself, not slantwise as he had done the last time. So, not to warn any targets by the sight of five men and seven horses, they proceeded along the

Abernethy Glen, well to the east, its track out of sight of the corries and the escarpment of both hills.

Halfway along the glen there was a detached eminence of some height, which allowed them to turn off and approach the main Binn Hill unseen from this direction. Cautiously rounding this they could look into the northern corrie, half a mile off still. They could make out no sign of deer as yet.

Exclaiming disappointment, the visitors were told not to give up hope. The corrie slopes were uneven, with hollows and pockets and burn channels. There could be beasts there, hidden from here. Also, even though there might be none, it was always possible that the stags David had seen the day before had gone over the summit, and could be grazing on the west flanks of the hill, above Glen Farg.

Knowing the terrain so well, David ordered the two men with the garrons to remain here, out of sight, and led the other two by a round-about hidden approach, still able to walk upright, for four or five hundred yards, until they came to the actual foot of the northern corrie. And there he himself crept off to scan the prospects, alone.

At first he feared that there was going to be no sport for them this day. But picking his cautious way northwards, further, suddenly he was able to see into a declivity of the corrie formed by a burn; and there, concealed hitherto in the hollow, were the three stags he had hoped for, one actually sitting by the burnside.

Here was a boon, not only that the creatures were present but that they were in a quite notable hollow, this fairly steep-sided. Which meant that, if they remained so, they could be approached unseen right to the edge of the dip, a great help. The only problem would be the wind, due west, and the stalkers would be moving up from the south, and the eddies and swirls caused by the broken and serrated hillsides might well carry the scent of them to keen nostrils in the little valley.

So it was back to the waiting couple with the news, to much excitement. David said that they could advance on foot for most of the way still, but keeping well downhill, that is, eastwards, lest the wind betrayed them; and then creep up to the edge of the gully, out of sight, until they could get within range. That is, of course, if the deer did not move off meantime. This looked like being one of the easiest stalks ever.

But even their upright approach to the burn's dell was not so easy for James Stewart, because of his knock-kneed gait, and over rough ground. He had to be given frequent warnings to be quiet, as he panted and spluttered and cursed, stumbling. But it was better than crawling, at least.

When they reached the south edge of the declivity, David left the others hidden while he crept on to the lip, among the heather, to peer. Whether he had misjudged, or the deer had moved further up, he discovered that he was considerably too low down now. To get within good range they would have to move fully one hundred yards higher.

Back at the king's side, he told them, a little worried now, because every yard higher brought them into possible wind eddies; although admittedly such might well carry their scent well over the heads of the stags, across rather than into the hollow. They had to pick their way on up, then.

Assessing the distance as accurately as he might, David crawled, belly-down, to the edge again. Thankfully he let out his breath. The beasts were still there, showing no sign of alarm, although the sitting one was now standing. They were only some fifty yards below him, well within even inexpert range. All were antlered, he confirmed.

Returning to his companions, he instructed them. Cross-bow strings to be tightened, arrows ready to be fitted. The shooting to be done with as little raising of the body and shoulders as was possible. Silence, and the greatest care.

Both to shoot at the same moment. Aim a hand's-breadth behind the creatures' shoulders. Let James go for the best head. Were they ready?

To nods, he led the crawl forward.

At the lip, lying flat, they gazed over, having to part the heather. The deer were still there, fairly close together, heads down, grazing. David was able to see that one head had eight-pointed antlers, the other two only six each. He pointed to the middle one.

"Yours!" he whispered to the king. "Keep down, as low as you can."

James was fitting arrow to bowstring, hand fumbling a little with his excitement.

"*You* ready?" David asked the Master of Mar.

That youth nodded again.

"Shoot together. Centre and right beasts. Now!"

The pair hoisted their shoulders higher than they ought to have done, to gain better view and aim. And this was enough to cause all three stags to raise heads, to gaze in their direction.

The two bowstrings twanged almost simultaneously.

The central stag gave a tottering leap sidelong, staggered, and then collapsed, forequarters first. The right-hand one leaped also, but then to stand still for a moment, head down. The third beast was off up the burnside in great bounds.

David, bow at the ready, sent another arrow into the wounded animal, and it fell alongside the king's one.

Yelling his elation and pride, James Stewart jumped up, threw bow aside, to go plunging, reeling over and down towards the burn, tripping and all but falling, Johnnie not far behind, although less ecstatic. David followed.

"Eight! Eight points!" the monarch cried. "I've done it! Eight! See, Johnnie! Yours only six."

"Excellent, Sire," David commended. "Good aiming. You

did well." He forbore to add that it had been the least difficult stalk that he could remember, as they gazed down at the two dead animals.

He did not have to instruct his companions on the necessary gutting and entrail-extraction process, for they were used to that in their horsed hunting. But James apparently did not like cold steel, and ordered his friend to do the belly-slittings, although he rolled up his sleeves and plunged hands into the steaming guts to draw them out eagerly enough, all but revelling in it.

David's extraction was of the three arrows.

Then it was trooping down to the waiting men and garrons, hidden behind that hillock, to send them up for the carcases, no difficult task for them or their horses. David would have ridden back to Balvaird at once, but the king was determined to wait there for his kill to be brought down to him, so that he had it in pride to show to the Murray family. He had never before slain an eight-pointer.

There were great congratulations and salutations at the castle, Dand even feeling constrained to join in, however reservedly. Quite a feast was provided for the stalkers, the Murrays seeking not to seem astonished at their young liege-lord's manners and behaviour, amiable indeed, almost excessively so as he was, his praise for David embarrassing.

The repast over, the monarch was for back to Falkland with his trophy. David saw them on their way as far as the edge of the Arngask border at the beginnings of Pitmedden Forest, where James, declaring him to be a most useful and admirable companion, said that he must come to visit him at Stirling Castle, and soon. He was going there in three days' time, to deal with all the papers and appointments that needed his decisions and signatures. Yon Ruthven was for ever at him over it all. Come, and he would show him some roe-deer hunting in the Carse of Forth, and hawking for wildfowl over the Flanders Moss, Davie Murray now become a favoured friend.

They parted, David at least in a sort of wonderment at this so extraordinary and unexpected development, and elevation to royal association and esteem. And all because of the tines on a male deer's antlers.

3

David did not delay overlong in heading for Stirling; after all, this visit was a royal command. And Sir Andrew was all in favour of his son making good use of the monarch's goodwill. It could possibly lead to great things.

So he rode off up Glen Farg and over the higher ground at its head to the west of those Lomond Hills by Milnathort and Kinross, heading for the wide strath of Glen Devon, or the Vale of the Black Devon or Avon as it ought to be called, round the head of Loch Leven (both these names a play on the Gaelic word *abhainn*, a stream). This was the loch where St Serf had brought young St Mungo before he founded Glasgow and where, in its islanded castle, King James's beautiful but unfortunate Catholic mother had been imprisoned by the Protestant Lords of the Congregation and forced to sign an abdication in favour of her year-old son. Poor Mary, now a prisoner in England, however unwise openly to pursue her Romish faith in her so militant Presbyterian Scotland, did not deserve all her grievous misfortunes.

Soon after Loch Leven, riding on past Dollar and Alva, Tillicoultry and Menstrie along the hillfoots of the Ochils, David could see Stirling Castle towering on its mighty rock ahead of him, a great fortress and main seat of the realm's monarchy. David knew it quite well, of course – at least the town below the rock, for he had never himself been inside the citadel. It was barely forty miles from Balvaird, placed at a strategic point where the Firth of Forth narrowed in to become a river, with the wide estuary to the east and the marshlands of the Carse on the west all the way to the mountains of the other Lomond, so that all who would cross from south to north, from Lowlands to Highlands must do so here, under the frowning battlements of the castle, from there to be inspected and, if so desired, halted. Here had been fought battles innumerable, from Roman times down to William Wallace's Stirling Bridge, Bruce's Bannockburn and James the Third's fatal Sauchieburn.

David rode across the bridge into the walled town, with its narrow streets climbing up towards the high tourney-ground approach to the citadel. Surely few realms could have such a dominant monarchial seat?

At the head of that small, level plateau famed for tournaments, the drum-towered gatehouse of the castle, behind a deep ditch, barred all access to the rock-top stronghold, with its magnificent views all around for endless miles. Here David's arrival was loudly challenged, and he had to shout that he was Murray of Gospertie, son to Sir Andrew of Arngask, come on royal orders to see His Grace. He was told to wait – as needs he must, for the drawbridge was only half lowered, and there was no crossing of that wide dry moat.

It was some time before the clanking and creaking of chains heralded the lowering of the drawbridge, this the only intimation of welcome. He led his horse over the timbering and through the gatehouse arch, past the watchful guards. And there, on the bare rock rise beyond was Johnnie Mar waiting for him, with easy greeting.

His mount was handed over to a groom, and he was led up the quite steep slope, past a square tower and into a courtyard housing the palace buildings, opposite a handsome Great Hall edifice erected by the king's grandfather, James the Fifth. There were more buildings higher, but Johnnie turned in at a door in the palace wing.

David found Jamie, of all things, writing poetry, to which it seemed he was very addicted. Glad to see his new friend, the monarch promptly rummaged about a great pile of papers on his table, official documents as well as his own scribblings, and managed to find a piece in verse celebrating his eight-point stag triumph, this making Murray and hurry and flurry rhyme, along with tine, fine and mine. Amused, the visitor read it, declaring it excellent, although he did not really judge it so – but then he was no judge of poesy.

The king said that it was too late in the day to go hawking or hunting; anyway, he was expecting Ruthven with more papers to sign, this before the evening meal. That man had a town-house down at the corner of Broad Street and St Mary's Wynd – a right plague he was, ever with his quill and ink-horn. But they had time to go and let David see the hurly-hackit brae, and have a go at it before the treasurer arrived.

Leaving all the papers, the three of them climbed further up to the summit of the eminence, to the north-east corner, where the formation of the rock underwent an odd change. Elsewhere, save the tourney-ground approach, it was all precipitous cliffs of hundreds of feet. But here there was a grassy slope, fairly steep, leading down to a sort of grassy shelf or terrace, this wide enough to allow cows to graze there, and be the castle's milk supply, half a dozen of them. It was apparently known as Ballengeich. James the Fifth had called himself the Gudeman o' Ballengeich in his secret amorous adventures. Below this was bare rock cliff again, of reduced height of course, but still unclimbable.

At the top of the grassy slope the two youths led David to a row of great skulls, of all things, ox skulls, these responsible for the name hackit, this a word for a cow bearing horns. These were, it seemed, to be sat on and used as a sort of sled to hurtle down the slope of short grass and bare earth, this being the hurly – hurly-hackit. The horns were to be clutched as handles on the bumpy way down the hillside, using the sitter's outstretched legs and feet to help guide the way over the rough course. Down there, just before the terrace with the cows, there was a slight bank to aim at, to halt the descent, this flanked by gorse bushes. And part of the challenge of the sport was to avoid crashing into these, with their prickles.

David eyed it all doubtfully, not greatly taken with the prospect. But his companions selected their hackits, and the king presented him with one, so there was to be no refusal. James said to watch him, and then follow on.

The slope was not very steep at first. The monarch, despite his wobbly legs, was obviously expert at this. He grasped the tips of the skull's horns and began to run forward, pushing it in front of him in shambling progress until it reached the steeper part, then flung himself somehow on to it, to sit astride where the neck bone and skull joined, as it began its bumping descent, legs outstretched forward, heels to assist in the steering. There was just room to sit and no more.

The sled gained speed quickly, and the others could hear James's gurgling shouts of glee as he plunged onwards, twisting this way and that to avoid outcrops, pitfalls and steeper drops, clearly quite an art on that unwieldy and cumbersome mount. But there were no overturnings or upsets, and after a couple of hundred feet or so, skull and rider ended up at that slight bank, to yells of triumph.

Then it was Johnnie's turn, and he set off in similar style if with rather less demonstration and elan, taking a more diverse route down, to avoid the evident hazards. He duly joined his royal companion, to gaze up and wave David on.

That man rather gingerly took hold of the ox horns, to push his skull over the lip of ground, and, when he judged that he had gone far enough, managed to sit himself down. But he found himself stationary. Using his feet to all but walk himself

31

forward, he wondered what he was doing wrongly, for the sled remained reluctant to slide onward. Was his footwork at fault?

He saw a steep area to one side, and made for that. And there, suddenly his strange mount took off, and he was sliding and slithering downhill, by no means in any straight or selected course but slewing this way and that according to the state of the ground. He sought to use hands to steer the horns to aid in his feet's efforts at control, but with scant success. Bumping and lurching, having difficulty in keeping his seat, he plunged on downwards with increasing velocity, out of all control.

The inevitable happened. Straight into that clump of gorse bushes he was flung, to come to a very jagged and spiky halt.

Hurly-hackit! Hurly-folly, more like!

The other two came to help him extricate himself from the jags and bristles, with much laughter and helpful information as to what he had done wrong. It seemed that he had committed nearly every mistake possible. Picking the thorns out of himself, he heard them somewhat sourly.

Then they had to carry the skulls uphill, an awkward business, especially for James with his unsteady gait, the sleds quite heavy. David did not offer his liege-lord assistance.

At the top, another descent was readied. The novice was told what to do and what not to do. He would have preferred not to do it at all, but felt that he could not refuse. James indeed declared that he would accompany him down on foot, as much as was possible, as guide, little as this was desired. He had jumped on to his sled too soon, it appeared. It should gain its own impetus before being sat on, the extra weight having the effect of grounding it. And the horns were not for steering, only for holding the rider in place, the legs and feet to do the guiding.

That second descent was rather more successful than the first, with James being left behind midway, but David still ended up in the gorse bushes, the wretched terrain seeming to propel him thither.

The king shook his head over him.

Mounting the hill again, there was to be a third attempt.

This time it was managed considerably better, and David was able to finish at the grassy bank beside the others, avoiding the prickles.

It was as they turned to face the climb once more that they saw a figure standing at the top, obviously awaiting them.

The monarch gabbled a curse. "Yon's Ruthven, for a wager! He's aye after me! Why can he no' be mair like Esmé Lennox? *He*'s Chancellor, but he isna ever at me."

Lord Ruthven, the High Treasurer of Scotland, was a stern man, greying of hair. He did not soften his critical expression as the trio came up to him with their skulls.

"Your Grace, much demands your attention downby," he said. "This of unprofitable diversion should not be at the nation's cost."

"Whaur's the cost?" James demanded. "Papers will no' flee awa', will they?"

"There are more than papers. The Earl of Bothwell awaits Your Grace—"

"Him frae North Berwick? The witch-maister! A right scoundrel him!"

"As to that, I know not. But he comes regarding the tolls payments for Hailes Castle, the crown's share."

"Payments, eh? Och, weill . . ."

Depositing their skulls, they accompanied the treasurer down to the palace.

Johnnie Mar took David to present him to his father, the seventh Earl of Mar, hereditary keeper of the royal castle and all but guardian of the young monarch, a kindly man, whose mother had been related to David, the Countess Annabella, a daughter of Tullibardine. There proved to be quite a large family of these Erskines of Mar, three other brothers and three sisters, their mother, the Countess Mary, a daughter of Esmé, Duke of Lennox, very obviously pregnant, so there was more to come. All had heard about the stag-stalking and were interested to hear more.

David was given a room, and told that the evening meal would not be long delayed, and that the king would not be held up over this of the Earl of Bothwell.

In fact when James arrived he brought the said earl with him, however unfavourably he had judged him previously. Perhaps the fact that he had brought quite substantial moneys with him for the treasury, from Hailes, had commended him now. A youngish man of aquiline features and darting eyes, he was not exactly related to the monarch but connected, his father having been one of James the Fifth's bastards. Why he had brought the money was because Hailes Castle which he held, directly under the steep isolated hill of Traprain Law in the shire of Haddington, was in a notably strong position between the slopes and the River Tyne, through the narrows of which the main road to the south and the border with England passed, right under the castle walls. This had great advantages in more than a fine defensive site, for Hailes was a barony, and one of the privileges of such was that, if the king's highway passed through its lands, the baron was entitled to charge tolls from all travellers, a proportion of which money had to go to the royal coffers. None could pass Hailes without paying, one of the busiest roads in the land. Also it could hold up any unwanted travellers, even quite large companies, so narrow was the way between steep banks on the one side and the river on the other. Those Hepburns, introduced from Northumberland by the old Earls of Dunbar, knew what they were at.

So David sat down to eat in distinguished company, the monarch, two earls, a countess, the High Treasurer and other lords, the Lyon King of Arms, and another well-known and renowned figure, Master George Buchanan, the great Protestant reformer, former principal of St Leonard's College, St Andrews, scholar and poet, Keeper of the Privy Seal and tutor and preceptor of the king, a tall but now bent old man, austere still, and eyeing all critically, including his former young charges, James and Johnnie. David sat beside the latter and his next-eldest brother, the younger members of the family having fed elsewhere.

After the repast, David did not see the king again before bed-going. It seemed strange how different and distant was the monarch's position here in the palace, among the great ones, than it had been previously, on the hill and indulging in hurly-hackit. Now he was surrounded by his lofty advisers.

However, in the morning, at breakfast with Johnnie and the Mar family in a private chamber, David was told that there was to be a hawking chase, at which he was to attend, this among the meanders of the River Forth north-west of the town. He would be provided with a falcon and the necessary gear.

No large parties were desirable for this sport. Presently David was led out to join a little group assembling with their horses on the tourney-ground, this consisting of James and Johnnie, the Master of Ruthven and the Master of Gray, the last a brilliantly handsome, personable and indeed dashing individual of whom David had heard, famed for more than his good looks and womanising. Each had a tranter allotted to him, whose duty was to retrieve hawks and prey after each kill.

So it was ten riders who set off down through the town and out north-westwards into the Kildean and West Haugh area of the extraordinarily coiling river, which made a long series of wide bends stretching for many miles right to the widening into the estuary, including the boggy ground to the east where the famous Battle of Bannockburn had been fought. Their present destination had its own fame, for Kildean was where William Wallace's victory had been won, at the original bridge, now superseded by the one nearer the town.

David was provided with a peregrine falcon, a tiercel, to sit on a thick padded leather glove to fit over his left hand and arm, its legs bound with thongs called jesses, which the sportsman had to loosen when the hawk was to be flown, with the hood that covered its head removed. David had gone hawking often before, of course, so he required no instruction in the matter. The tranters allotted to each had dogs with them, to pick up fowl that fell into water.

Reaching the Kildean bridge but not crossing it, the company swung left along the riverside, and almost immediately they went into action as a couple of herons rose up, to flap heavily away westwards. David did not unhood his tiercel, recognising the king's right to the first prey, James and the Master of Gray flying their hawks. Herons, large birds, do not soar high nor fast, and the falcons swiftly were hovering above them, to stoop, dropping fast as hurled stones down on to their targets, with a force sufficient to break the creatures' necks.

David was watching this when a couple of mallard ducks burst from the reeds close by, and, glancing at Johnnie, who nodded, he whipped off the hood from his peregrine and loosed the jesses tying its legs. Without any waiting, the keen-eyed bird was off into the air after the fowl, these flying much faster than the herons and in the other direction, eastwards; and forthwith his tranter and dog were away, and in haste, for it might well be some distance before a kill might result.

Another pair of ducks had the Master of Ruthven freeing

his falcon; so all five sportsmen were thus promptly involved.

The king's and Patrick Gray's hawks and prey were quite quickly retrieved, for the herons' heavy flight did not carry them far before they were killed; but the ducks were a different matter, and David, Johnnie and Ruthven had time on their hands, awaiting their tranters and hawks. They rode on westwards, past another great bend of the river, where another heron rose, and James was able to fly his tiercel again.

They came to a point where the River Teith entered the Forth, from the north; and it came to David to wonder why the streams were so designated. For the Teith was a much larger water than the Forth, coming from further away, from the Doune and Callander and Leny area of the southern Highlands, the Forth from not half that distance. Why was the resultant river and its estuary called the Forth and not the Firth of Teith?

He asked Johnnie, who said that he did not know, but that it had always been so.

His tranter and dog returning with a mallard duck for him, David did more wondering. Why was this of hawking considered to be so worthy a sport? After all, *he* had done nothing at all but released and unhooded his falcon. It, and the tranter and dog had performed what was necessary, the sportsman's part feeble indeed.

There was some stir when the Master of Ruthven's falcon killed a wild swan, an unusual occurrence; but otherwise the day's bag consisted of more herons and ducks. James seemed quite pleased with it all, David less so.

Back to Stirling for another evening similar to the last.

Next day it was a different programme, hunting roe-deer in the Carse of Forth. This was a very contrasting sport, larger numbers taking part, mounted again, with hounds to rouse the deer from their coverts and hiding-places, the riders to chase the fleet-footed, graceful creatures. The carse extended westwards for many miles, a sort of strath of level ground on either side of the Forth, averaging some four miles in width, ending eventually in a vast boggy area known as the Flanders Moss, presumably because it resembled the Low Countries wetlands, before reaching the large Loch of Menteith, this name again emphasising the superiority of the Teith over the Forth, since it meant the high ground or Mounth of the Teith, and even gave name to a royal earldom.

The carse was only partly tilled land, the rest rough and bush-strewn, excellent roe country. The hounds for this hunt were very different from the previous day's tranters' retrievers, long-legged, bounding, slender animals, necessary for chasing deer. Roe were much smaller than the red deer of the mountains and forests, very graceful and lightly built, with short three-tipped horns which could not be called antlers, paler brown with white rumps, their meat more tender than the stags' venison, juicier. They did not gather in herds either, but dwelt singly or in pairs. Chasing them, therefore, was very different from the great deer hunts, with individual animals fleeing off, with one or two sportsmen after each, with their hounds. So, although many men set out on the chase, the actual pursuit of each beast was irregular, fitful, hunters breaking away in various directions to follow chosen quarry. Therefore there was no great horn-blowing and hue and cry as in the red deer drives, but a much more scattered hunting. David much preferred it, a challenge not a slaughter, more resembling stalking, for the roe were nimbler and swifter than the horses, and could flee over soft and broken ground and amid bushes which riders had to avoid.

That day he enjoyed, the company quickly disintegrating into individuals and pairs, although, because it was all over open ground, not woodland, the others could be seen, far and wide. There were plenty of roe-deer to provide sport, but making a kill was far from easy, for the creatures darted and swung away capriciously, chased by the hounds, usually giving little opportunity for the hunters to get crossbows and arrows into position to shoot.

David managed to kill only one deer, however many he sought to chase. Others were even less fortunate, however plentiful the game. And the slain beasts had to be left plainly evident for servants following on to pick up, these nowise called tranters.

The movement of it all westwards was therefore dispersed and scattered inevitably, hunters occasionally crossing each other's paths, even sometimes chasing others' deer in error. But it made lively and exhilarating activity.

It was when they all eventually got to the more boggy, bushy and wild area of the Flanders Moss that the hunters had to temper their enthusiasm with caution, for this terrain was noted for its wild boars, and these could be dangerous, apt to attack intruders, and making horses very alarmed and ready to bolt. It was of course considered to be a great feat if one of the riders managed to slay a boar; but most were concerned to avoid any such contacts, and the servitors coming along behind considerably more so.

In the event, David reached the shore of the Loch of Menteith without seeing a boar, but managing to kill another roebuck with a quite good head. Others arriving *had* seen the dangerous beasts, but none had been charged by one, and no attempts had been made to slay one. Boar hunts and deer hunts had to be quite distinct, spears required for the former as well as bows.

King James claimed to have killed four roes, all bucks, and was well pleased, Johnnie Mar three, but the Master of Gray no fewer than seven – this having the monarch sniffing. The afternoon was well advanced by this time, and they had almost fifteen miles to ride back to Stirling. So a start was not delayed to await the arrival of one or two of the still absent hunters. James had David ride beside him and Johnnie on the road down the carse, and was very voluble, if thickly so.

In the morning, with the king having to go to Edinburgh for a meeting with envoys from England, the Duke of Lennox turning up to accompany him, David was for home to Balvaird. When they parted, James told him that he would be back at Falkland in two weeks' time, and that Davie should join him there and accompany him on a deer drive, *red* deer not roe; and they might have another go at the stalking on the Lomonds; this before winter set in, and the like became unseasonable.

David was evidently to remain the king's friend, for better or for worse.

4

Two weeks later, then, David set off eastwards for Falkland, calling in at Gospertie on the way to see that the drainage was going on well. He was spending much of his time at that small lairdship of his, superintending this of drainage of quite an area of marshland to make it capable of growing grain and becoming profitable. He judged this more worthy than the mass hunting of deer hinds and calves in forests.

At Falkland, however, he discovered that the king had gone off further north, a dozen miles or so, to Creich, at the invitation of Beaton thereof, or Bethune as it should be spelled, of the family of the late and famous, or notorious, cardinal. A sister of Beaton's had been one of James the Fifth's numerous mistresses, mother of the Countess of Argyll, and sister of one of the present unfortunate queen's four Marys. David would as lief have gone back to Gospertie, but these royal commands . . .

So he rode northwards. The barony of Creich was situated near the Fife shore of the Firth of Tay, opposite the Errol area, set among low hills. His route was through what was known as the Howe of Fife, crossing the River Eden, and on among the modest hills of Lindifferon and Collairnie and Moonzie, pleasant but not dramatic country however prominent its lairds. Presumably the monarch had been invited to hunt in these hills.

Creich Castle, David found beside a hamlet rather than a village or a castleton, and named not Creich but Brunton although the parish was called Creich, its church nearer the Beaton seat than the community. David actually called at the wrong castle, Montquhanie, by mistake, only a mile to the east of his true destination, an unusual circumstance to find two fortalices belonging to different families so close together. He wondered at there being no sign of any large party about the place, and discovered that this was a Balfour establishment. The lady of the house informed that, yes, the king was hunting from Creich, she understood on the hills of Norman's Law and Fliskmilan, and her husband was with the royal party. Creich was a couple of miles to the west.

Riding on, he found that castle on the north face of a hill looking across to the Tay and the Carse of Gowrie beyond, a moderately sized fortalice in a strong position half a mile north of the hamlet of Brunton. There was little sign of activity about the establishment; but then, most of its menfolk would be off with the hunt in one capacity or another.

Dismounting in the courtyard near the stables and byre, he decided against presenting himself at the castle door, a single unknown visitor. He had ridden at least twenty-five miles already that day, and had no desire to ride further and to get involved in a hunt over hills in the late afternoon and his mount already tired. He would just go for a walk on the hillside and stretch his legs after the long riding, and await the monarch's return.

However, tethering his horse, a servant lass came out of a byre with a pail of milk and, greeting him, declared that she would see her mistress and inform her of this late arrival. Was he one of the young king's party?

He said that he came at the royal command, yes, but not to trouble the lady of the house. He would take a stroll, awaiting King James's return.

He was making for the gatehouse and out when another young woman emerged from the castle and came over to him, a very different female this. The servant girl had been sonsie and quite bonny; but this one was strikingly good-looking, dark of hair and eyes, quite tall, slender but well formed and with a graceful carriage. She came over to him, eyebrows raised but smiling.

"You have left the hunt?" she enquired. "Your horse failed you?"

"No, no, lady. I have but come here from some distance. Late. At royal behest. Too late for this day's hunting. Come from Balvaird, near to Glen Farg."

"Ah! A Murray, I think? Of Tullibardine?"

"Only kin to Tullibardine. But of Arngask. My father."

"Sir Andrew, is it not? I have heard of him. I am Elizabeth Beaton. Come you within."

"I do not wish to cause you inconvenience. I am for a walk until the hunt returns."

"No inconvenience at all. If you have ridden from Glen Farg you will be weary, I judge. And would be the better of some refreshment, no?"

"No need."

"You have sustained yourself some way, on the journey?"

"No. But . . ."

"Then need there is. Come, you." And she gave his doublet sleeve a little tug.

However reluctant he may have sounded, David was by no means unwilling to go with this lovely creature, he cherishing that tug at his sleeve. She led him indoors, and up the turnpike stairway to a withdrawing-room off the hall on the first floor.

"Sit you, and I will fetch you some suitable cheer, friend. You have not told me your name, apart from Murray?"

"David, just. David Murray." He wondered whether he should add "of Gospertie". But decided not. It was too small a holding, of but a large farm and a piece of moorland.

"And that young king had invited you here to join him at his hunting? A strange young man!" Turning back to David, hand up to mouth, she made a face. "Oh, forgive! I have a foolish tongue – that I am often told. That sounded as though King James was strange in asking you here! I am sorry."

"No need. It is just that I taught him how to stalk stags. On the hill. Not just hunt them, as today, ahorse, and with many men. Stalk, alone. He did not know how. And learning, he managed to kill a beast with quite a good head. He was grateful for this. So . . ."

"So you are now in the royal favour. Over slaying a deer! Strange creatures men are! For ever killing! But at least killing deer is better than killing their fellow-men, as they have been doing down the ages." Another face, but not apologetic this time. "Wait you, David Murray, and I will supply your needs. Or some of them!" And smiling, she went gracefully off.

David gazed after her in a sort of wonder. He had never met a young woman quite like this, in her converse and behaviour as well as in her looks.

She was not long in returning, bearing a tray with wine, cold meat in the shape of partridge legs, with scones and oatcakes spread with honey.

"This is scarcely a feast," she said. "But it may keep you from starvation while you await the return of all the other hungry men. We women seem to have to spend much of our time satisfying the other sort of the Almighty's creation, and not only in food!" Elizabeth Beaton raised an eyebrow at him. "Heed me not! I know that I have an unruly tongue. I am told of it often enough. Eat you, while I go see to the provision for the multitude. When my good father invited the king and all his company here, he and my two brothers just took it for granted that I would cope with them, play hostess to the host." Another grimace, if such it could be described on that so comely face. Then she was gone.

David was quite overcome by this hostess he had landed upon – and hostess she evidently was, no mother or other female, by her words, responsible for this Creich establishment. How old would she be? Hard to tell, her aplomb and self-assurance contrasting with her moments of self-reproof. Probably about his own age.

Eating his welcome sustenance, his thoughts were busy if somewhat complex. He could hear much activity going on in the hall adjoining, the moving of forms and chairs, the clink of tableware and the like, and occasionally his hostess's voice upraised: preparations for the hunters' return. It occurred to him that he possibly could be of help in this, for it was female talk that he could hear. He rose, and went to the communicating door.

There he saw only the one man, elderly, carrying a bench to one of the three lines of tables stretching down the hall from the dais platform. Elizabeth herself was up on this, arranging matters there. He went to relieve the old man of his burden and carry it to where directed.

A voice, raised, called, "David Murray, you are guest, not retainer." This to giggles from the women busy there.

He continued to help in the furniture arranging.

Presently he found his hostess at his side. "I may be a mere female, but I am mistress of this house," she told him. "Go you back to yonder chamber." And taking his arm, she gave him a push in the direction from which he had come. That was the second physical contact with him. "I will rejoin you shortly."

He bowed. "I do as I am told, Mistress Elizabeth."

"I am usually called Lisa," she told him. "And I am no man's mistress."

When she came back to the withdrawing-room, it was with another glass of wine for him.

"I have been admiring the hangings and tapestries here,"

45

he said. "They are very fine. We have none so good at Balvaird."

"I can claim no hand in any of these," she declared. "Although I do tapestry work on occasion. Some of mine hang in my bedroom. But these are older. Beaton women can have their talents, other than in entertaining men! One of these, I forget which one it was, was woven by my aunt, another Elizabeth, who entertained King James the Fifth, the Gudeman o' Ballengeich, the present young James's grandsire – and sufficiently to give him a daughter, who is now Countess of Argyll! Poor soul, married to a Campbell! And the one beside the door there was by my great-aunt Janet, who wed Scott of Buccleuch in the Borderland. And when he was murdered – you know the ways of these Border mosstroopers – she led his clan to avenge him, as tough as any of his reivers. Yet another aunt, Griselda, also married the next Scott of Buccleuch, and when he too was killed wed Murray of Blackbarony, a different tribe of Murrays, I think? Those Border marriages tended to be of short duration!"

David was hearing more of female Beatons, who clearly had been, and still were apparently, a lively lot, when noise and shouting from without heralded the return of the huntsmen, and an end to converse.

The company seemed pleased with their day's sport, this area to the west of Creich, especially that of Norman's Law and Glenduckie, well populated with deer, the reason for the king's invitation here, his favourite pastime well known. There was much talk and discussion, particularly once the wine started to flow, scores of the incomers setting the castle in turmoil. Elizabeth became more than busy, David now very much in the background.

Eventually King James found him, and greeted him in very comradely fashion, telling of the day's successes, also sundry mistakes made by various individuals. But soon there was a summons to the tables. James remained in the withdrawing-room, to make his monarchial entrance on to the dais, this when all others were seated according to accepted precedence. So David had to go and find a lowly place near the foot of one of the lengthwise tables.

From there he watched the notables file in to sit in due locations on the dais platform, Elizabeth, as hostess, showing them where, all carefully arranged beforehand. David noted that three seats were reserved in the centre, the middle one with an extra tall back, clearly to serve as the throne. He noted that the Lord Ruthven, the treasurer, occupied the position next to it on the right, and Patrick, Master of Gray, alleged to be the most handsome man in the land, next on the left one, he, as ever, looking assuredly amused at all the proceedings.

At length David Beaton, with his daughter, appeared from the withdrawing-room which backed the hall, he to act as host and announce the entry of His Grace the King. This seemed to David to be rather ridiculous, when that youth had been mingling with them all that day in comparatively casual fashion. So all had to rise, and James came in at a sort of ungainly trot, grinning, and Elizabeth conducted him to his central high chair, she then remaining standing on his left, her father on his right. All were now standing, as required.

A gong was clanged, to intimate that the provender was to be brought in.

And fine provision it proved to be, witness to Elizabeth's prowess as hostess. It started with soup, thickened with white sauce and flavoured with spirits, David judging it to be of a partridge base, from which perhaps those partridge legs he had nibbled had come. This James gobbled down with gusto, demanding more.

There followed Tay salmon, garnished with lettuce and parsley and mint. Then a choice of roast venison, duck or heron, the servants busy indeed, Elizabeth heedfully attending to the young monarch's requirements, with occasional words to the Master of Gray on her left. Why *he* should be placed there, David did not know, since there were earls and lords present whom he judged should have occupied such prominent placing; presumably he occupied some important position at court.

This over, there were sweetmeats a-many; and, of course, wine and spirits glasses and tankards to be replenished.

When the eating was over, although the drinking continued, musicians and singers from the minstrels' gallery entertained the now somewhat noisy company.

David found himself watching for, and somehow resenting, Patrick Gray's quite frequent touchings and strokings of the bare forearm of his hostess. That repast and entertainment took long to finish, by which time David, like others, was yawning after the day's much riding. Some fell asleep at table, to be awakened by servants and escorted to their rooms in the castle itself or in the courtyard outbuildings, much accommodation required, Elizabeth superintending all, despite Gray's attentions.

David was uncertain as to what he should do, and where to go. His was a very humble status compared with so many of the magnates present, he recognised, although he was here at the monarch's invitation. James had disappeared fairly early on. He decided that he could bed down on the straw of the stable where he had left his horse, quite comfortable if wrapped in his plaid. He was preparing to rise and go thither when none other than Elizabeth Beaton came down to his side, to inform him that the King's Grace required his attendance, this said with those expressive eyebrows raised. Follow her.

He was led, wondering, past snoring men, and upstairs to a quite handsome chamber on the second floor. There he found

James, with Johnnie Mar – but not the latter's father, who was one of the earls at the hunt. Pushing him within, Elizabeth said goodnight, and, with a pat on the shoulder, left him there.

Astonished at this development, he was hailed by the monarch. "Och, Davie, I saw you doon there, by your lane. I telt yon woman, Creich's daughter, to fetch you. She's bonny, is she no'? Pate Gray has an eye on her! You'll bide here the night wi' us. Yon's a fine big bed."

"Sire, I, I do not know what to say!"

"I'll dae the saying, Davie! See you, we spied a richt guid stag this morn. It sped awa' up the side o' a hill ca'd Ayton, a bit spur o' yon Norman's Law. We were for the woods o' Glenduckie beyond. It had a fine heid. There's to be another hunt the morn. But I'd hae that heid, if I can. We'll let the ithers dae the hunting, and we'll hae a go at it. The stag I saw. Stalk it, eh?"

"If it is your wish, Sire. Just the three of us?"

"Aye. The ithers'll no' see the like, doon in yon woods. We'll no' get that many chances o' stalking afore the snows set in for the winter."

Sharing a bed with his liege-lord and the Master of Mar made an extraordinary night for David Murray. But there was no fuss about it. The usual tub of steaming water to wash in was before the fire, but James ignored it, tossing off his untidy clothing and jumping into the bed after gulping down one more glass of wine, Johnnie following suit. David did wash himself, and then joined the other two. It was, as James had said, a big bed, so he was able to keep himself well apart.

Despite the oddity of it, he had an undisturbed night.

James announced to all, when the next day's hunt was being prepared, that he would not be accompanying the others. He was going stalking, on Ayton Hill, and he did not want any others bar Johnnie and Davie to be there frightening the stags.

The trio had only a three-mile ride, round the quite steep Norman's Law, to the lesser hill. David would have expected the best beasts to be on the higher and more extensive summit, even though it was no mountain, but James declared that it was on this Ayton that he had seen the quarry he wanted. So, dismounted, they started to circle the lower slopes carefully, keeping themselves as inconspicuous as possible while still able to scan the upper heights and hollows – these could scarcely be called corries.

They had made almost three-quarters of a circuit and were beginning to fear that no sport was to be theirs when, rounding an isolated knoll, there, up near the summit plateau, they spied not one but three deer, the king's disappointment changing into elation.

David, scanning the terrain, pointed out to the others that Ayton, unlike its neighbour, was a fairly smooth-surfaced hill, offering little or no cover for an approach. He judged that their only possible course was to go back and round to the further side, climb there, and make their attempt from above. This could have its problems, admittedly, because of wind currents which might eddy round hilltops and possibly give the deer warning; but he saw no other alternative here.

So it was a return whence they had come, to a point over half a mile off, where they could make an unseen ascent, and still be well eastwards of the stags, so that the south-west wind would not betray their presence.

At the flattish summit they had to creep cautiously north-westwards. As they neared the lip, they had to go belly-down. There was some short heather, but it was mainly deer-hair grass, which did not provide them with much in the way of concealment.

At length, peering over, they saw the three beasts none so far below, and seemingly unalarmed. Nevertheless, the young monarch groaned. None of these three had the fine head he had looked for; antlers, yes, but nothing of particular worth.

Lying flat, they debated. Should they make an attempt on these? Or assume that the fine-headed one had drifted over to the higher hill, Norman's Law, and themselves go back and head for that?

But it had taken them some considerable time to get thus far, in their necessarily cautious progress, and to give up and start an entire new survey and possible stalk would demand much more. And these *were* stags, after all, whatever their antlers. David pointed out that it would still be valuable practice to go for them.

Scanning the hillside below, he thought he saw a way by which they could get even nearer to the animals than their present position. So it was back, and out of sight, and then along northwards and over into the genesis of a burn channel, down which they could work their damp way unseen, David assessed, to well within range of their quarry.

Johnnie Mar grumbled about getting his clothing wet, but James did not.

They hoped that there would be no down-draughts of wind from the hilltop.

When they had gone what they thought would be about the right distance, David crawled up to the rim of their declivity, to peer. Then, backing, he waved the other two up.

"All well," he reported, in a whisper. "Sixty yards, no more. They graze each a few yards apart. We are close to them, so we may not have long to aim. The least whiff of us and they could be off. Exertion can cause sweat, and that means a scent of men. So – three beasts. One each. And to kill, not to wound, see you. A hand's-breadth behind the shoulder. The best head, the right-hand one, yours, Sire. Johnnie the middle one. Right?"

They readied arrows into their crossbows, and edged forward.

They were only just in time as they gained view and raised themselves sufficiently to aim and shoot, for the deer sensed their presence, lifted heads from their grazing, and stood momentarily at gaze. The three bowstrings twanged almost simultaneously.

At only sixty yards, to miss would have been shame-making. All three deer staggered, lurched, tottered and fell to the ground, to jerk and kick.

James whooped his triumph, however modest the trophy, the head with only the two top points on each antler, above the brow tines, Johnnie's and David's merely the bare spikes of young beasts.

They did the gralloching there and then, the king seemingly enjoying the messy business. The carcases could be left for servants to collect.

Back at the castle, they found the hunt party already back. James was loud in his accounts of his exploit.

The monarch was not having Davie isolated down at his distant place at table, and, on entry to start the meal, sent Elizabeth to inform him so. She came, to tap his shoulder, and to point to the dais and beckon, wordless but smiling.

Distinctly embarrassed, he followed her up, past all the interested guests. As he climbed on to the platform, James called to him to fetch himself a chair from the withdrawing-room and place it at the end of the dais table, his throaty-worded instructions heard by all, and no doubt wondered at. Ill at ease indeed, he did as he was told, finding himself having to sit next to the Lord Gray, the Master's elderly father, who eyed him unspeaking.

With so many prominent folk placed down in the body of the hall, David felt some sort of interloper. The monarch's favour had its discomforts, at least to him.

James was not one to linger at table for long after the eating was over, the entertainment of little appeal to him. When he rose, and all others must stand also, he came to grab David's arm and point, clearly a command to follow him. That man caught Elizabeth's eye, and she nodded.

Johnnie Mar at his side, they climbed up to the second-floor bedchamber.

It was the same procedure as the night before, save that they sat by the fire sipping wine, James gulping it down indeed, there discussing the day's stalking, and wondering where the fine stag seen earlier had got to. The monarch was much concerned, for he had to leave Creich next day, to return to Stirling to receive the papal nuncio, however theoretically Protestant James might be. Which meant, of course, that David would depart also.

In the morning, Creich Castle was delivered from its invasion of guests. Throughout, David had barely exchanged a word with his host, Beaton thereof; and his two young sons had been very much in the background; but the daughter had made a major impact on him, and he was already wondering how he could contrive a return visit.

James clearly assumed that David would accompany the royal train much of the way back on the road to Stirling, so he had no opportunity for any private converse with anyone. But Elizabeth did come to his side as he mounted to the saddle. She reached up a hand to him.

"It has been an active day or two for me, as for others, David," she said. "Busy. I have had little time for aught but playing hostess of this house and provider of as fair hospitality as I was able. So we have not had opportunity for much of . . . association."

On impulse, he bent to kiss that hand instead of merely taking and shaking it. "To my loss, Elizabeth," he said, and meant it.

"Loss? Surely not. What had you hoped to gain?"

That was a poser. "Just, just a little more of your time, Elizabeth," was the best that he could do.

"My friends call me Lisa," she reminded him. The cavalcade was beginning to move off. "Haste ye back."

"You mean that? Come back?"

"I usually mean what I say, young man!"

"Then I will have to think of an excuse for coming."

"No excuse required . . ."

He had to leave her there.

5

Despite Elizabeth Beaton's assurance that there was no need for excuse over a return to Creich, such did occupy David's mind considerably from then onwards. What could he use as a valid reason for visiting the area, enabling him to call in at the castle, as it were in passing?

Meantime, he had much to keep him busy at both Balvaird and Gospertie. This of the drainage development at the latter had prompted his father to point out that they had marshland nearer home, especially at Conland, and his son could well spend some time in making that profitable, Dand seemingly assessing such work as beneath his dignity. Winter was all but upon them, and heavy rain, frost and snow no conditions for that sort of labour.

No word came from King James, either from Stirling or Falkland.

Strangely anough, it was the weather, however unsuitable for drainage, that solved at least one of David's problems. A particularly cold spell, as December succeeded November, had the effect of freezing much standing water, this including Loch Leven at Kinross. And that large but fairly shallow sheet of water, or rather its ice, was famed for curling tournaments or bonspiels, the landed gentry in particular vying with each other at the sport. This consisted of skimming rounded, polished stones across ice to reach targets, rather similar to skittles or bowls. Some years the ice was never sufficiently thick to bear the weight of scores, even hundreds of men; but this early frost was severe and maintained, and the word

55

was that curling was the order of the day. And Sir Andrew Murray was a keen curler. So it was south by east to Loch Leven – and that lake was only a dozen miles from Creich.

The male Murrays moved down to Kinross.

Lochleven Castle, where the king's mother had been so grievously ill-used, although once a royal seat now belonged to the Morton Douglases, with whom Sir Andrew was at odds. So they found lodging in the town, but with some difficulty, for many others had arrived for the curling.

David was not so keen on this sport as was his parent, but he felt that he had to put in one day at it before making a sally further east into north Fife. And there, on the ice next morning, he found Beaton of Creich himself among the many other notables come to compete.

All sorts of folk went in for curling, many working men, wrights, millers, ploughmen and of course the burghers of Kinross and Milnathort, quite as expert as were the nobility and gentry, one of the few sports thus general. All had to bring their own two stones. These had to be of a more or less exact size, ten inches to a foot in diameter and weighing between thirty and forty pounds, rounded save for the flattish base, and highly polished. The competitors brought sweeps, brushes, to clear the ice of any least obstacles in the path of their stones, even tiny objects and scraps of ice itself enough to divert the stones as they neared the end of their impetus. The recognised course, or rink as it was termed, was one hundred and thirty-eight feet long by fourteen feet wide, all most standardised. Usually the stones had handles attached for more effective impelling.

Sometimes individual players competed, but more usually teams of four co-operated. The objective was to get the stones as close to what was named the tee, a small circle marked on the ice at the centre of wider circles, these gaining lesser marks; and one man's stone was allowed to knock another out of its position – a situation that could sometimes improve the last's score.

It was not thought to be a sport apt for women, much muscle needed to propel the heavy stones for such distances, with much stooping, and the wielding of the sweeps necessary, this last of course only possible when teams were competing.

Sir Andrew was good at it, and practised, when he could, on the little Loch of Pitlour.

The Balvaird group formed a team of four, Patrick, the youngest, having to watch, he not yet strong enough to send a stone the required distance. After a few trial runs, they chose to compete first with their Tullibardine kinsmen, and despite no very brilliant efforts, managed to defeat the others by a small margin. Then they challenged Lord Lindores, from not far away, and again won. But in a contest with Balfour of Monimail, they were soundly beaten, as perhaps was good for them.

The days were short now, and the curling had to stop, to be succeeded by recourse to the local inns and taverns for warming regalement of chilled sportsmen, this tending to develop into further contests of a different and wordy type.

David had wondered whether the king would make an appearance at Loch Leven. But no; perhaps his ungainly frame and limbs did not lend themselves to propelling heavy stones; or he might have found frozen water nearer to Stirling.

In the morning, David announced that he had a matter to attend to connected with his drainage activities, which commended itself to his father, this at Collairnie just south of that hill of Norman's Law and the missing fine stag. This was not entirely an invention, for he had sat next to Barclay of Collairnie at dinner at Creich, and they had discussed methods of improving infertile and wet land, of which apparently Collairnie had more than its due share. So he sought exemption from more curling that day, and rode off north by east the fifteen miles on icy roads and tracks.

In due course he had a fairly brief chat with the Barclay laird, to ease his conscience, and was able to continue the further few miles to Creich thereafter, in hopeful anticipation. What would his reception be? She had said to haste him back, but that could have been only a polite parting.

At that castle he was heartened by his reception. Elizabeth greeted him warmly, with no indication of surprise at his arrival, giving him a kiss, admittedly only on the cheek, and declaring that she had wondered when she was going to see him again. Her father, and James, the elder of the two brothers, were at Loch Leven, so that she and young Robert had the house to themselves. By this time it was mid-afternoon, and with the early December dusk it was evident that the visitor would be spending the night there – which was satisfactory, although David rather wished that the ten-year-old Robert had had his brother with him, and so was not dependent on his sister for company. It was to be hoped that the boy would be packed off to bed before the evening was well advanced.

Elizabeth reminded the new arrival, when he so named her, that her friends called her Lisa, which was a hopeful sign.

"I think that we will not put you into the large bedchamber that you shared with the king and the Master of Mar," she said. "A smaller room, more readily heated in this cold weather, would be best. Up on the third floor. Come you, and we shall see."

They climbed the winding turnpike stair, Robert accompanying them, also two hounds.

There were three apartments at this level in that tower, one pointed out as the boys' room, one Lisa's own, and David shown into the third. It had a smaller bed than the great canopied four-poster below, two chests, two chairs, hangings on the walls, and a fireplace. Also the usual sanitation garderobe in the thickness of the walling, and deerskins on the flooring.

"Will this serve you?" she asked. "I will have the fire lit."

Risking boldness he answered, "Most kind. And, next to your own, the better!"

"Ah, is that the way of it! As well, no, that I can keep my door locked!"

"I, I did not mean that," he told her hastily. "Just that it will be the more companionable. All admirable."

"I see that David Murray is concerned for his conveniences."

"No, no. I was just grateful."

"Well, we must not disappoint, must we? See you, I will have hot water brought up for you to wash with, in yonder tub. After your long riding. And will prepare a meal adequate to sustain the inner man."

"Do not put yourself to so much trouble."

Trouble or not, after the washing and settling in, it was a very adequate repast to which the three of them sat down in due course, young Robert earning a ticking-off from his sister for remarking that it was all better than usual.

Thereafter they sat by the well-doing withdrawing-room fire, in very pleasant fashion, the boy asking about the curling and saying that he wished that he had been taken to see it. He was sure that he could push a stone well enough.

Lisa asked whether David would like to have a little music? She could strum a lute just sufficiently well to cover the failures in her singing. Did David sing?

He did not claim to be any sort of minstrel, but he could chant in tune with a lute or clarsach after a fashion. Robert said that *he* was a good singer, and knew many lays and ballads. So Lisa fetched her six-stringed lute, and proved to be an expert with it, and to have a fine and melodious voice as well. She encouraged David to join in, his baritone harmonising and the boy's treble completing the accord. They sang together quite a number of traditional chants and ballads and lyrics, the man humming his contribution when he did not know the words. Altogether it made an enjoyable interlude, the intimacy of it all much to David's gratification.

At length, with the boy beginning to yawn, Lisa announced that it was past his bedtime and that he must be off. He grumbled, but she took him by the hand and led him upstairs.

David sat by that log fire and thought his thoughts.

When the young woman came down again, she asked if he had had enough of music for one evening? He said that he had enjoyed the singing with them both, but his part had been the least of it. If she wanted to continue he would be well content. It made for a pleasant association.

"Association?" she commented. "Yes, I suppose that is true. We do seem to be associating quite companionably."

"It is my hope that we may continue to do so, Lisa!" He was picking his words quite carefully. "I would so wish it."

She eyed the flames of the fire. "Association," she repeated. "That is a word that could mean much, or little. How do *you* mean it?"

"I mean it much, not little." He paused momentarily, and then added, "My dear."

She transferred her gaze from the fire to his face, and took her time before speaking, while he all but held his breath.

"This is unexpected! Scarcely looked for! You mean it seriously? Or is it gallantry of a sort?"

"No." He leaned forward, towards her. "I do. I mean it. With all that is in me. From my heart, Lisa. It is all of me, my desire, my need, my longing." He shook his head. "How can I say it, tell you, lass?"

"But you have not known me for long. Seen but little of me. Do not truly know me, David."

"I know *myself*! And know you sufficiently to want you, ache for you. I have done, almost from the first day. You struck right to all that is me, my heart, my want, my desire . . ."

"A man can desire a woman, see you. And many a woman! But that is other. But . . ." She left the rest unsaid.

He all but reached out to her. "Hear me, my dear – for that is what you are, dear to me. Whatever you may think or feel or would have. I had not meant to speak so, to tell of it now, so soon. But I have known it, lived with it, since our first meeting. Is that crazy-mad? It has come out. Perhaps over-soon. But you must know it, understand it."

She drew a deep breath. "David, my friend. This is all too unexpected. I knew that you liked me, yes. Thought well of me. As I did of you. But this is different." She rose to her feet. "I think, I judge, that we should say no more on it. Meantime." She took the poker to push a smouldering log deeper into the fire. "Would bed-going now suit you? There is more wine in your room."

"My thanks. Shall I douse the lamps?"

"If you will." Lisa waited for him at the stair-foot, and they climbed the steps together.

At the bedchamber doors they paused, she opening hers.

"I hope that you are not upset? By my telling you. My, er, confession!" he said. "But you should know how it is with me. May I wish you a goodnight, a night of no worries, no ill thoughts?"

"*Ill* thoughts, no. But thoughts, yes. Many thoughts. Sleep well, David." She took his arm, leaned forward, and offered him a kiss, brief but with her lips, before entering her chamber and gently closing the door on him.

He stood there for moments before going into his own.

In the morning, after a night in which the man had done almost as much thinking as sleeping, or so he reckoned it, at breakfast Lisa, not referring to the evening's discussions, announced that she proposed to take him to a favourite haunt of hers, which it was improbable that he had visited. They would take Robert, of course, the boy lonely without his brother.

David was well pleased at thus being taken to somewhere that apparently meant much to his hostess – although he could have done without her young brother's company.

They rode eastwards, parallel with the south shore of Tay, rocky and bare, for about five miles, the air chilly although the sun shone hazily through thin cloud. Lisa explained. The area they were heading for held three places of interest, all within half a mile, this near the Hay castle of Naughton. There was St John's Well, its waters reputed to have healing qualities. There was Battle Law, the site of a defeat of the heathen Danes who had desecrated the well, this by the Hays of Naughton in 990, after the greater Battle of Luncarty at which the Hays had distinguished themselves. And a still more venerable site, that of a Pictish Culdee cell at a spot called Dolhanha, the monks of which had founded the well in the name of the Baptist, whom they particularly revered.

David observed that Lisa was clearly much interested in historical matters. Or was it religion? Or both? She told him that she probably was less religiously minded than she ought to be, but that the land spoke to her, somehow, of the past, and this greatly captured her.

Passing the devastated Cistercian Abbey of Balmerino, sacked first by the English and then again at the Reformation, Lisa told him that it had been founded by Queen Ermengarda, widow of William the Lion, three hundred years before; and Ermengarda herself had actually been slain therein, before the high altar, a few years later. Then they came to the site of the Danes' defeat, called Battle Law, near the village of Gauldry, where those marauding Vikings had been punished by the Hays for defiling the holy well. This little victory, she said, was apt to be confused with the greater one of Luncarty, north of Perth, because it too had been won with the help of the Hays, when King Kenneth the Third had been sorely pressed by the said Danes or Norsemen. For their services the Hays were granted the barony of Errol, just across Tay; and the Bruce made Sir Gilbert of Errol Hereditary High Constable of Scotland for his great aid. Now they were Earls of Errol, as David would well know. The nearby castle of Naughton was held by a branch of the family.

Then the trio came to the site of the early Culdee chapel, the young woman explaining that the name came from the Gaelic Keledei, the Friends of God. There was only a grass-grown mound of masonry left of what had evidently been but a modest small religious establishment, nevertheless important, at least to Lisa, as the most ancient Christian relic of all the area. She came here often.

Then on to St John's Well, now no very dramatic feature, significant as was its story, set among bushes from which rags of clothing hung, these what remained of offerings left by poorer folk who had come to drink of the holy and healing water; the better-off pilgrims usually put silver or copper moneys into the well itself, as in so many another similar shrine, whence came the phrase "coins in the fountain", meaning small payments for large benefits.

David was much impressed, not so much by what he saw as by Lisa's fund of lore and knowledge, not something which he had associated with beauteous young women. When he complimented her on it all, she brushed his praise aside as quite unmerited; it just happened that she was interested in the like.

Young Robert, however, was bored with it all.

Finally they made a call at Naughton Castle, but found the Hays amissing, they also having gone to Loch Leven for the curling. Lisa hinted that she was not altogether disappointed, for the son of the house tended to be somewhat pressing in his attentions in her direction. This made David the more thoughtful.

Back at Creich that evening, when Robert had gone to bed, by the fire David thought to revert to that remark made about the Hay young man's attentions. "You, Lisa, will attract the advances of many men, I think. I saw how that Master of Gray concerned himself with you on the dais on that royal occasion. Which makes it the more difficult. For me."

"Difficult? What mean you by difficult, David?"

"You know my feelings for you. And with many seeking your favours, what chance have I?"

"What favours do you seek?"

He hesitated, as well he might. "You are very kind to me. Treat me as your friend. Entertain me in your house. And, as this day, take me to places that mean much to you. This I greatly esteem. But . . ."

"But you seek more?"

"Can you wonder at it? You are so kind. And your person so lovely. I would be no man if I was not eager for more. For your closer . . . generosity!"

"Ah! So we are back to this of association! You would have me yield my person to you in some measure? Is that it?"

Confronted with so frank a question, he swallowed. "I, I would not wish to be a worry and distress to you. When you are being so good to me. But you must be aware how greatly you appeal to me. You, all of you."

"Poor David! Do I tempt you unduly with my womanhood? Alone with me while the family is absent, apart from Robert? Must I make some slight amends? We shall see. But" – she waved a hand – "some music, meantime? We can associate in that, at least."

So the lute was brought forward, and they sang together,

6

Back at home, David found concern for the peace and well-being of the realm prevailing, curling superseded by fears. It seemed that the factions that largely contested the control of the young monarch, and therefore the government of the kingdom, these headed respectively by the Duke of Lennox and the Lord Ruthven, High Treasurer, had all but come to blows, and over religion, or at least Church government. Scotland had had a sufficiency of religious strife at the Reformation, it could be judged; but now the successful Protestant cause was itself split between the Episcopal and the Presbyterian sections, the bishops versus the divines; and Lennox and his supporters backed the bishops, and Ruthven the Presbyterians. There had just been a General Assembly of the latter, and its members had been incensed by the appointment of one of its own ministers, Robert Montgomery, to be Bishop of Glasgow, this contrived by the Duke Esmé, who had, as senior representative of the House of Stewart, under the monarch, arranged that this new prelate should receive an annual stipend, but that the revenues of that great diocese should come to the ever-empty royal coffers. The divines declared this to be wicked and unlawful, Ruthven backing them, and poor young James was torn between the two.

Sir Andrew Murray, not in any way fanatical about religious differences, feared that there could be outright civil warfare, as in a return to the Reformation period. And if there was, would he and his have to become involved? And which side was likely to win? Which control the king?

It had occurred to him that his second son's odd relationship with James might be useful in finding out how the situation balanced as between the two factions. David should go to Stirling and try to discover what was the likely outcome.

His son, although not wishing to be mixed up in any conflicting issues, was quite prepared to attempt this, his mother urging it also, her family, the Montrose Grahams, being episcopally minded.

Two days later, then, David rode for Stirling, the rain persisting.

He had no difficulty in gaining access to the fortress-citadel, the Earl of Mar, its keeper, ordering admission. There he found James and Johnnie playing cards, no weather for hurly-hackit. They were glad to see him.

They told him that there was bad blood between the duke and Ruthven; there always had been, but now worsened over this of the bishops, and they very much feared that it would come to blows. James, of course, was for his kinsman, Lennox, but recognised that Ruthven had the greater following, especially among the churchmen; and as treasurer, he held the purse-strings, even though not those of the royal privy purse. Keeping the pair from outright clash was a problem indeed; and the result of such open enmity could be dire for the nation. But what could be done to prevent it? The crown must not seem to take sides.

David wondered whether there could be some favour offered to Ruthven to sweeten him? Some token that would appeal to the man, and persuade him to come to some agreement with Lennox, for the realm's sake? The duke was Chancellor and he High Treasurer; but was there not something else? Some added position?

None, James thought, that he could bestow without parliament's agreement; and the last thing that was wanted was a parliamentary battle to add to the religious dispute.

"A title, then?" David suggested. "Ruthven is a lord, yes. But an earldom? Your Grace can make earls, no? That might please him. Dukes are for the royal blood, but earls are the next in degree. In Scotland, at least. The English have their marquises, but not here. Your father is an earl, Johnnie. As is my Montrose uncle. An earl, then, on condition that Ruthven and the duke come to terms?"

The other two eyed each other.

"It might serve," Johnnie said. "And nane could stop you, Jamie. Nane ither can make earls. Only you."

"It's a notion, aye. If he'll hae it. Earl o' Rivven! We'll see, Davie, we'll see."

David spent the night in the castle, and dined with the Duke of Lennox who had quarters there. He was a friendly man, with his French accent, formerly Stewart d'Aubigny, easy to get on with, even if Ruthven did not find him so, the latter having his own house down in the town. Nothing was said of the earldom proposal, of policies or affairs of state, these not to be discussed at table.

Allotted a room to himself here, he wondered whether he would come face to face with the awkward Ruthven, or Rivven as James called him.

He did, when the king, saying that he had spoken to the duke, who was not opposed to this of an earldom, summoned the treasurer up to the castle. With Lennox at his back, James made the offer, this including some of the royal lands of Scone, these none so far from Ruthven Castle, but on condition that he and the Chancellor settled their differences in amicable fashion, for the good of the kingdom – this all declared in burbling diction and in braid Scots tongue. David, the Earl of Mar and Johnnie waited in the background.

Ruthven, surprised, looked round at all, stroked his pointed beard, cleared his throat, and eventually nodded. "As Your

Grace wills!" he said, but it was at Lennox that he looked, and less than amiably.

The duke stepped forward then, and held out a hand to shake, this accepted with a single jerk.

The bargain was made, however doubtfully, James glancing over at David, and grinning.

Later, the king informed that the treasurer did not wish to be styled Earl of Ruthven but Earl of Gowrie. This because the lands of Gowrie had belonged to the abbey of Scone, which he now held in part, and where he wished to expand his properties, there being more scope for territorial advancement there than at Ruthven. He had five sons and seven daughters, and was eager that they should all spread themselves across the lands. This change of the style of the earldom was of no matter to the king.

The duke spoke to David afterwards, saying that he understood that it was he who had suggested this of some sort of compact between himself and Ruthven and the granting of an earldom to facilitate it. That was of notable devising, in especial for so young a man, and was not to be forgotten, whatever the outcome.

James was quite pleased with himself in having appointed his first earl, although he had signed charters giving earldoms to three or four nominees of his late and detested regent, the Earl of Morton. Now he had actually created one – not that he liked the man, but that was not the point.

There was nothing to keep David at Stirling. In the rain, reduced to a mere drizzle, he rode back to Balvaird.

His priority, of course, was an early return to Creich. But now Lisa's father and brother would be there, and conditions not as he would wish them. How could he contrive to be alone with her?

He thought of a device that might possibly serve. The king

had been talking about a family and castle called Fernie, in Fife. The Fernies of that Ilk had long been hereditary foresters of his Falkland, and constables of the royal burgh of Cupar. Their line had fairly recently died out in an heiress, and Fernie had been bought by another landed family's son, Arnot of that Ilk. He could now claim these appointments, and James had wondered what sort of character he was, and whether he would make a worthy forester and constable. Fernie being only some six miles south of Creich, it now occurred to David that he could go and investigate the situation in the monarch's cause – and seek Lisa's help with it. That might work to his purpose.

At Creich, then, he had no complaints to make over his reception, Beaton having learned of his friendship with King James, and recognised possibilities of advantage in this. If he was in any way concerned over his daughter's association with their visitor he did not show it. And when David spoke of Fernie and the Arnots, Lisa declared that she knew them well, indeed the sister of young Arnot was her friend. So there was no need for excuses for her to accompany him to Fernie. Fortunately the weather had improved.

They rode off together, by the village of Luthrie, to circle to the west of the Hill of Lindifferon, which was known as the Mount locally; and although there were mounts by the thousand in Scotland, this one was quite famous as giving title to that renowned character, Sir David Lindsay of the Mount, who, among other poems and plays, wrote *The Satyre of the Thrie Estaitis*, mocking some of the follies of the Scots parliament and its members, Lisa mentioned. David, interested, said that he had often wondered which mount this so distinguished man had owned.

Fernie lay just south of this hill, in Stratheden, the central Fife vale, an ancient castle which had once been the seat of the MacDuff Earls of Fife, so prominent in Scotland's story.

It had passed to the Balfours and been enlarged and updated. It now made a fine place.

David found Walter Arnot easy to deal with, which was as well, for his visit was of his own devising, not the king's ordering. So he had to be careful what he said. He explained that he had the great privilege of being on friendly terms with the young monarch; and James had mentioned that the Fernies of that Ilk had always been foresters of Falkland, and questioned, now that their line had ended in an heiress, whether the new laird of Fernie desired to be appointed to that position? And if so, whether he would be a suitable incumbent?

Arnot admitted that he had thought on this, and wondered whether there was any possibility of thus gaining the royal favour. Would the king consider him? And what were the duties of the forester?

David had to confess that he was uncertain as to all that it entailed, but that in the main undoubtedly it meant overseeing the sporting rights and conditions of the royal forest, famed for its deer hunting. To see that there were no unauthorised hunters, and to punish any poachers. That was all fairly obvious. And there was also the constableship of Cupar. Just what this implied he did not know, but no doubt the provost of that royal burgh would inform.

The other declared that he would be much honoured to be allowed to take on these responsibilities, if the king would so agree.

No problems having arisen over this visit, and Arnot's sister Alicia having provided refreshment, the callers started off on their return to Creich, David wondering how best to advance his cause with Lisa. Somehow he must get her dismounted in order to gain the more physical contacts he sought. That Hill of Lindifferon, then? Their horses could take them most of the way up; but the final approaches to the summit looked as though they would require foot-climbing. Lisa however had not come very suitably clad for such.

He suggested a ride up the hill, to where Lindsay might well have conceived his project of the *Thrie Estaitis*.

Lisa voiced no objections, provided it did not take overlong, for the December dusk fell early.

It made no difficult riding, and as they climbed the views were far-reaching and rewarding. But David aimed for other rewards.

With outcrops of rock becoming prevalent as they neared the crest, he suggested dismounting. They tethered the horses to scrub, to go afoot for the short distance remaining, after he aided her down from her saddle and making something of a feature of it, which had her smiling. And he continued to hold her arm as they picked their way upwards, she having to hitch up her skirts somewhat.

At the summit they gazed around them. They could not actually see Creich because of the intervening hills, modest as these were. But they could glimpse both the Tay and the Forth estuaries, Lisa pointing out the various places of interest and naming them.

But there was a chilly wind up there, and hand in hand they began to retrace their steps.

They went only for a few yards however, to find a slight hollow, out of the easterly breeze, where David gestured.

"We can sit for a little time. Recover our breath," he said.

"I wondered when it would come to this!" she told him, wagging that head of hers.

"We have earned a rest, have we not?"

"Is that what it is to be?" But she sat down beside him. "You require rest?"

"I require *you*!" he declared. "As I have told you. You, all of you!" And he drew her to him.

"Is this the place for requiring? And giving?"

"Would you give?"

"I have already given somewhat, have I not?"

"I ask for more, Lisa. I have not hidden it."

"No. But there is a time and a place for all things. This scarcely it. On a hilltop on a winter's day."

"Would I be more fortunate elsewhere?"

"I judge so."

"How fortunate?"

"Wait you, and see."

He eyed her questioningly, and then rose. "At your home your family are . . . very much present," he said, as they went down to their horses.

"There are places where they are not."

"Mmm."

They spoke but little on the ride back to Creich.

As they drew near to the castle, she pointed over towards the orchard, this on a level stretch to the south. "I do not think that you have ever seen our pleasance? I spend much time there, tending the fruit trees. And the bushes. I make apple wine. Honey wine also, for we have bee-skeps there. I have a press for the apples in a shed there."

He did not fail to turn his mount to head for where she indicated.

"At this time of year there is little to see," she told him, but reined round with him.

Among the apple, pear and plum trees and the berry bushes they dismounted and, leaving the young woman to tether the horses, David headed straight for these sheds.

"The left-hand one is the apple one," she called after him. "It is the more . . . convenient."

Entering, he saw what she meant by convenient. There were rows of shelving laden with apples. He had seen straw covering the plant-beds against wintry weather as he came.

Now he saw that the far end of this shed was stacked with bundles of the straw. He went promptly to sit on that comfortable base, and facing her as she followed him in, held out his arms to her, wordless.

"No family here, meantime," she said, and sat down beside him.

"At last!" he exclaimed.

"Better than a hilltop," was as far as she got before her lips were sealed by his.

The man's embracing was as comprehensive as it was eager, Lisa not repelling him, even when busy fingers opened her bodice. His kissing of her bosom at least freed her lips to speak.

"Desirous one! Like any child at the breast!"

"Would that I could give you one, a child!" he blurted out.

"Ah! So that is it? Not today, my friend!"

"One day?"

"Who knows what might be?"

"You are my need, my longing, my hunger, my whole life's demand, the object of my wishes and thoughts and dreams!"

"Needs, desires, hunger, longings? I seem to have heard this before, David! But—"

"But you never say how *you* feel! You are kind. Kind, yes, as now. But I get no further! I never hear of my love returned. The love that is breaking my heart, woman!"

"Love!" she exclaimed. "Do I hear aright? *Love*?"

"What else? What else but love?"

She grasped him, all but shook him. "David! David, you love me! You are saying it, at last. Love! Is it true?"

"Lord, Lisa, what have I been telling you all these days, these weeks?"

"You have never said it. That one word. Love! The word

I needed. Oh, you foolish man!" She buried her face on his shoulder. "David my heart, my dear!"

He sought for words to express the tumult, the chaos, but the joy also, which was all but consuming him. Then, shaking his head, he stroked her hair, deep-breathing. What need for speech now? She loved *him*, or she would not be acting thus.

They rocked each other, there on the straw.

At length he got it out. "You will be mine? All mine? For aye? Mine!" he demanded.

"I have been for long, David Murray! Only, you did not say the word, the required word. So brief. But four letters. Love!"

"Did I not? Have I never said it? You must have known? I have not hidden it. But . . ." He gripped her, in sheerest possession. "We shall wed? Wed, woman!"

"What else? If we are each other's." She nodded her head, twice, thrice. "Then we shall be one. For all time. And hereafter."

He paused. "I am no great match, see you. No lord. No laird of great lands. Only a second son."

"Still you are foolish! Think you that I care for that?"

"Your father may!"

"I am my own woman. And now yours. Fear not. We shall wed. And the sooner the better, no? Impatient one?"

"It cannot be too soon for me!"

Oddly, now that he had her declaration and promise, David no longer continued nor went further with his love-making. All had suddenly become different. He was for up and acting, of another sort. All was changed. And all must know it. Eager otherwise now, he rose, taking her hand to hoist her to her feet.

Lisa laughed at this masterful change in him, as she buttoned that gaping bodice.

The approach to David Beaton presented none of the problems the prospective son-in-law had feared.

"I wondered when you were going to come to me with your quest, young man," he was told. "Delayed, no? Lisa seems to favour you, so why should not I? Even our young liege-lord is not averse to you, I hear. Which may be no disadvantage for your wellbeing. And therefore for my daughter's."

"I . . . I have your permission to wed her, then, sir?"

"I scarcely could withhold it, even if I wished! Lisa has a mind of her own – as you will discover, my friend! And she is of age. She has been directing all in this household since her mother died. Now she will direct yours. We will miss her."

"She will be none so far off, sir. Gospertie is but a dozen miles from Creich. It is no great house, I fear. But she will grace it."

"She will do more than that, if I know Lisa!" He shrugged. "But I wish you both well. When will you wed?"

"That is for her to decide."

"Like so much else, I judge!"

And that was that. David was accepted – and warned. How soon could he contrive the great day?

7

As it happened, despite the would-be groom's impatience, marriage had to be postponed, this on account of two very different factors. First, Lisa's father fell ill, seriously ill, of a lingering disease, a sweating sickness with the lungs and breathing much affected and fluxes resulting. Since the Reformation and the dispersal of the monks who had generally served the ailing, there had been a grievous loss of care in matters medical. Now Lisa's constant attention was demanded, her ministrations all that was available, this a long-drawn-out preoccupation. And second, there were monarchial troubles, in which David became involved. So the spring and summer of 1582 were not what the couple had looked forward to, with matters outwith their desires and control.

Lisa was kind to her lover in the interim, to be sure, granting him intimacies and attentions to ease his ardour; but generous and ample as these might be, she always stopped short of full possession, declaring that this must await their wedding night – or what would they have to celebrate? Grudgingly David had to admit the worth and truth of this.

His own preoccupation over these weeks commenced with the arrival at Gospertie of Johnnie Mar, who came much upset. Jamie had been taken, abducted against his will, a sort of prisoner, this by that scoundrel the new Earl of Gowrie, taken from Stirling off to Ruthven Castle, despite his protests. It was a scandal, shameful, all but high treason. Gowrie said that it was in the king's and the realm's interests, and that the Duke of Lennox was seeking to convert Jamie to

78

the bishops' cause, Episcopacy, to the hurt of the Kirk and God's true religion. Johnnie's father, the Earl of Mar, had objected, but to no effect. Gowrie, the High Treasurer, was adamant, and his senior, the most powerful man in the land other than the Chancellor, the duke. Jamie must be rescued.

David was appalled. But what could they do? Was Lennox not able to deal with this?

Apparently not. He was the Chancellor, yes, and presided at parliaments and the Privy Council. But he had been reared a Catholic in France, and was known to be strong for the bishops. So if he acted in this it could be seen as a move against the established Kirk – the reason Gowrie gave for taking Jamie out of the ducal influence. Lennox must not seem to be involved.

What was to be done, then? David demanded. They could not leave the king a prisoner at Ruthven.

"My faither said to come to tell *you*. My mither was a Murray o' Tullibardine. And you are kin to them. My mither's sister is wife to Tullibardine. And Tullibardine is scunnert wi' Rivven, aye has been, baith strang kirk folk as they are. Aye, and the Drummonds are close to the Murrays and against Rivven. Jamie Drummond, the Lord Drummond's son, is King Jamie's and my friend. We three were taught togither by yon Maister Buchanan. So – a bond. Between your Murrays, the Tullibardine ones and the Drummonds. A' in Strathearn, in the shire o' Perth against Gowrie. How say you?"

David, distinctly bemused by all this of kin and relationships as he was, had no doubts as to the need to rally to the aid of King James. He agreed that a united front of the enemies of Gowrie might well achieve the royal freedom. He would approach his father. He might even have got the Beatons into it, but unfortunately Lisa's father was a sick man.

So it was Balvaird for him, to seek to persuade his father to join in the rescue effort.

Sir Andrew was not hard to convince, even if Dand was less in favour. He was no friend of the Ruthvens, and duly concerned for the young monarch. He would do what he could.

Then on to Tullibardine went David, a score of miles westwards up Strathearn. There he found Sir William Murray strong in his condemnation of the king's removal by Gowrie, and more than ready to act. His sister was married to Patrick, third Lord Drummond, at Strathallan only a mile or two away; and he volunteered to take David there to seek to enrol that powerful family, descended from Maurice, the Hungarian shipmaster who had brought St and Queen Margaret to Scotland five centuries before, taking name from Drymen, near Loch Lomond, which she had given him.

Lord Drummond, like Sir William a man of middle years, heard of the situation grimly. He was prepared to do something about it. He suggested that their best course was for their group of magnates to present themselves at Ruthven Castle, request audience with the monarch; and if this was refused, demand James's release, or they would assemble their combined forces to achieve it. That threat ought to be effective, especially if they intimated that they would enrol other potent folk to join them. If not, then nothing for it but to muster their men in arms, and proceed to assail the castle. They did not want to bring Chancellor Lennox into it meantime, for fear of arousing religious contention.

This was accepted as the best procedure, and they left Strathallan.

David felt that he had made a fair start.

It took time to arrange a day to suit all the great ones who were to approach Gowrie; for David and his father had enrolled others to emphasise authority, including the Earls of Mar, Montrose and Glencairn, the last Lisa's uncle.

So they made an impressive group to present itself at the gatehouse of Ruthven Castle, two miles north-west of Perth, on a November day.

The fortalice was a handsome one, consisting of two great keeps, one ancient and one less so, these linked by a more recent and slightly lower building, to make a most commodious establishment, all within a courtyard surrounded by a high curtain wall and dry moat. So this was the young monarch's place of confinement. The drawbridge was raised, making access impassable.

Tullibardine hailed the guards at the gatehouse, who must have wondered at so numerous and lordly an approach. He shouted that they required audience with the King of Scots. He named the earls and the Lord Drummond.

It was called back that the lord of Gowrie would be informed although it was almost certain that the occupants of the castle would have observed the arrival of the visitation.

They had quite a wait, nevertheless, before a voice from the gatehouse parapet addressed them.

"I am Gowrie," it declared. "What seek you?"

"Audience with His Grace," Tullibardine returned.

"His Grace is engaged in . . . affairs."

"*We* come on the *realm*'s affairs! And must see him."

"What affairs?"

John, Earl of Mar spoke up, probably the most senior there, seventh of that title. "I am Mar, keeper of Stirling Castle and His Grace's former guardian. There are matters of state that require the king's decision, signature and seal."

"Then leave them with me. I will put them before His Grace."

"They require explanation and advice."

"I will see to that. I am High Treasurer. And of His Highness's Privy Council."

"As am I," Patrick, Earl of Montrose, David's kinsman

added. "And I demand to see His Grace, as an earl of Scotland, as are others here. *You* may not be aware, Gowrie, as a new earl, that we have this right. Ever since Scotland was, and before that, in the days of Pictish Alba, when the earls were styled the *ri*, the lesser kings, they had the right of audience at any time with the Ard Righ, the High King. Now we, Mar, Glencairn and Montrose, demand that audience." That made long shouting.

Silence.

Glencairn raised voice. "I, Glencairn, so require."

Again no reply.

"I am Drummond," that lord called. "My mother Lilian Ruthven was your aunt. I urge you, pay heed!"

The voice that answered was different. "My lord of Gowrie has retired," it said. "He bids you begone, my lords."

All there eyed each other, in anger, frustration, all but disbelief. So that was Gowrie. What could they do? Nothing, it seemed, meantime. Action there would have to be, but clearly not here and now.

David Murray, from the rear, shook his head, all his efforts fruitless. And Jamie in the grip of that man . . .

Back at Gospertie, David was not long in making his way to Creich to tell Lisa of it all. She declared that Gowrie should be hanged! He could not keep the king imprisoned indefinitely. He would have the entire nation against him. His time would come.

She was able to report some improvement in her father's condition, enough, she judged, for them to plan their marriage. A Yuletide wedding? Or just before?

David was all for before. Had they not waited sufficiently long? For himself, it could be on the morrow or the next day. No need for any great ado and fuss.

She would have a meet and worthy wedding, she declared.

After all, God willing, it would be her only one. And she had her woman's condition to consider, let him not forget. How about St Drostan's Day, a good Scots saint, 14th December? That would be suitable for her.

He said that he could probably wait for just that long.

So it was decided, the man at least starting to count the days . . . and the nights.

8

The local church, which Creich shared with the neighbouring hamlet of Brunton, was small, really only a chapel, and clearly incapable of holding all the folk who were to attend the wedding. The ceremony might have been held in one of the large churches of Cupar, ten miles distant, but Lisa's father was still frail and in no condition to travel. So the problem had to be solved. If it had been a summertime event, it could have been held outdoors, in the courtyard of the castle; but in mid-December this was out of the question. So the parish minister was besought to bless and consecrate the large barn of the nearby mains, or home farm; and this, for the occasion hung with tapestry and plaids, and decorated with holly and other greenery, had to serve. So David Beaton was able to be present, much amusement being expressed by all concerned over this unusual venue.

Odd as the site and scene might be, the nuptials proceeded satisfactorily enough, with Lisa looking at her most lovely, the target for all eyes, superbly gowned and most obviously happy and assured. David, for his part, although clad in his best, was a deal less confident, particularly as he had to have his brother Dand as groomsman, with whom he got on only doubtfully, and who on this occasion contributed much more of flourish and display than did the groom who was in a state of some bemusement. Indeed he was scarcely aware of the details and significance of much of the performance, although he kept telling himself that this was it, this the great event to which he had looked forward, the most important and vital day of his entire life, long awaited.

He was in due course nudged by Dand to cope with the ring-fitting, Lisa beaming smiles and squeezes of fingers which accompanied his fumbling, and pressing him down on his knees to receive the final declaration and benediction of man and wife. He rose and clutched her, wordless. *His* time would come.

At the barn door it was all salutations, congratulations, good wishes and some advice, not all of the last welcome. Then back to the castle hand in hand for the feasting.

Thereafter, with many of the guests tending to become drink-merry, Lisa, anxious to avoid the popular bedding ceremony, had arranged that they should quietly slip away, to make for her friends' house of Fernie, seven miles, where they were promised peace and privacy, although the Arnots remained at Creich.

The ride, despite the darkening, was no concern, at least for David, who was much more at home in the saddle than among wedding celebrations, their finery wrapped in cloaks.

They rode in silence much of the way, although now and again they moved close, to reach over and clasp each other.

At Fernie the servants were well instructed and understanding. They had prepared a repast for the newly weds, but this was declined, save for the wine, and there was no delay over proceeding upstairs to the warmed and thoughtfully decorated bedchamber. There, closing the door behind them with his first real flourish of the day, David held out his arms. Lisa flung herself into them.

"Dear heart! Beloved! My adored! My all, all! And now all *mine*! My wife!" he got out.

"Yours . . . for long!" was all that she managed to respond, before being picked up bodily and carried over to the canopied bed.

There he delayed only long enough for her to discard her riding-boots before commencing to undress her, she aiding him where helpful and murmuring endearments. Soon she was naked, and lay there in the lamp- and firelight, all the superb, shapely and inviting femininity of her.

He stood back a little to gaze, to devour her loveliness with his eyes, as she held out open arms to him, no shy and bashful maiden this.

They were both silent now, deep-breathing, the stirring of her splendid breasts a gift and giving in itself.

He began to throw off his own clothing, then thought better of it, and knelt beside the bed in his shirt-sleeves, to start kissing her, all of her, from hair and brow and eyes, to white shoulders and neck down to the welcoming thrusting breasts, lingering there, and on to rounded belly and the dark triangle at her groin, the so provocative invitation to the ultimate goal and climax. Then further down her long white legs, which she spread wider for him, until he could delay no longer with these preliminaries, delightful as they were, and had to make the final challenge and take possession. Lisa's welcome of him into her was as warm as all else about her, even though she could not refrain from gasping and jerking at his forceful entry, virginity abandoned. Her fierce clutching of his back, nails digging in, were her inevitable reactions to his masculine urgency and thrusting.

This did not, could not, last long before David convulsed in an ecstasy of fulfilment, while she gazed up at the bed's canopy, lip-biting, until, in a few moments, he sank limply heavy upon her, panting his gratification.

"I hope . . . I hope," was all that she said.

"Yes. Yes, lass," he mumbled against her heaving bosom. "You will, you will. Give me . . . a little time. And I will pleasure you. I do promise it."

He rolled off her, and they lay side by side, silent, save for their sighs.

It was not overlong before the man was able to begin the discharge of his pledge to her. But now he was more gentle, less hurried, caressing, kissing, fondling and seeking to stimulate, arouse and please. And with some degree of success, before once more he came to male culmination, however much he sought to restrain himself.

Shaking his head, and mumbling, he sank down on her again.

"That was . . . better," she declared. "I am learning. I think that I will come to relish it!"

"You will, you will! You are . . . all woman!" he told her, his voice already becoming drowsy.

They lay there, on their backs. Soon he slept. But Lisa took much longer, holding his hand and thinking, thinking.

They slept late into the morning, and thereafter waited for the return of their Arnot friends from Creich. In the afternoon they rode for Gospertie's modest laird's house, no castle, more of a hallhouse or large farming manor, but Lisa making no complaints. She would make a worthy home of it undoubtedly, not long in pointing out adjustments and improvements and possibilities. She behaved in most friendly fashion towards the elderly couple who had kept it in order for David, and who now would move to a cottage nearby, as arranged.

While somewhat apologetic about the premises to which he had brought his bride, David was proud to show her his extensive drainage developments, and the waste land that he had bettered thereby and made cultivable. He claimed that, if adopted more generally by other lairds and farmers, this could greatly enhance the value of their properties and tenancies, this including Creich itself, where there was much heath and morass. Lisa was duly impressed. For her part, she was all for bettering the state of the orchard at Gospertie, this somewhat neglected. She declared that she would have a row of beehives therein, to provide honey for their table, and honey wine, of which she was fond. Also wax for candles, which she knew how to make, and for polishing panelling and furniture.

Their arrival at Gospertie coincided with the start of the Yuletide festive period, and Lisa was determined to make their first Christmas together a memorable one. So busy she became forthwith. David had never spent a festivity of any sort at his inherited property, and much applauded her efforts.

They visited Balvaird, of course, where David's mother, the Lady Janet, was delighted with her new daughter-in-law, asserting that her second son was a fortunate young man indeed.

His father, however, had other matters on his mind. With the king held prisoner, Mar and Tullibardine were planning a full-scale assault on Ruthven Castle within the next few weeks, when they could muster a sufficiency of loyal folk for the challenge.

So a rewarding Christmastide was spent at Gospertie, with the anticipation of action soon to free King Jamie, Lisa almost as concerned for the youth as was her husband.

9

It was all but an army that assembled at Perth, to march westwards the short distance to Ruthven, Mar leading the great assembly of lords, lairds and even some Kirk ministers, Johnnie well to the fore with David at his side. Siege-machinery was outdated and not available, but they had scaling-ropes with anchors attached, and no lack of arms.

They surrounded the castle and a trumpet was blown. Mar shouted.

"I, sixth Earl of Mar, demand audience with His Grace the King. Tell the Earl of Gowrie so."

There was no reply from the gatehouse.

"Heed well!" he went on. "Disobey, and you are all guilty of treason, high treason. And will be dealt with accordingly."

Still silence.

"Have the Earl of Gowrie speak."

He got an answer to that. "My lord of Gowrie bids you be gone."

"So! Very well. He pays the price!" Mar turned and raised a clenched fist to the great company behind him, and a mighty yelling and cheering arose and continued, all around the perimeter walling. Time for talk was over, action now on that high bank above the River Almond.

David and Johnnie were more than ready. Each had a long rope, knotted at intervals a foot or so apart, tied to a three-pronged iron hook to serve as anchor. The walling surrounding the courtyard was a score of feet high, topped by a parapet and wall-walk for guards. The objective was to hurl up the ropes sufficiently high for the anchors to drop over the parapet, to be tugged this way and that until hopefully caught in some projection of the masonry and held, so that the throwers could then climb up the rope, using the knots as hand- and footholds, to reach the parapet and over, there to be ready with swords and dirks drawn to meet any guards. The walling was extensive, to be sure, following the contours of the terrain, hundreds of yards of it, and the defenders could be only scattered. So the more numerous attackers had good chances of their anchors not being flung back upon them, and not being countered on reaching the wall-walk.

David's first throw of his rope-ladder did not find a grip, and he had to dodge the descent back of his own hook. But Johnnie was more successful, his anchor gripping, and he clambering up agilely. Meeting no opposition, he was able to tether David's second throw securely, so that his friend could mount to join him.

They did see guards and other attackers fighting a score or so of yards off to the right. Drawing swords, they ran along the walk to aid their colleagues. The two defenders here involved were hurled, screaming, over the parapet, to crash to the ground below.

Greatly outnumbered, the guards were soon disposed of, some abandoning the wall-walk and hurrying down to the courtyard below, with its stables, hay-sheds and storehouses, making for the doors of the two great towers of the castle.

Following them down, David and Johnnie rallied some of their fellows to proceed to the key point of the outer defences, the gatehouse and arch guarding the drawbridge spanning the dry moat outside, this presently raised. Attacked from the rear as they hid from arrows aimed from beyond, the men here were quickly overcome, and the all-important draw-bridge clankingly lowered, the wheels of its chains turned, to cheers from outside. Another set of wheels raised the iron portcullis.

Once these defensive devices were down and up, the main strength of the attackers surged into the courtyard. Now for the two linked keeps themselves, the major and ultimate challenge.

All the leadership knew where the possible weakness was. The massive thick-walled towers themselves were all but impregnable, standing separate, the doors up at first-floor level reached by detached stone steps, the platform tops of which could be reached only by plank gangways pushed over from the doorways themselves. So there was no access possible there. But Gowrie's father, Patrick, Lord Ruthven, had deemed it convenient to join those two keeps together by erecting a linking and lower building, and this had its door at ground level. Convenient it might be, but this constituted the only weakness of the main castle. The massive door would undoubtedly be well guarded, however.

This was quickly emphasised when the first of the attackers went to inspect it, and were promptly a target for missiles hurled down upon them from the open bartizans of the two keeps high above.

David, who had been eyeing it all from the first, shouted, "A battering-ram! A ram for it. A ram!"

That was well enough. A lengthy massive hammer of some sort which could be propelled by a team of men to smash down the door, long enough for the wielders to be some way back from those missile-throwers above, or at least under some protective cover.

As the leaders asked themselves what could possibly be used for a battering-ram, it was David again who suggested the answer, for he had been interested by stories of sieges in the past since his boyhood.

"The drawbridge! The drawbridge timbers!" he cried. "Use

one of those. Long enough. Break up the bridge. One of its beams."

At least there were plenty of men to tackle the task of part-dismantling the bridge, David directing, and a sufficiency of battle-axes and maces for the work. He pointed out that some of the planking could be used to provide a covering roof for the ram-wielders. It might be rather extraordinary that, with all the great ones present, everyone seemed prepared to accept this young man's orders. Clearly he knew what he was at.

It took time to detach one of the main bridge supports, but time was not greatly important. No one was going to come to the rescue of Gowrie. In one of the courtyard sheds they found carts, and smashing off the upper works of one of these, they were able to use the undercarriage and wheels on which to base their lengthy battering-ram, the bridge timber being fully thirty feet in length, this to span the wide moat.

There were ample volunteers to push the ram. They found better boarding in the stable block to use as cover over the rammers' heads, raised on lances, and this ought to be sufficient to protect them from anything flung down by the defenders.

All ready, David, with Johnnie Mar, gave the signal to start, this after manoeuvring their heavy and unwieldy weapon on its carriage into due position. To the cheers of the onlookers, the rammers bent to their task. Their first push was not successful, the positioning of the cartwheels wrong, too much to the rear, so that the nose of the ram rose at too high an angle, and was going to strike the stone lintel of the doorway, not its timbers. So an adjustment had to be made. A second thrust, and the dozen men, driving forward with all their might, smashed the ram-head against the massive door fairly enough. One of its vertical planks was shattered, but the others held fast. Stones and other objects rained down on them from aloft, but the boarding cover was enough to protect the rammers.

Back they pulled, and well back, to give an added impetus to their drive, and at a shout from David the third assault was made. And with a splintering crash the door collapsed, torn off its bolts and hinges.

David and Johnnie led the entry rush, swords and dirks drawn. Thankfully they saw that the stairway within was a straight one, held by a group of the garrison. Had it been one of the more ancient twisting turnpikes, only one man, part hidden behind the central newel, could have barred the way with a sword single-handed, so narrow were these ascents. But the straight steps, however convenient for everyday use, did not provide such cover. Facing the defenders, David shouted for lances, spears, and these were quickly forthcoming. Their length, greatly outmatching the swords, drove the opposition back and, both sides stumbling on the steps, the attack proceeded slowly upwards.

In the lead, David was well aware of the problems ahead. This linking building looked like being captured; but the two massive keeps on either side presented a different challenge. They could not bring their battering-ram up here. The need was to prevent the escaping steps-defenders from getting within the doors and slamming them shut and bolted. The lances again, however unwieldy, must be used for that, to jam them open.

This worked, and the backing-away Ruthven men were unable to keep their assailants from following them into the left-hand keep, which was the one they entered, the opposite door remaining unopened. In after them David, Johnnie and the others drove.

Once inside the large tower's narrow vaulted passages, with streams of men coming on behind them, a halt was called. A muster, David urged, a muster. Numbers were needed now, to penetrate and explore and to enter the various chambers on the different levels. They would vastly outnumber the occupants. Let them do so effectively. Presumably this was the keep being used by Gowrie.

Once sufficient men had gathered, it was a matter of splitting up, following the defenders and searching the rooms up and down. David led one group, with Johnnie, Tullibardine, Mar and Drummond likewise.

Where would Gowrie and young Jamie be? The main hall would be down on the first floor, as was normal. There could assemble the greater numbers of the garrison. So it was down the twisting turnpike for most of them, some defenders retreating hurriedly before them. Other chambers opened off at different levels, and David was investigating one of these when loud yells sounded from just below, and continued. Presumably these signified something important, and he led his group out and down.

The noise proved to be coming from a lesser second-floor hall. And reaching this they entered. And there was Johnnie Mar embracing the king, with Gowrie standing nearby glowering, arms folded, confronted by Drummond and Tullibardine, wild rejoicing going on all around, the fighting over.

David ran forward to grasp Jamie's shoulders, unsuitable behaviour towards a monarch as this might be. The king was babbling, they all were.

Great was the excitement. Gowrie was hustled away, to be put into one of his own dungeons, and the large family of no fewer than five sons and seven daughters, his wife being dead, told to remove themselves to the other Ruthven castle of Dirleton, in Haddingtonshire, south of the Forth.

David found himself being hailed as something of a hero, his efforts over the battering-ram in especial acclaimed. When James heard of it all from Johnnie, he was grateful indeed, and declared that Davie must be rewarded. He would think of something suitable. He told them how he hated Gowrie, who had forced him to sign a paper awarding him indemnity for taking him and holding him captive, as this being for the good of the realm. He had got on well enough with the Ruthven girls, but the boys had been unkind, mimicking his speech and gait, calling him King Lickspittle because he tended to dribble somewhat, ever at him, mocking. The youngest, Patrick, was the best of them. He would be thankful to get back to Stirling Castle and Johnnie's companionship.

The attacking force was dispersed, with congratulations, leaving Tullibardine in charge at Ruthven, his seat only a few miles off, and his people numerous enough to provide a garrison, Gowrie removed to Stirling.

David and his father and brother returned to Balvaird, Dand less than happy over the other's popularity. David did not enquire what part *he* had played in the proceedings.

King James released from his captivity was to find that there
had to be major changes at court, and urgently. His kinsman
and friend, Esmé, Duke of Lennox, had gone over to France
to deal with some matter of his estate of Aubigny, when he
suddenly fell ill, and died. This dire happening produced more
than mourning, for he had been Chancellor of the realm. A
successor had to be appointed, and swiftly. His son, Ludovick,
who followed him in the dukedom, was considered to be too
young and inexperienced in affairs of state to take on the
office. So another of the Stewarts, James, Earl of Arran, was
given the chancellorship, a younger man who had gained the
Hamilton earldom of Arran through his heiress mother. This
office, needless to say, was a vitally important one, for as
well as presiding at parliaments its holder had the task of
convening the Secret or Privy Council.

And now a parliament was promptly required to decide
on what to do with Gowrie. He could not be tried for high
treason in the normal courts of justiciary because he was
High Treasurer of the kingdom and a member of the said
Privy Council. It would have to be a parliament itself that
judged him.

David's father, as Baron of Arngask, had a seat in parliament, this one being held in the great hall of Stirling Castle, as
so often; and David went to watch from the minstrels' gallery.
Arran presided, with the king sitting on a throne on the dais,
and Mar alongside. It was a crowded assembly, this one.

Arran, bowing towards the throne, declared that this was

an especial session, and the commissioners must bear with him as it was his first as Chancellor. They were there to consider the position of the Earl of Gowrie, who had unlawfully and by force taken the person of His Grace the King into custody at his castle of Ruthven, and there held him for many months. Now His Grace had been freed, and Gowrie apprehended. Parliament must decide on the consequences. He ordered William, Earl of Gowrie to be brought before the assembly.

That man was led in, looking haughtily indignant, and, before any further announcement could be made, loudly declared that this was a travesty of a trial and justice, and quite unlawful. That he was Lord High Treasurer of this kingdom, and as such had taken His Grace James into his protection from the machinations of those who were seeking to enforce Episcopacy on the nation, contrary to the established rule of Holy Kirk and Christ's true religion. His actions had been for the weal of the realm. And it was to be noted by all that he who would have been presiding here this day had been the leader of that grievous confederacy, and had been taken to final judgment in France.

Uproar arose in the hall, with Episcopalians and Presbyterians shouting at each other and shaking fists, Roman Catholics looking on bemused, and non-aligned members protesting at this bringing up of religious bias to the proceedings.

Arran banged his gavel on the clerks' table for silence.

When he had gained it, he announced that such behaviour was unseemly, and must end. The Earl of Gowrie was in error in addressing the assembly before the offences with which he was to be charged were fully declared, speaking much out of turn. He was here to be tried by parliament. He, the new Chancellor, now called on the High Justiciar of the realm, Colin, Earl of Argyll, to detail the charges.

From the earls' benches, Campbell of Argyll rose. "I accuse William, Earl of Gowrie of high treason," he announced. "The assault on the person of the monarch, the taking of His Grace into custody, the holding of him against the royal will for months, whatever his proclaimed reason, this constituting treason of the most grievous sort. No valid excuse nor explanation is possible for such offence. And the penalty for high treason is known to all!"

There was more shouting.

Arran had to bang that gavel again. "You have heard the charges, my lord of Gowrie. You may now speak."

"This is folly," Gowrie declared. "I acted for the realm's and the Kirk's weal. Someone had to do so. And I have His Grace's written pardon and indemnity for any inconvenience occasioned to His Highness."

There were gasps at this, as all gazed at the young king.

"He made me do it!" James cried thickly. "He forced me to it. He did!" It was seldom that a monarch intervened thus in a debate.

Mar, at his side, tapped the royal arm and shook his head.

Argyll spoke up. "Nothing that the accused has said reduces the offence. Does any here, save himself, say otherwise?"

"I do," the Earl of Rothes announced. He was married to Gowrie's sister, and was strong for the reformed Kirk. "As High Treasurer the Earl of Gowrie had a duty to perform. If he did it over-zealously, that is unfortunate. But that is not high treason. And he was aiding the Kirk."

"To take the king by force and against his royal will, *is* treason," the Lord Drummond asserted. "That is not to be denied. And he must be punished. Or the realm is in chaos."

There were shouts for and against, commissioners jumping to their feet, the Chancellor hard put to it to maintain order.

"The issue before parliament is simple," he said, when he

could make himself heard. "Was the Earl of Gowrie guilty of treason, or was he not? The matter of religion must not come into it, solely the issue of taking his liege-lord by force and detaining him against his will. I put it to the vote. Who moves that the accused is guilty?"

"I do," Argyll from the earls' benches called.

"And I second," Tullibardine from among the barony-holders added.

"And I move against. No treason committed," Rothes declared.

"I second." That was the Lord Colville of Culross, another of Gowrie's brothers-in-law.

"So – vote. Those in favour of the accused, no treason, show hands."

A fair number of hands were raised, but clearly nothing like a majority of those present. The clerks did not require to count.

"Those who declare treason committed?"

Fully two-thirds of those present voted against Gowrie.

"So be it," Arran announced. "Guilty. Now, the punishment? The recognised penalty for high treason is death, execution. But . . ." He left the rest unsaid.

The High Justiciar, Argyll, rose. "I advise otherwise. My lord of Gowrie is, or was, High Treasurer, and of His Grace's Secret Council. He acted wrongly, yes. But he could have intended less so, conceived himself as serving the realm. I say no execution. Instead, banishment. Banishment from the kingdom."

Again shouting for and against.

Mar spoke up, his first intervention. "Execution could be over-severe. He is paying the price. Dismissed from the treasurership. And from the council. Forfeited. Let it be banishment. Let him leave Scotland. Go to France, or otherwise. Will that not serve?"

There were murmurs from all over the hall, mainly in agreement. Argyll nodded. It was accepted.

Arran used his gavel. "I declare that it is the decision of parliament. The Earl of Gowrie forfeits all position and power in this land, and departs into exile. And that forthwith. To France, or where he will. But not to England or Wales or Ireland. So I pronounce." He paused. "With Your Grace's royal permission, I declare this session of parliament now adjourned."

The Lord Lyon King of Arms, waiting near the throne, signed to a herald, who blew a trumpet-blast. "Stand for the King's Grace," he ordered.

All rose, as Mar took James's arm, raised him, and led him from the hall.

Guards took Gowrie out by a rear door.

From his gallery, David drew a long breath. So that was that. Gowrie was to meet his deserts, although not execution. It was enough. Or was it?

It was not long before Scotland learned that it was *not* enough. Conducted to Dundee to take ship for France, Gowrie had managed to escape from his guards, and entered the castle of Dudhope in that town, presumably with the connivance of Sir James Scrymgeour, constable and provost of Dundee, who had been one of those voting in favour of Gowrie at the parliament. There he summoned Lord Colville of Culross, his brother-in-law, to bring men to his aid, and ordered all his tenantry of Ruthven and the Carse of Gowrie to flock to him, armed. One of the Carse lairds, however, a Hay, was more loyal to the crown than to Gowrie, and hastened with word of it all to Stirling; and Mar, with Lord Drummond and Tullibardine and others from Strathearn, was able to march on Dundee in sufficient numbers to forestall any assembly of the rebels; Gowrie was captured and brought to Stirling once more, and securely immured in one of the stronghold's dungeons.

And now the situation demanded another sitting of parliament, in order to renounce the decision of the previous one as to banishment. All close to the king agreed that there was nothing for it but execution. So long as Gowrie lived he was obviously going to seek to control the king and the kingdom, his ambition insatiable.

The custom was for forty days' notice to be given for the calling of a parliament; but in this crisis such must be dispensed with, on the royal authority. So it was a small and sparsely attended assembly which was held at Stirling again, this quite lawful in that Chancellor Arran had declared the last meeting adjourned, not actually terminated, a fortunate chance; so this was able to be declared merely a resumption of the earlier sitting.

David was there again, in the gallery with Johnnie, James actually waving to them from his throne. So they heard the doom of execution passed on the so troublesome Gowrie, and this ordered to be without delay by Argyll the High Justiciar, whose attendance had been possible at short notice because he was tending to reside these days at Castle Campbell none so far off, at Dollar in Clackmannanshire, rather than on his ancestral estates up in the West Highlands.

David had no desire to witness the actual beheading; but Johnnie Mar did so, and later described the scene to his friend. Gowrie had behaved, in the end, with dignity and seeming composure. He asked for the scaffold to be decked in scarlet cloth, and from its platform, after a brief private prayer with a kirk minister, announced that if he had served God as faithfully as he had done the king, he would not have come to this end. He believed, however, that their merciful Father would accept His unworthy servant into His peace. Then, rejecting the usual performance of the headsman to tie a kerchief over the victim's eyes, did so himself, then opened his doublet to bare his neck, and knelt, actually smiling, to lay his neck on the block. A single blow of the axe severed head from body. The corpse was then wrapped in the scarlet cloth, and taken for burial.

So died William Ruthven, even Johnnie praising the manner of it.

Scotland would be very different without him, to be sure.

Part Two

11

David, rejoicing at being able to live normally at Gospertie with Lisa, with peace in Scotland, was not long in becoming involved in great changes in the realm, even though these were not occasioned by treasonable and rebellious activities that summer. The Earl of Mar suddenly died, to the distress of loyal folk, as of family and friends, and Johnnie became seventh Earl of Mar. King James, greatly saddened by the loss of his all but guardian and long-time mentor, decided to celebrate his eighteenth birthday by assuming full rule of his kingdom. Arran, the new Chancellor, supported him in this, as did the rest of the Privy Council.

There were great official ongoings to mark the event; but the monarch summoned David to Stirling for a more private proceeding, with just himself and Johnnie involved. And in a privy chamber in the royal quarters, he poured plentiful drinks for the three of them, and then raised his tankard high.

"Here's tae us a'!" he announced. "Tae mysel' in taking ower the rule. To Johnnie, noo Earl o' Mar. And tae Davie, to be gien a richt weel-earned place in this kingdom o' mine. I've been aiming to dae this, for lang. Noo we'll hae his guid works right marked. Here's tae Davie!"

Johnnie also drank, even if David could not.

"I have done nothing in especial, Sire," that one said. "Helpful in a small way against Gowrie at Ruthven. Taught Your Grace how to stalk the stags . . ."

"Hear him! A sma' way! Yon o' the battering-ram was

richt remarkable, aye remarkable! And much ither. Johnnie, fetch you yon sword," and he pointed to a garderobe in the thickness of the walling. "Kneel you, Davie lad."

Blinking, David shook his head, but had to obey the royal command.

Somewhat gingerly, James took the sword from Johnnie, for he had a dread of cold steel, said to be the result of the slaying of his mother's Italian secretary, David Rizzio, before her eyes, and she pregnant with James, and that by none other than Gowrie, then the Lord Ruthven, Darnley her husband looking on and urging. Gripping the weapon tensely, unhandily, he brought the blade down first on one of David's shoulders and then on the other, narrowly missing his head in the so doing.

"Davie Murray, I hereby dub thee knight," he gabbled. "Thus and thus! For services richt weel rendered. Be thou guid knight until thy life's end. Aye, so! Arise, Sir Davie!"

Speechless, David got to his feet, James promptly getting rid of the sword, and punching one of the newly knighted shoulders.

"Hoo's that, then?" he demanded. "*Sir* Davie? Aye, *Sir* Davie! And yon lassie, Lisa Beaton, the bonny yin, to be *Lady* Murray."

"Sire, this is, this is too much! I, I thank you. But . . ."

"Hae done wi' this o' Sire and Grace, man, when we are alane. Just Jamie and Davie. Aye, and Johnnie. And it's no' too much. I'm no' done yet, see you. I'm haeing you at my court, here. You're to be my Cup Bearer, so's you can be richt close to me. And bonny fichter as you are, Captain o' my Royal Guard. No' only that, but because of the stalking and the hunting, you're to be Maister o' the Horse. What say you to that, eh?"

David was too bewildered to say anything.

But the monarch was not finished even yet. "You'll need

a seat in the parliament, no' just up in yon gallery," he went on. "Sae you've to hae ain o' yon Rivven's forfeited estates, the barony o' Collace, in Gowrie. You ken it? Dunsinane is on it, whaur yon MacBeth had his bit castle. Yon's no' there noo, mind. But there's a richt enough ha'hoose. You're to be the Baron o' Collace."

David looked from James to Johnnie. He wondered whether their liege-lord had taken leave of his senses.

"Better than yon Gospertie, eh?" Johnnie observed.

"It is all, all beyond belief!"

"You'll get used to it, man Davie!"

"Enough o' this, then," James declared. "We'll awa' and eat. And you can play my Cup Bearer at table, Davie. Wi' plenties, plenties. And I'll tell you if you dinna dae it richt, never fear! And after, you can go oot and inspect the guards, as their captain. I'll keep you busy!"

That June night, David rode back to Gospertie, his mind in a whirl.

Lisa was much impressed by all her husband's royal favours and appointments, wondering whether she would play the Lady Murray of Collace adequately. She recognised that they would have to spend much of their time at court, but hoped that it would not be too much, for she wanted their married life not to be spoiled by overmuch public activities. Presumably they would be leaving Gospertie for this Collace? She was eager to see it.

David was uncertain as to how often he was expected to be present at Stirling, and how much he would be able to be master of his own time. He understood that there was a deputy captain of the Royal Guard, one William Stewart, so perhaps his own duties would not be too onerous in this respect. Cup Bearer would be more or less honorary, to allow close contact with the monarch. As to Master of the Horse,

James had said that this was to be concerned with hunting mainly. So perhaps no very protracted attendances at court would be demanded of him.

Meantime, he and Lisa would go to inspect this new Collace barony before the next call to Stirling came.

They had some twenty-five miles to ride, through Glen Farg and into Strathearn, over Moncrieffe Hill and down to Perth to cross Tay; then north-east another eight miles, by Bonhard and Balbeggie, on the skirts of the Sidlaw Hills. They saw the two tall summits of Dunsinane and Black Hill dominating the landscape ahead of them, and knew that they were nearing Collace.

Just when they entered their barony they could not tell; but reaching scattered woodland they came to a cottage, and asking the woman there where they were and what this was called, they were told that it was Bandirran Wood, that they were a mile or so south of the village of Kinrossie. They knew that Kinrossie was in Collace parish. It was strange to be riding through this their own new property without knowing it.

Before they reached the village, they came to the church of the parish, not in either of the villages but midway between them, with the manse and a few houses. They called in at the manse, met the Reverend Ogilvie, who eyed them somewhat warily when he learned their identity, well aware that Sir David Murray had been much involved in the bringing down of his previous lord, Gowrie. However, Lisa's friendly good looks reassured him, and he became more amiable. He had not heard that Sir David was now Baron of Collace, and was duly respectful. Asked where was the seat of the barony, he told them that it was Dunsinane Castle, this lying a mile or so west of the Kirkton, and not, as might have been assumed, near Dunsinane Hill, which lay in the opposite direction.

So it was on through more woodland, and past a small

loch, to a quite handsome hallhouse, defensive but not any real castle or tower-house, set on a sort of terrace, with fine views southwards.

Lisa fell for it at once, declaring that it looked worthy indeed, and if it was as good within as it seemed without it would make a pleasing home, a deal finer than Gospertie, David reserving his judgment. She approved of the loch and the views.

They found the keepers or caretakers of the place as guarded as the other residents they had met thus far, as was not to be wondered at in the circumstances, on property forfeited to the crown by its executed lord's misdemeanours, all unsure of their position now. But the new owners sought to put them at ease. Apparently this house had previously been occupied by an aunt of Gowrie, now departed to another nephew's establishment in Fife.

Dunsinane House, when examined, quite came up to Lisa's expectations, with much character, commodious and comfortable. It would make an excellent residence, she declared. King James had done them well, although almost certainly he had never visited the place.

They spent two days and nights at Dunsinane, climbing the hill of that name, steep on three sides, less so on the other, to visit the so-called MacBeth's Castle, although this was in fact an infinitely earlier structure, a large Pictish fort of green grass-grown ramparts and ditches, the vistas magnificent, particularly north-eastwards up Strathmore, that vast vale, right to the sea, and north to Coupar Angus, Blairgowrie and even Alyth, famed for its links with King Arthur's Queen Guinevere and Sir Lancelot. The Black Hill nearby, still higher if less renowned, was also rewarding. They visited Collace village itself, the Milton thereof, the Witches Stone and its stone circle at Cairnbeddie, St Martine's Chapel, the former monastery of Friarton near at hand, and of course the little loch, which attracted them both. Lisa said that she could swim therein, which she had not done since she left Creich near Tayside, and David, seeing trout jump, recognised opportunity for angling. Altogether they esteemed Collace as a most notable acquisition, and blessed King Jamie for it, whether he knew of its attractions or not.

Back at Gospertie, they found the half-expected summons from the monarch awaiting them – but for David to go to Falkland, not Stirling. The Master of the Horse was to perform duties there.

At the little palace beneath the East Lomond Hill, David found James in something of a state. There had been poaching of his deer, he announced. Some wretched scoundrels had been killing them. Parts of carcases had been found over quite a wide area, haunches and legs cut off but heads left, venison the objective obviously. Many beasts slain. This must be stopped, the culprits found and punished. Falkland was a royal hunting-forest. Let such miscreants seek their venison on the Ochil heights if have it they must, not on *his* bailiwick. Let the Master of the Horse see to it.

David promised to do what he could. It seemed a strange task for the monarch's Master of the Horse, but then James was a strange monarch.

So instead of joining in next day's hunt, he set about this duty. A little thought convinced him that local men, that is the folk of Falkland, would not be likely to kill the king's deer, this to endanger their situation and wellbeing. And this poaching was being done on a large scale apparently, so it was not just for family feeding. It must be for profit. So the venison would be for selling. And not to the Falkland people, who would be suspicious. Another community, then. But not too far away, with the problems of transporting the meat. There were two fairly large villages near Falkland, Freuchie and Kingskettle, three and five miles to the east. Markinch and Windygates were probably too far off.

Freuchie and Kingskettle first, then.

At a junction of roads and tracks, Freuchie was as large a place as Falkland. Leaving his horse at the mill on the burnside, half a mile from the village, David went on foot. He seldom was grandly dressed, especially for riding, and he would not be known here. He would speak in the broad Lowland dialect.

Choosing one of the larger houses in the main street, he rapped on the door, which was opened by a heavy elderly woman, who eyed him enquiringly.

"I'm frae Kirkforther," he announced. "I was telt that folk here were selling deer-meat, venison. Cheap. I could dae wi' some. D'ye ken whae sells it, mistress?"

"Kirkforther? Yon's a couple o' miles. You've cam a lang way for your meat, my man!"

"My wife's birthday. It's the morn's morn. She could dae wi' a change frae mutton. She has a taste for the venison. I was tellt try Freuchie. A friend frae Muirhead had won some frae a man here."

"Aye, weel, there's twa-three whae get their hands on the venison, some way. There's Pate Shaw. And Dan Henderson. Aye, and Hal Kemp. They a' whiles hae venison to sell. Try you them."

"Whaur dae I find them?"

"Och, Pate Shaw's just four doors up by." She sniffed. "But if I ken them, they'll a' three be in Jukie's tavern at this time o' day! But they'll no' hae the meat wi' them there!"

"They'll can get it. Whaur's this tavern, then?"

"No' far off. Doon the vennel, just off the Green yonder. You'll find it easy."

"My thanks, mistress."

David had no difficulty in locating Jukie's tavern, the noise coming from it aiding. Entering, he found many men there drinking. He saw a buxom female having her bottom slapped as she bent at a rough table to fill tankards from a great jar, and judged her the one to ask.

"Mistress, can ye tell me o' Pate Shaw and ..." He hesitated, trying to remember the other names. "And Hal somebody?" he said.

"Whae are you, my fine lad?" she demanded, eyeing his garb. "I dinna ken your face."

"Och, I'm frae Kirkforther. MacAndrew's the name. New come."

"Is that so? Weel, yon's Pate and Hal. Wi' Dan and Chairlie." She pointed.

He went over to another table where four men sat. "Is it you I'm efter?" he asked them. "I'm seeking a bit venison for my wife. Her birthday, just. She likes it fine. I was telt to seek it here."

"Oh aye? You'll hae the coin for it, eh?" one asked.

"Aye. But, no' that much, see you."

"Six pence for a haunch. Three for a foreleg. Twa for ribs."

"That's richt costly!"

"No' for venison. It's no' mutton, see you. And it taks a deal o' winning, mind."

"I'll tak the ribs."

"Let's see your coin, man."

David should have thought of this. He did not want to bring out his purse, with more silver than base coin in it, unlikely wealth for such as he was pretending to be. He turned his back on them sitting there and took a pace or two away, so that he could open the purse unseen. He extracted a couple of pence, and went back to proffer them.

One of the drinkers rose. "I'll get him it," he told the others. "Come, you."

Together they went out into the vennel and turned up to the Green and the main street. At one of the houses the man went in, leaving David at the door. He came out, after a minute or two, with three ribs of venison wrapped in some ragged cloth.

The coins changed hands, without thanks.

David was turning away when he looked back. "If a friend wants some, whae dae I tell him tae ask for? Your name, man?"

"Hal Kemp 'll find me."

"Aye, weel . . ." With his trophy, he strode off and out of that village, well pleased. He had what he wanted, proof and names. He had been a little worried that his clothing might have made these folk suspicious. But evidently not. He rode back to Falkland and the king.

That evening, after only a modestly successful hunt, James was told of the situation, to royal satisfaction.

"Guid for you, Davie!" he declared. "We'll hae them paying for their wickedness. Fine, we will!"

David raised brows. "Payment?" he asked. "What payment do you suggest?"

"I canna just hang them. For the poaching," the monarch admitted. "But I'll clap them in jile. And for lang, sae I will."

David felt uncomfortable about this. These men were not such villains that they should be imprisoned for long. They had to be stopped from poaching, yes, and punished. But not so direly.

"Payment?" he said. "Imprisoning them would gain you nothing, Sire. But if they were to *pay* for their sins. Coin. You could benefit, no?"

"How pay? Wi' what?"

"These men must be able stalkers, killers of deer, stags and roe. And have a market for the meat. There are sufficient deer on all the hills and in the woods other than in your royal Falkland forest and the Lomonds. If they were to use their skills elsewhere, and paid you part of their gain, as their punishment, would not that be better than gaoling them? And having to feed them in gaol."

"Man, Davie, that's a notion! Aye, *pay* for their wickedness. I can aye dae wi' some siller! But hoo can we hae it paid into my royal coffers?"

"They could pay it to me. Say month by month. As your representative."

"And you keep a wheen to yoursel', eh? Man, you hae the rights o' it. I'll mak you Royal Ranger o' the Lomonds, and keeper o' Falkland. And you can see to it. Aye, and can better it a'! The deer we kill on my hunts gie little profit tae me. Maist o' the venison gets taken by ithers, the hunters and their men. If it was to be gied to you, as ranger and keeper, or the bulk o' it, we could baith benefit."

"Mmm. Yes." Nodding, David slapped the table. "See you, these poachers! They could sell it. Like their own meat. They have the market. Make them helpers, not just folk to be punished. Your, or *our* venison for them to sell to the folk of Freuchie and Kingskettle, of Markinch and Leslie, and otherwhere. They could carry it on garrons. Or in carts. Pay some of the moneys to me, and so to Your Grace. Make of your Falkland a gainful place, not just a sporting location. Your treasury gaining from it, not costing you."

"Guid, guid! Man, you hae it. You're a right wunner, Davie. See you tae it. As ranger o' the Lomonds and keeper o' Falkland."

So it was agreed. David had a new responsibility. And source of profit. Collace, and now Falkland. What would Lisa say to this? Teaching the young monarch to stalk stags had led a long way . . .

12

Their settling in at Collace's castle of Dunsinane was pleasing, rewarding, but very interrupted, for David had to spend much time at court at Stirling and on occasion at Holyroodhouse in Edinburgh, this as well as at Falkland; and Lisa quite enjoyed accompanying him frequently, not a stay-at-home wife. King James, not normally very interested in womenfolk, became fond of her, and indeed named her his lady-in-waiting.

The venison trade flourished, the former poachers becoming all but servants of the ranger-keeper, in fact progressing to be merchants of venison in a large way, using garron-drawn carts to transport the meat as far as Kirkcaldy and Cupar and Dunfermline, this at considerable profit for David and the king, as well as themselves. There was no lack of deer, so more Freuchie and Kingskettle men became involved in the process, and venison grew to be almost as popular in Fife as was mutton and beef. Indeed the need to preserve the meat became important, and David, learning from Lisa how the fisherfolk along Tayside used smoke-houses to keep their catches edible, experimented with this device, and set up a smokery at Freuchie, fed by peats cut up on Purin Hill. This proved to be a success, and smoked venison became acceptable, and could of course be kept in bulk and in private houses for lengthy periods.

A parliament had to be held that autumn, at Linlithgow, the first at which David attended as a commissioner, sitting on the barons' benches; and it was Lisa who occupied a gallery to watch, interested.

The need for this session was great, urgent, developments in international affairs remarkable and with a major impact on Scotland, particularly in financial matters; the which made David's and the king's concern over the venison trade modest indeed, all but laughable. Religious contentions came into it too, in a big way.

Pressures came from three main quarters: France and Spain in Catholic alliance; England in Episcopal; and the Kirk of Scotland Presbyterian; and the first two sought to advance their causes with money, much money, even if the third could not. King James's treasury was notoriously empty, especially since the death of Treasurer Gowrie, and this was well known and acted upon. The Kirk, unable to compete with gold and silver, did so with eloquence and dire injunctions, this against both the other forms of worship. James and Arran inclined towards the bishops; but the Catholic lords were strong, led by the Earls of Huntly and Erroll, and what was being called the Counter-Reformation was aggressive. This parliament was a markedly divided one.

Arran started off by declaring that they had most distinguished visitors with them this day, from the Queen of England and from the Kings of France and Spain, and an emissary from the Pope at Rome. All had proposals to make to parliament. He would call upon the Master of Gray to speak first, with Queen Elizabeth's message.

David had met Patrick Gray, heir to the sixth Lord Gray, and he was a man not to be forgotten, that handsome man. In his early thirties, he was not only of brilliant good looks but courtly, all but graceful of bearing, with a sense of humour and highly intelligent – and was known to be ambitious. King James thought highly of him, and had sent him to be his envoy to various courts, including Queen Elizabeth's. It was on her policy and behalf that he rose to speak now.

"My Lord Chancellor, my lords and fellow-commissioners," he said, smiling. "I bring the Queen of England's warm good wishes to all in this realm, and in especial to His Grace her very dear kinsman, whose regard and favour Her Majesty much esteems. In token of which she authorises me to announce that she is prepared to pay His Grace a pension, and to make a donation to his treasury of some thousands of pounds."

There was much vocal reaction to that, approving and otherwise, by no means all present in favour of closer links with England, ever in fear of one more attempt to take over the rule of Scotland, which had been the English monarchy's aim for centuries.

But James, from the throne, beamed.

"Her Majesty, recognising His Grace's attainment to full manhood, seeks his further wellbeing, and recommends the blessings and comforts of a queen, to provide him with royal company and kindness. She suggests marriage to one of the daughters of King Frederic of Denmark and Norway, which union would be beneficial in many ways, not least in trade between the nations, for King Frederic has much influence with the Hansa League at Lübeck, the greatest merchanters of Christendom."

More murmurings and comments from his hearers, men realising that this could be of advantage to England also. James however looked doubtful.

"Queen Elizabeth applauds His Grace's support for the Episcopal form of worship, and offers every help to the bishops of Scotland in the establishment of the true faith."

Needless to say, that produced all but uproar. But smiling genially and waving a courteous hand, the master bowed to the throne, and sat down.

Arran had to beat his gavel loudly to gain silence.

"We have other notable guests here present," he went on.

"The ambassadors of the Kings of France and Spain. Heed them well."

After the Master of Gray's eloquence and practised flourish, the two royal envoys from across the Channel, with their halting English and odd intonations, could not be expected to make the same impact. But the French ambassador did hold the attention of all present nevertheless, for he announced that King Henry the Third was prepared to double whatever contribution Queen Elizabeth Tudor made to King James's treasury, and more. This in the hope that His Highness would aid the Roman Catholic faith in Scotland by giving its adherents every encouragement and goodwill, and in preventing attacks and condemnations from the ministers of the so-called Reformed Church, and any further plunder of Church of Rome lands and properties, and granting of commendatorships, His Holiness urging this likewise.

The Spanish ambassador had difficulty in making his agreement and backing heard in the clamour. Among those who rose to their feet to protest was one who was present in an especial capacity, the Reverend Andrew Melville, Principal of St Andrews University, the premier seat of learning of Scotland and, with the privilege of being represented in parliament. He had previously been Principal at Glasgow, one of the foremost divines in the land.

Arran had to point at him, although in no friendly fashion, his unique position calling for it.

Melville spoke well and in statesmanlike rather than pulpit-hectoring style. He pointed out that the Reformation had been very much the expressed will of the Scottish people, and the Reformed Church, both Presbyterian and Episcopalian, ought not to agree to subsidies, any more than advice and instructions, from Catholic monarchs, especially with the papal blessing. He moved that such be rejected herewith.

Andrew Stewart, Lord Ochiltree, governor of Edinburgh

Castle, a strong Presbyterian, seconded. He declared that donations to the royal treasury should be accepted gratefully but only with no conditions in matters religious attached.

So this, proposed and seconded, called for a poll, for and against, the first so far in this session. David was uncertain as to how to vote. He had been reared in no very religious family, but himself rather favoured Episcopacy. And Lisa was so inclined, the Beatons strong for the bishops. While accepting that Catholics should be free to worship as they deemed fit, he was against them gaining great power in the land, as this French, Spanish and Popish gesture and funding seemed probable to lead to. He voted for Melville's motion, his first parliamentary action.

So did a majority of those present, seeing it his way.

Arran, as Chancellor, looked well pleased, nodding towards the throne. He called upon Ludovick, Duke of Lennox, the only duke in Scotland, the late Esmé's son, who was concerned to put forward a motion.

That personable young man rose. "This of the governance of Holy Church in this realm," he said. "His Grace King James is in that position and status by royal birth, not by any will of men, his subjects. Therefore by God, as are other monarchs, by divine right. I say that, for the settled weal of Church as of state, he, the king, should be leader of both in this his kingdom. Head of state and of Church. I so move."

"And I second, with all approval," the Master of Gray added. "His Grace is born to that position, by right."

David felt that, in all loyalty and friendship to James he would have to vote in favour, although he really did not see the young monarch as the religious leader of the nation. He looked up at the usual minstrels' gallery of this palace of Linlithgow, where many folk were watching, most of them women. Lisa, catching his glance, nodded. There was much shouting down in the hall, for and against.

The Reverend Melville moved rejection, and he was seconded by many jumping up, even some Catholics.

The vote taken, it was almost equal it seemed. Twice the clerks counted, the first assessment in favour but by only two, the second against by one.

Melville intervening, declared that the Reformed Kirk could accept only Jesus Christ as its head, however loyal to the King of Scots. He challenged all good Christians to maintain so. He advised a third count.

David, in doubt, abstained, as did not a few.

The vote counted was in Melville's favour.

There was something like pandemonium in the hall.

Arran himself showed his disapproval, and anger indeed, by banging his gavel again and again on the clerks' table. "I say that this is folly!" he cried. "Worse, disloyalty. Sin, even! You, Melville, are presumptuous! Speaking against your liege-lord, and in his presence!" He waved that gavel in the air. "Although your head may be as big as a haystack, I could make it leap from your shoulders!"

This extraordinary outburst from the Chancellor of the realm in full parliament, had the attenders all but dumbfounded. Never before had any heard the like, such statement and language from he who presided over the session. Men stared at each other.

Arran himself appeared to realise that he had grievously erred in this. He grimaced, laid down the gavel, turned to look at the king, and then shook his head.

"I, I apologise!" he got out. "I spoke in error. Tempers have arisen in the assembly. So much of controversy, dispute. There should be other business. But it has been a long session, and difficult to maintain fair judgment. For all, myself included. It is a sufficiency, no? With His Grace's royal agreement, I would declare this session adjourned." He looked at the throne.

James obviously was only too glad to nod his head.

"I so declare, as Chancellor, then. Routine business and appointments can wait. Adjourned."

The Lord Lyon signed to his herald, who blew the required blast on his trumpet, and the monarch rose. So all had to rise also. Wagging his head over it all, James hesitated, as though for guidance, and then shambled out from the dais.

David's first active parliamentary attendance had been an extraordinary one.

13

That parliamentary outburst of the Earl of Arran had eventual results far beyond what might have been expected. The Master of Gray used it to convince the king that the man was quite unsuitable to be Chancellor and as such be behind the governance of the realm. With the help of Sir Thomas Randolph, the English ambassador, he had Queen Elizabeth's backing. They persuaded Ludovick, Duke of Lennox and other influential lords to urge Arran's dismissal by the monarch.

David was in some measure embroiled in this situation through an odd development. There had been an unfortunate affray at the annual meeting of the Wardens of the Middle March of the Borders, Scots and English, this intended to be an amicable exchange of views and the ironing out of the many problems thrown up by the behaviour of the awkward mosstroopers who dwelt in the Debateable Land on either side of the borderline. But on this occasion matters had come to blows for various reasons, not handshakes, and the young Lord Russell, heir of the English Earl of Bedford, who was there as the guest of the English warden, Sir John Foster, was slain. This unhappy affair was held to be the responsibility of the Scottish Warden, Sir Thomas Kerr of Ferniehirst, who, it was claimed, ought to have controlled the Scots who killed Russell. Queen Elizabeth was much upset by this, and her ambassador, Sir Thomas Randolph, was demanding redress. For some reason, King James seemed to consider that this was a matter for his Master of the Horse to enquire into. So he was to proceed down to Teviotdale in the Borderland and take the necessary steps.

Less than eager, David set off southwards.

Riding by Stirling to Edinburgh, he then went by Dalkeith and Pathhead Ford of the Lothian Tyne, to climb over the pass of Soutra and down Lauderdale, to reach the River Teviot and Jedburgh. Ferniehirst Castle stood on higher ground two miles south-west of the town, in a strong position above the Jed Water, and none so far from the actual borderline at the Reidswire itself where the trouble had taken place, these Kerrs clearly apt to be very much involved in cross-border ongoings. David did not relish his present mission. Why had James sent him, instead of Francis, Earl of Bothwell, successor of Mary Queen of Scots' third husband, who was Lieutenant of the Borders and Chief Warden of the Marches?

He found Sir Thomas Kerr, a fine-looking man of later middle years, hospitable and friendly. While agreeing that the trouble at the Reidswire meeting had been most unfortunate and deplorable, he pointed out that it had arisen quite fortuitously in a bicker between a group of Scots and English mosstroopers, into which the young Lord Russell had intervened for some reason, and had been struck down by the angry squabblers in the process, it was uncertain by whom. All later denied responsibility, and he, Kerr, was still trying to discover the slayer, for due punishment, as was Foster, the English warden.

David pointed out that something had to be done about this. The Earl of Bedford, father of the victim, was a favourite of Queen Elizabeth, and she was demanding dire retribution, and naming him, Sir Thomas, the Scots warden, as ultimately responsible. And Walsingham, the English Secretary of State, was implicating Arran in the business, declaring that he had some hand in the murder, and had given instructions to Kerr to arrange it. All might be no more than an excuse to damage

Arran, who was for some reason hated by Walsingham and the English, but that was the wretched position. Sir Thomas Kerr was a friend of Arran's, it was said, and it was being claimed had co-operated in the slaying.

Kerr admitted that he was friendly with Arran, had been for many years, when he was just Captain James Stewart; but declared that the earl had in no way been involved in this Reidswire affair. It was all an unpremeditated and almost accidental killing, Border riders being quarrelsome and hard to control, ever ready to draw sword and dirk. But he would find the slayer eventually.

David could not but believe Sir Thomas. He found him and his wife, the Lady Janet, friendly and excellent hosts. He would go back to Stirling and tell King James that Kerr was entirely innocent, and to be trusted. And that Arran was not involved in any way.

The king accepted his findings, and all ought to have been settled in this unfortunate affair. But Queen Elizabeth, and therefore her emissary Randolph, was not satisfied. It seemed that she wanted James to be rid of Arran, and saw this death of Russell as a means of attaining it. Just why she was so much against Arran was unclear, for he was not in any way anti-English, whatever his ambitions and indiscretions. Randolph announced erroneously that Foster, the English warden, was convinced that Arran was behind the death of Bedford's son, and suspected that Kerr of Ferniehirst might be in the plot, however untrue this allegation. The queen in London was insistent that they both be punished. The implication was that if this was refused by James, his pension from Elizabeth would cease.

This of the money was of the utmost importance to the young king. He was obsessed with fears of financial insecurity and an empty treasury, despite all those funds donated by the rival seekers of Scotland's favour. A pension was a recurring benefit, and must not be endangered. Arran and Kerr had to be chastised, or seen to be by the English. They must both lose their positions, as Chancellor and as Warden of the Marches, and given some sort of banishment. Nothing very dire, perhaps, but enough to satisfy Randolph and his royal mistress. He would send Arran away, to St Andrews Castle perhaps, meantime; and Kerr further, to Aberdeen, he declared. That ought to be sufficient. So now there would require to be a new Chancellor and another warden.

David was not happy about being in some measure involved in this of alleged statecraft and intrigue, Lisa urging him to distance himself from it all. He had just a suspicion that the Master of Gray was in some way behind it, even possibly in Elizabeth's pay; and he was rumoured himself to be seeking the chancellorship, Johnnie Mar of that opinion. Together they urged James to appoint his kinsman, Ludovick of Lennox, to that vital position, Scotland's only duke, and an honourable man. None could counter that. James was prepared to do this, but Lennox refused it. He was insufficiently experienced in affairs of the realm, he said, nor had he any desire to become a statesman. But he suggested that, to prevent the Master of Gray obtaining the office, whom he mistrusted, Sir John Maitland, the Vice-Chancellor, should be promoted to it. He was a most able, reliable and talented man, of wide experience, who would make an excellent Chancellor, and no schemer like the master, nor likely to have higher ambitions. He was the second son of Queen Mary's Secretary of State, Lethington, had been made Keeper of the Great Seal and Vice-Chancellor, and was also a Lord of Session – that is, a High Court judge.

Johnnie Mar and David, among others consulted over this, agreed with the proposal. It would be a welcome change to have such as Maitland, non-aspiring for still higher things, presiding over parliaments and councils.

Maitland did not take long to demonstrate his abilities, and to the realm's advantage. He arranged, with Thomas Randolph, a great meeting to be held at Berwick-upon-Tweed, between commissioners of both Scotland and England, to secure, and if possible to finalise, the good relations between the two nations, and to ensure King James as agreed successor to Elizabeth's throne, should she herself not produce an heir – which was unlikely in the extreme, since she was now of fifty-three years and unmarried. This, and to agree to the mutual support, in arms, of the realms in the event of invasion by France and Spain in favour of the Catholic cause. And to confirm that Elizabeth's pension to James, as her heir-apparent, should continue.

Since Elizabeth herself would not attend, it was deemed unsuitable for James to do so. But he wished to be in close touch, for consultation. So it was arranged that he should lodge at the Home castle of Paxton, only three miles from the town. And as was seemly, he would take a little court with him, this to include Maitland's wife, the Lady Anne, daughter of the Seton Earl of Winton, and Lisa Murray, still his only lady-in-waiting. So David did not have to leave his beloved at Collace.

The actual meeting was a success, managed by two very effective men, Maitland and Thomas Randolph, many as were the lords and even bishops who took part. First, it was established that James should eventually succeed to the English throne, and that the English pension was therefore to be continued, and if necessary increased, in token. Second, that the Episcopalian form of Church government should be maintained in both realms. Third, that mutual armed aid should be instituted, this in especial against possible Catholic uprising backed by France or Spain; Scotland to contribute two thousand horse or six thousand foot, but at English expense. And if invasion took place within sixty miles of the border, King James would muster all possible force. Fourth, all active rebels on either side to be apprehended and delivered up. Fifth, James's mother, Mary Queen of Scots, in long captivity, was to be warned against any links with the English Catholic cause – marriage to the leader thereof, the Duke of Norfolk, Earl Marshal of England, was being rumoured – Scotland actively to counter any of the talked-of plots to have Elizabeth assassinated to enable Mary to take her place as Queen of England.

David was not actually a commissioner at this meeting, although attending, but Johnnie Mar was. They both felt sad that James should seem to be acting against his own imprisoned mother in this matter, but recognised that her strong Catholic leanings endangered both realms. Always this had been at the heart of Mary's problems, with the Reformation coinciding with her coming to the Scots throne, and indeed the reason for her defeat and imprisonment. And, of course, James did not really know her, she having been parted from him when he was one year old.

The advised marriage of James was also discussed at this meeting, and the Danish–Norwegian match approved. King Frederic had two daughters, Elizabeth and Anne, and it had been assumed that if James did indeed marry one, it would be the elder. But the news was that Elizabeth had now been wed to the Duke of Brunswick, a German grand duchy strongly linked with the Hanseatic League. So if there was to be a marriage, it would have to be with the younger sister Anne. And fairly soon, or she too might be paired off to somebody else. This alliance was deemed to be valuable, over King Frederic's strong connection with the said Hansa merchanting confederation, the greatest trading organisation in Christendom, much mercantile benefit resulting, even though James himself was in no haste to wed. But an heir to his throne, and therefore Elizabeth's also, would be welcomed.

So the meeting ended with agreement on all points, Maitland and Randolph both satisfied, and their positions strengthened.

14

The Murrays were not long back at Collace, from Berwick, when the news came that Queen Mary had been transferred from her place of confinement at Chartley to a much more secure and stern establishment, Fotheringhay Castle, this under Sir Amyas Paulet, a man of harsh reputation. This, needless to say, worried her many sympathisers. The reason for this removal to Fotheringhay was not announced, but there had been a scare over the possible assassination of Elizabeth, being called the Babington Plot, allegedly linked with efforts to free her kinswoman.

However, there were less worrying matters to engage the Murrays' attention that Yuletide. Johnnie Mar, after various affairs with young women, had found one very much to his taste, proposed marriage, and had been accepted, even though formerly he had paid some attentions to her elder sister, Jean. This was Anne, one of the five sisters of Patrick, Lord Drummond, whom he had known for some time but who had now blossomed out into a very lively and attractive young woman.

The wedding was to be held at Stobhall, eight miles up Tay from Perth, the original Drummond seat, although the lordship also had Drummond Castle near to Crieff, much to the west. The Drummonds were a Catholic family, which did not prevent Johnnie marrying into it, for he was not notably concerned with religious distinctions. And because of this, the wedding was to be celebrated at Stobhall itself, in the private chapel thereof.

David and Lisa had been there before, but never in the chapel. The castle stood on a ridge, with the Tay on one side and a deep, steep glen on the other two flanks, its enclosing courtyard necessarily being erratic, following the contours of the site. It was highly unusual in that it consisted of four distinct and unconnected buildings, the chapel central, with a keep, a kitchen and store block, and what was known as the Dowery House which also comprised the gatehouse.

There was a great concourse for the occasion, for the Drummonds were linked with many of the most prominent families in the land. King James, needless to say, had wished to be present, but had been advised and persuaded not to go, this by both Maitland and English Randolph, in the circumstances, since it was to be a Catholic ceremony and the monarch's attendance thereat could be construed as looking favourably on that dangerous faith. He had sent gifts and good wishes, however.

Less offput by such considerations were the Earl of Crawford, senior earl of Scotland, whose son, the master, was married to Anne's sister Lilias; the Earl of Montrose; Murray of Tullibardine married to another sister, Catherine; Ogilvy of that Ilk, husband of Sibylla; as well as innumerable other great ones; so the chapel, large as it was, was crowded to overflowing.

It was indeed a remarkable edifice, with priest-rooms, chambers above and dungeons below – just what the latter were for not explained. The church part itself was magnificent, panelled in carved wood and with a richly painted heraldic ceiling and deep-set windows of painted glass.

The Bishop of Dunkeld and two other priests conducted the service, which was more elaborate and prolonged than some present thought necessary, but certainly gave the impression of a very effective joining together of man and woman to be one in the sight of their Maker. Johnnie looked highly pleased with himself throughout, his bride a picture of bright-eyed and confident femininity, guiding him through the ritual and the nuptial mass that followed, this last stood through – for there was insufficient seating for all present – with a sort of patient forbearance by most of the congregation.

The feasting thereafter, in the great hall of the towering keep, called for no reservations by non-Catholics, and was sumptuous and, like the nuptials, prolonged, with various entertainments, including a masque, minstrelsy, gypsy dancing with the women discarding their topmost clothing in the process, a tame bear also dancing, in more ponderous fashion, and even a rider entering the hall on a horse, having somehow mounted the stairway, to blow a trumpet to signal the eventual departure of the bride and groom to one of the other three buildings of the disconnected establishment, where they would spend their wedding night. There was no suggestion of a public bedding ceremony, such as most couples abhorred but was apt to be popular with guests; earls of Scotland were thankful to be spared that.

Lisa and David enjoyed their evening, and wished their friends most satisfying and prolonged fulfilment. They themselves passed a rewarding night after distinctly belated bed-going.

Next morning all saw the newly weds off on their way to the Erskine homeland, west of Glasgow across Clyde where, despite the Mar title – which of course related to Aberdeenshire – and their long hereditary captainship of Stirling's royal castle, they still had ancestral properties. Johnnie was ever proud to recount their descent from a hero in the reign of Malcolm the Second, around the year 1010, who slew a Viking commander called Ernic single-handed at the Battle of Murthill, and with his bloody dagger cut off the raiding Norseman's head and presented it to the monarch, who congratulated him. He declared that he intended to perform still greater services than that for his liege-lord, whereupon King Malcolm named him Earis-Skyne, in the Gaelic, that is *earnach-sgian*, bloody dagger, whence came the surname Erskine, the dagger held up in a clenched fist still the crest of the family above their coat of arms. They were also granted local lands. And a descendant thereon helped, in 1225, to found Paisley Abbey. They became the Lords Erskine; and the twelfth of the line inherited the title of Earl of Mar through marriage with that ancient northern house's final heiress. Johnnie said that, on the way, he would present his bride to King James at Stirling, and eventually take her over to the Isle of Arran, where the Erskines had long had considerable sway. Just where they would spend Christmas remained to be seen.

That festive season was marred for many in Scotland and England, even in France and Spain, by the news that Queen Elizabeth had given Paulet at Fotheringhay authority to execute Mary Queen of Scots, claiming that it was her kinswoman's life or her own, plots for her assassination common knowledge, and her nation's Protestant religion depending on *her* survival. Execution of a woman and a monarch: it was scarcely to be believed, and after eighteen years of captivity. All Christendom was shocked.

King James's reaction to this terrible pronouncement was diverse. He had no love for his mother, saw her as a Catholic menace, and a possible impediment to his eventual attainment of the English throne. He would not greatly mourn if she died, and she was known to be in a poor state of health now, crippled with rheumatism. But *execution*, and of a crowned sovereign – that was all but unthinkable, the divine right of kings presumably including queens-regnant. He wrote an indignant letter to Elizabeth and sent it by Sir William Keith, of the family of the Earl Marischal, who was instructed to express himself without reserve to Walsingham and Cecil and the other English lords, and to Elizabeth herself if he could gain audience; and to co-operate with the French ambassador to the English court, who would be strong in defence of Mary. This was in early January; and in three weeks Keith was back, to inform that Elizabeth had told him that, swearing by the living God, she would give one of her own arms to be cut off if any means could be found for both of them, queens, to live in assurance! Walsingham however had spoken very differently, actually shaking his fist at Keith, and had to be calmed down by Cecil, Lord Burghley, the English High Treasurer, this a grim indication.

It took ten days thereafter for the dire tidings to reach Scotland. The king's mother was dead, executed on a stage in the great hall of Fotheringhay Castle, her head cut off with an axe, she kneeling to confess her sins and holding to the Catholic faith, crossing herself even as the blow fell.

Scotland, and indeed much of Christendom, was devastated, not only Catholics. The like had never been known before for a queen to die on an executioner's block, and presumably with the consent of her fellow-monarch, whatever the latter's disclaimers, for Elizabeth Tudor ruled her realm with a very strong and positive hand. The Dean of Peterborough, who had stood on the scaffold beside Mary to hear her last confession, when the executioner held up the severed royal head, had loudly announced, "So let all Queen Elizabeth's enemies perish!"

It was some weeks later that the Murrays heard fuller details of the Queen of Scots' last days (this from Lisa's aunt Mary Beaton, the four Marys having been allowed to return to Scotland). It seemed that the queen had taken the announcement of her fate and her execution very calmly, declaring that she had had enough of captivity and looked forward to her onward progress, God willing, to a better land than this England or even Scotland or France. She had told her attendants not to mourn. She would die gladly for her Catholic faith, and would wish for her body to be buried at Reims beside that of her mother, Mary of Guise. She had written farewell letters, despite her hand being all but cramped by rheumatism, to the Pope and to her nearest blood relative, Henry of Guise, to see to the wellbeing of her friends and servants after her death.

To all this the attendants were witness, and were desperately concerned, the queen herself much the most calm and assured, her caring for *their* futures much on her mind, this maintained right to the end, when she gained promises from Paulet that the lady attendants would be free to go where they would after she was gone. She had bestowed such gifts as she could upon them, giving away her royal rings and her pen. It was recounted to them how, at her actual execution, the queen had taken her renowned string of forty black pearls on a gold chain, the only such known to exist, and which she sometimes wore entwined in her hair, and had placed it round the neck of one of her ladies and told her to take it back to the vicinity of the River Tay from where the black pearls, so rare, had come.

The execution of the queen produced a strong anti-English reaction in Scotland, even among the fervid Reformist faction, for she had been crowned Queen of Scots, queen-regnant, a hitherto unknown situation, the only other heiress to the throne having been the infant Maid of Norway, all those centuries ago, and she had died before she could be crowned. That Elizabeth Tudor should have ordered this was held to be beyond belief – even anti-Catholic belief. Oddly, this resulted in James's increased popularity in the nation, and the reverse for those known to support Elizabeth, such as the Master of Gray. The national anger was exemplified by the Hamiltons, Lord Arbroath and Lord Claud, who offered to raise three thousand men for an invasion of England; and the Borderland chiefs, Scott of Buccleuch, Kerr of Ferniehirst and Ker of Cessford, proclaimed themselves ready to lead in fullest force; and indeed many of the freelance reivers of the Debateable Land were already conducting their own vengeance southwards. Sir Thomas Randolph, Elizabeth's man in Scotland, was sent packing back to London.

Maitland the Chancellor sought to keep some sort of statesmanlike control of the situation, his monarch uncertain as to how to act in the circumstances.

The year of 1587 was a testing one for Scotland, and, to be sure, for England also, for the Kings of France and Spain were loud in their condemnation of the slaying of a queen, and threatened their own armed reaction.

David and Lisa, at Collace or Stirling, waited anxiously.

15

The turmoil in Scotland that year was more than equalled in England, with France and Spain, long antagonistic, seeing their opportunity to put their enmity into action in order to restore Catholic power in a kingdom disgraced in the eyes of all Christendom. They announced that they would indeed invade. Spain was the greatest naval power in all the world, and would provide the ships, a huge fleet.

Word of it all reached Scotland by various means and bit by bit. As many as one hundred and thirty great vessels were assembled at Lisbon, with thousands of men, and these were to pick up similarly large numbers at the French port of Calais, and more from the great army in the Spanish Netherlands. Elizabeth Tudor and her advisers were to pay sorely for their behaviour.

James and his advisers were worried by these tidings, for if indeed England succumbed to Catholic invasion, Protestant Scotland would not be likely to escape attack, or at least powerful pressure, despite the Auld Alliance with France. And over one-third of the Scots lords were still Catholic, as were most of the Highland chiefs and their clans.

However, as well as anxiety there was celebration at court, for on 19th June the king reached full age; and although he had acted as of such since becoming eighteen and assuming full rule, his twenty-first birthday was to be signalised with no little flourish, for this age of consent was still looked upon as of much importance in certain matters, even for a monarch, especially by the churchmen and in legal circles. Even King

Frederic of Denmark had been delaying any possible marriage of his daughter until James reached this milestone.

So Stirling became agog, great ones ordered to attend the festivities, Johnnie and Davie of course to the fore, their wives among the few women present.

After the banquet that evening, James announced that Johnnie Mar was now High Treasurer, and given the barony and lands of Fintry for his good services. And then that Sir Davie Murray, in addition to his other duties, was to be Comptroller of the Household, with especial responsibility for the good keeping and provisioning of the royal coronation quarters at Scone Abbey, with care of the Moot Hill there, the crowning-place, which ill scoundrels had been damaging. And to support him in these additional responsibilities, he was to be given the lands and barony of Auchtermuchty, in Fife, available after the death of the previous holder. So now David was to hold two baronies, this last being a richer one than Collace and Dunsinane, with much of the rents of the burgh payable to him, although he and Lisa had no difficulty in deciding to continue to make Dunsinane Castle their home, it suiting them well.

Being royal favourite was a profitable privilege; but its duties and obligations were turning out to demand much of time and energy.

After a very late night of it, James, apparently none the worse for the quantities of liquor he had consumed – unlike some others – was not going to allow the celebrations to pass without a manifestation of his favourite activity, the hunt. It was noon next day before most of the company had recovered sufficiently from the evening's ongoings to participate in the chase, and by no means all of them even then; but eventually a start was made.

It was over-late to head for the best area for deer and wild boar reachable from Stirling, the Flanders Moss at the western end of the Carse of Forth, so they had to make do with the area around Frew and Coldoch, where there was much open pasture and little woodland and bushes. This called for an especial contribution by the deerhounds, always important in the hunts in locating the quarry; here on the open levels they had to act more like sheepdogs, in locating again, but also rounding up and driving over the game towards the huntsmen.

On this occasion, and on this terrain, it was mainly roe-deer that were to be found, and in twos and threes, not in herds as were the larger red deer. This provided a very different sort of sport, much more diverse and scattered, with spurring after little groups in all sorts of directions as the graceful creatures bounded and drifted this way and that, with the horsemen having to dash off hither and thither, the hounds in continuous action. David at least found it more enjoyable than the normal chase, even though he still preferred stalking stags on the heights.

It all became a confused but hilarious afternoon, with the dogs enjoying themselves in their barking pursuit and efforts at gathering as much as did the huntsmen; whether the horses did was another matter, with all the reining round, the rearing, twisting and turning. The king's favourite hound, old Tell True, distinguished himself particularly, and brought more deer his royal master's way than did any of the others, James continually having to fit new arrows to his crossbow, however erratic his actual aim. Johnnie shot two roe, David only one, but the king claimed four, although one of these already had an arrow projecting from its haunch when he finally brought it down.

When eventually they had to call it a day, with the surviving deer disappeared and no fewer than thirteen slain and the monarch exulting in the best score, David had seldom seen him so gleeful. He almost always carried a leather flask of wine at his saddle-bow, as did many, and, as he surveyed the collected carcases, and the servants extracted the arrows, each with its marksman's identifying sign, he beamed round at them all, and raised that goblet.

"Here's to auld Tell True!" he cried. "Tell True, I drink to thee, above all my hounds! Aye, and would sooner trust *thy* tongue than even my chaplain Craig's or Bishop Montgomery's!"

It was surely one of the oddest royal salutes ever. Fortunately there were no clergy present.

Roe venison was juicier, more tasty, than red deer's. In the warm June weather David hoped that his meat would keep until they got back to Dunsinane, three days hence.

The long-awaited news resounded through Scotland. The Spanish fleet had sailed from Lisbon in May, it being called an armada, and had duly picked up the French reinforcements and Netherlands contingent; but thereafter had become a total failure, a disaster indeed. Laden, over-laden with troops, the host of vessels had been intercepted in the Channel by English squadrons under Howard of Effingham, Sir Francis Drake and Sir John Hawkins, these much fewer in number but better handled. Drake used fire-ships to send into Calais harbour, which badly damaged much of the French allied flotilla waiting there, and Howard barred off the western mouth of the Channel, preventing dispersal into the Atlantic. The Spanish vessels, overcrowded with troops, came off worst in the subsequent battle, and their commander, the Duke of Medina, was lost.

Disheartened, the ships not burned or wrecked or sunk sought to return home but, denied the exit to the west, turned northwards up the English east coast, pursued by their foes, seeking to round Scotland and reach the Atlantic that way. How many actually gained the Pentland Firth between

Caithness and Orkney, and eventually turned down into the Sea of the Hebrides was not known, but an uncustomary summer storm hit them off the Isle of Mull, and seeking shelter in the sound thereof, a number were driven ashore and sank in the Bay of Tobermory, allegedly these including one laden with Spanish gold intended for the hire of pro-Catholic English troops. It all made a sorry tale, however exciting was the thought of all that money lying below the Islesmen's waves. How many men died in all this catalogue of woe was uncountable. Twenty-seven thousand men had set sail from Lisbon, and the French and Netherlands contingents, however depleted, added to that. If five thousand won home, that would be an optimistic estimate. And Pope Sixtus had given it all his blessing!

King Philip would be an unhappy man, and innumerable of his people mourners, Elizabeth Tudor triumphant. The Catholic cause had suffered a dire blow. Johnnie Mar's countess grieved.

David Murray, like so many another in Scotland, did not know what to think of it all. While not favouring the Catholic coalition, he judged that England in the ascendancy was no cause for rejoicing, and could be highly dangerous. And James Stewart was thinking the same way. He was grievously disappointed with Elizabeth. She had sent an envoy, William Ashby, to inform him that she was disposed to strengthen him in his anti-Catholic attitude by settling on "her good brother" an English duchy and its revenues, plus a further pension of £5,000. However, she evidently changed her mind and rescinded this proposal for no declared reason, and no more was heard of it. James was, needless to say, disappointed, announcing that he had been duped and dandled like a boy!

Then, in December, they heard that the Tudor's position had been still further strengthened by the assassination of the Duke de Guise and his brother the Cardinal of Lorraine, two of her most consistent and able opponents, the nephews of Marie de Guise, queen of James the Fifth, and therefore cousins of her daughter Mary Queen of Scots. They had been summoned to King Henry's palace, and were stabbed to death by the royal bodyguard, the monarch apparently fearing their power and influence.

It had been a dramatic and eventful year, 1588, not only for Scotland and England. What were the chances of 1589 being less so? Few were prepared to prophesy.

16

It was as well that no more forecasts were made, for early in the New Year an especial envoy arrived at Stirling from London with Elizabeth's latest urgings, these that James should marry not Anne of Denmark but the Princess of Navarre. Her father, the Huguenot-Protestant hero Henry, had just succeeded the last of the Valois Kings of France, Henry the Third, and was now monarch there; Elizabeth saw this potential alliance as of great advantage to the English and Protestant cause. Her new representative, du Bartas – a poet whom she judged might well appeal to poetry-conscious James – all but demanded, in her name, this change in the King of Scots marriage arrangements. He alleged that Anne was not a sound Protestant. Moreover, her father, King Frederic the Second, was said to be a very sick man, and with only a twelve-year-old son to succeed him, so the future there was uncertain.

James was much angered by this new dictate from London. He had built up in his mind a picture of Anne – he had been sent a portrait of her by her father – and told everyone that he was going to wed her. He had even composed a poem about her. He was not going to have his whole life controlled by the Tudor woman. And the Scots people in general, especially the merchants and trading fraternity, were much in favour of the Danish match on account of the Hanseatic League and its possibilities.

Then the news came: King Frederic had died, Anne's father. And the new King of Denmark was her young brother, Christian. Would this alter anything? Why should it? Denmark remained a potent realm, governing Norway and much of Sweden; and the Hansa links would not die with Frederic. James, with Maitland's advice, decided to send a delegation to Denmark, to see the young woman and her brother. And if, as seemed highly probable, she was deemed suitable, and her dowry adequate, a vital point for James, to come to some of the required arrangements with her brother. Some great magnate had to lead the party, Johnnie Mar's wife was expecting a baby any day, so *he* could not conveniently go. The choice was therefore George Keith, Fifth Earl Marischal, one of his senior Privy Councillors. Davie should go also; and since it was a matter concerning a young woman, Lisa should accompany him, to see and advise. He had composed a poem for Anne, a fine, long poesy, which Davie was to present to her. It was entitled "The Fond and Earnest Suite and Smoking Smart of James the King".

David suggested that some other gift should accompany this oddly named effusion, since the young woman might well not know sufficient English to appreciate it; and rather reluctantly the king gave him one of his mother's brooches.

In mid-July, then, the pair from Dunsinane left to join the Earl Marischal at Leith, to sail for Copenhagen.

Their vessel, the *Falcon*, was large necessarily, and laden with wool, whisky and salted meat, including venison, David was glad to note, this bound eventually for Lübeck and the Hansa merchants of the Baltic. They found the earl, a handsome man of much presence, recently become a widower. They had known him, of course, at court. He had with him his brother-in-law, Alexander, sixth Lord Home, and *his* wife the Lady Margaret, a daughter of the late regent, the Earl of Morton. She made friendly company for Lisa.

Their destination was some five hundred miles off across the Norse Sea; but with the prevailing south-westerly winds they ought not to take much more than three days to it. Coming back would take longer, to be sure.

They settled in comfortably enough. It was Lisa's first lengthy sail, and in summer conditions should make for pleasant voyaging, despite the Norse Sea's reputation. Their only complaint was the strong smell from the oily unwashed wool.

Two days and nights brought them in sight of land, this actually Lindesnes, they were told, the southern tip of Norway. Now they had to begin by turning north-by-east into the Skagerrak before they could pull round southwards into the Kattegat, a distinctly narrower strait, which had the *Falcon* heaving and tossing in the conflict between the tides of the Norse Sea and the Baltic, meeting here, this tending to prevent the passengers enjoying their meals. Their shipmaster pointed out to them various landmarks, from what he called the Skaw, the northernmost point of Denmark on the west, and the Bay of Gothenburg in Sweden now on the east. They proceeded on their upheaved way down some thirty miles of this Kattegat, to pass the tip of the great isle of Zealand, on which lay Copenhagen, the Danish capital.

In the calmer waters of the Sund, whence came the word for the Hebridean narrows called sounds, they observed that Denmark was a flattish land, lacking the hills they were used to in Scotland. The country was obviously highly cultivated, even the tiny islets they passed bearing crops. David, with his concern over drainage for land improvement, was interested in this; perhaps he could learn something of value here.

Copenhagen reached, proved to be a large and clearly prosperous city, covering a wide area, with innumerable canals and tidal inlets, these lined with quays, piers and docks, much shipping in evidence. Obviously Denmark was a busy, well-doing realm, alliance with which should be rewarding.

Landing at one of the few vacant berths, their skipper,

who knew the city well, told them that there was more than one royal palace, but King Frederic's favourite had been the Christianborg Slot, or castle, and presumably his young son and daughter would be apt still to dwell there. The visitors ought to find their way easily, for it was none so far from where they had docked; and even though none of them spoke Danish, impressively clad as they were in their best, passers-by would direct them to the royal palace.

This proved to be the case, and they quite quickly found the huge and magnificent establishment, even though it was no castle, all pillars, columns, porticos and wings, like nothing they had ever seen in Scotland, nor England either. Most evidently wealth was abundant here.

However, imposing as this might be, the group found that it was not in fact their desired destination. It seemed that the new King Christian and his sister had removed to Uppsala, in Sweden, and were dwelling there meantime, this because, while Norway was securely under Danish rule, Sweden was less so, with many of its nobles and magnates refusing to accept overlordship from Copenhagen. So Christian's advisers had recommended that the young monarch should set up his court for the time being at Uppsala, which was the best centre for dominating the populous southern area of that country, and close to the great port of Stockholm, where Danish armed forces could quickly be got at his command, should this prove necessary.

So it was back to the docks, where thankfully they found the *Falcon* not yet departed for Lübeck. The master agreed to take them as near to Uppsala as a ship could sail. There were two ways of reaching this renowned city: by Gothenburg and overland eastwards; or northwards by sea to Stockholm and then on by road in round-about fashion through a great cluster of lakes, this the quicker way from Copenhagen, especially with the *Falcon* on its way to Lübeck.

They sailed without delay, first out of the Copenhagen Sund and southwards, to round the Malmö cape of Sweden, then northwards for about two hundred and fifty miles, past the long island of Öland, to reach the great port of Stockholm, the largest city of the country. Here the earl arranged that the *Falcon* should pick them up again on its return voyage from Lübeck, which would be in about two weeks, by which time surely they ought to have completed their mission. Uppsala was about fifty miles off, it seemed, as the eagle might fly, or the wild goose perhaps, since it was so very much a watery way, which involved travelling twice that distance around all the lakes.

They had no difficulty in hiring horses at Stockholm, and a guide to lead them northwards on a journey that would take them two days, halting overnight at a small town called Sigtuna. It was good to be in the saddle, after all the sailing.

There was considerable traffic on that coiling road, this indeed probably the busiest highway in Sweden. It wound its way through great pine forests and by reedy lake-shores, a very scenic route, which their guide said was always very icy in winter.

They found some difficulty in gaining accommodation at Sigtuna, for although there were innumerable inns, these tended to be full. But eventually they found one that squeezed in the five of them, plus their guide. The Swedes were proving to be very friendly people.

Reaching Uppsala the next afternoon, they were much impressed by this ancient city, so very different from bustling, busy Stockholm. It was all fine old buildings, a castle and palaces, a cathedral and many churches, the religious centre of the land, seat of Sweden's archibishop, its university renowned throughout Europe, its castle the seat of the kings, this monarchy presently in abeyance, with the Danes in control.

They made their way to the castle, more palace than fortalice, and declared to the guards there that they had come from the King of Scots to visit King Christian and the Princess Anne.

Conducted to a great panelled hall, they were presently joined by a large lady of genially authoritative bearing, of middle years, who beamed on them, and quite casually announced that she was Queen Sofia, mother of King Christian and the Princess Anne, the widow of King Frederic. Was she correct in hearing that they had come all the way from Scotland, and ladies with them? She spoke fair English.

The earl introduced them all, and said that they had come with King James' salutations and good wishes, and his sorrow at the death of King Frederic. They had sought the royal family at Copenhagen, and learned that they were meantime dwelling here. They had gifts for the Princess Anne.

The queen nodded. "I have heard that King James is a very learned young man," she said. "I would wish that my son and daughter were equally so! But I do my best with them. Your James is also a stout defender of a form of God's true faith against the follies of Rome?"

The Marischal stroked his chin. "The Church in Scotland is reformed, yes, although some of our people still adhere to the Catholic faith. We have two main orders of worship, Episcopalian and Presbyterian, the former none so different from your Lutheran tradition, we understand, with bishops. King James adheres to it."

"So! If my daughter was indeed to marry your king, she would be able to continue to worship in her accustomed way?"

"That would be possible, and agreed. Although there is at present no Lutheran Church in Scotland."

"This is important. King Frederic would have wished it.

Not that Anne is overly religious, I fear! I have more hopes for Christian."

The earl glanced at his companions. There was no comment they could make to that. They had not anticipated that the matter of religion would be so evidently important in this mission. James had not given them any instructions as to this.

"Princess Anne would be free to worship as she chooses, I am sure."

"I hope so. Such assurances would be required."

"We will so inform His Grace."

"Then come and greet my daughter. She awaits you. My son Christian is presently at his studies at the university, but he will return shortly."

They were led by corridors to a sunny chamber where two young women sat stitching tapestry, while a man strummed on a lute for their entertainment. The girls rose at the entry of the queen and visitors.

David, for one, scanned their faces keenly. Neither was such as to rival his own lovely Lisa, but one was quite comely, while the other was long-featured with a notably lengthy nose, but with the better figure. Which?

It was the latter who stepped a pace or two forward, looking enquiringly at them all.

"Anne." The queen nodded.

The men bowed, and their two women curtsied.

"We bring you gifts from the King of Scots," the earl began. "Also a poem which he has composed for Your Highness." And he produced a package to hand to her.

The princess, glancing at her mother, took it doubtfully, turned it this way and that, but did not open it. "Poem?" she said.

"Yes, His Grace is fond of poetry."

"Grace . . . ?"

"Majesty, we say," the queen observed. "Thank them, Anne."

The young woman – she was only of sixteen years – handed the package to her companion. "I . . . thank . . . you," she got out. Her English was clearly not so good as her mother's.

"His Grace, or Majesty, sends his warm greetings. As you will see when you read the poem," the Marischal assured. "As you will see, it is lengthy."

It was a less than comfortable meeting. The others of the party were introduced.

"Anne will have to learn your tongue better. If she indeed goes to your Scotland," the queen declared. "Come. We will drink to the friendship. We eat more fully before long."

They all trooped through to another chamber, save for the lutist, where liquor of a fiery strength was served, Lisa trying not to screw up her face at the bite of it.

Converse was halting, to say the least, although the queen talked readily enough, and Lisa and Lady Home sought, as it were, to bridge the gap. It was unfortunate that none of the visitors knew any Danish. No one at court in Scotland had been in a position to teach them even the rudiments of the language. For his part, David wondered what sort of a Queen of Scotland this giggling girl might make?

Queen Sofia told them that rooms would be prepared for the guests, and hot water to wash in after their long riding. Meantime, more schnapps, or aquavite.

Presently they were led by servants to a wing of the palace. There was ample and comfortable accommodation, at any rate. Lisa and David had a room to themselves, where they were able to relax, wash, and discuss the situation. They had been sent to assess the suitability of this Anne as a bride for James. What were they to say? David was not greatly impressed; but Lisa said that it was too early to make judgments. The lass was young. She was scarcely beautiful, but she might be quite cuddlesome, no? David admitted that she had a well-rounded figure.

Sommoned to an evening meal, they met the young King Christian, a solemn-featured boy, very much under the thumb of his mother, somewhat wary as to the visitors. They dined notably well among a noisy company, far from subdued in the royal presence, which got noisier as the repast wore on, and the plentiful supply of beer and schnapps had its effect. The Scots would have to get used to this heady liquor, even stronger they judged than their own whisky, and quaffed with gusto by these Danes and Swedes.

Ere they eventually slept that night, David and Lisa asked themselves how they were going to survive the two weeks of Swedish hospitality until their *Falcon* arrived back for them at Stockholm? These Scandinvians were convivial hosts to a degree, but . . .

In the event they came to enjoy their stay at Uppsala better than they had feared on that first day. Their hosts were active in more than eating and drinking, hunting and hawking popular, and much bathing and swimming in those lakes, no modesty about nakedness in evidence whatever age or sex. This took a little getting used to, Lisa not so embarrassed as Lady Home at first, older and concerned with her dimensions, David actually proud of his wife's evident impact on all beholders after his first doubts about nudity. They both swam a lot in their own loch at Dunsinane, to be sure. And at least it ensured that they could inform King James that the proposed bride was attractive physically.

As well as the bathing, those lakes provided much sport for hawking from boats, something the visitors had not tried before, for the waters were alive with waterfowl, ducks, geese, herons and swans. Dogs were very necessary for retrieving both hawks and prey, and the sportsmen and women were apt to get soaked from the creatures shaking themselved inboard – which called for more schnapps as ensurance against chills. King Christian was fond of fishing, angling, the lakes being full of trout; and David joined him in this more than once.

Altogether the days passed with as much activity as did the evenings with their eating and drinking. These Scandinavians were enthusiasts in all things obviously. There was much extravagance in evidence, prosperity not hidden, and the Scots came to realise that this land was, by comparison with their own, affluent. The Swedes, like the Danes, were great traders, not only through the Hansa merchants, and demonstrated their enjoyment of their profits. There seemed to be much less of pride of ancestry, family possessions, broad acres and the like.

So the time passed pleasantly enough. And two days earlier than anticipated a rider arrived from Stockholm to announce that the *Falcon* had docked there, from Lübeck, and was awaiting them. Farewells then to the Danish royal family and new friends whom they had made, and to horse for the south. They would have plenty to tell King James in due course.

The voyage home, the wind in their faces now, took longer, much tacking called for once they reached the open Norse Sea.

17

James listened to his envoys' account with more interest in conditions in Denmark and Sweden, trade opportunities and the size of the dowery offered – and that was considerable by any standards – than in details as to the Princess Anne, his concern with women not major, capacity for producing an heir his main objective after the financial aspects. He was well enough satisfied with their reports, and declared that he would go himself over to Denmark, or wherever, to inspect this princess and, unless much offput, marry her and collect the dowery. He would go before the winter storms made voyaging hazardous. It was now almost September, so no great delay. Early October would serve.

David and Lisa discovered that they were expected to accompany the monarch back to Scandinavia. James would take a large train with him to mark the occasion.

So the Murrays did not have long to attend to their own affairs at Dunsinane and Gospertie, and to visit Creich, before it was more sea-going.

One matter was concerning them both quite deeply. However enthusiastic and frequent was their love-making, Lisa gave no signs of becoming pregnant, to their disappointment, although perhaps more hers than David's. She was anxious to start a family and provide him with an heir. Whose failing was it? They both were sufficiently sexually active. They could only hope.

Johnnie and his Anne had produced a fine son, to be Master of Mar. The proud father offered to give them lessons.

On 22nd October, then, the royal company embarked at Leith, not in the *Falcon* this time but in a still larger vessel, necessary to transport all the party – and not loaded with oily wool and other goods. Johnnie came with them this time, although not wife and child.

James was in fine fettle, very much playing the monarch, and eager to demonstrate that his Scotland was a proud realm, the most ancient in all Christendom, compared with which these Danish, Norse and Swedish kingdoms were mere upstarts, descended from the Goths and Vandals. *He* could trace his ancestry practically back to Noah, and frequently bored his listeners by reciting them in chronological order, how accurately none could tell.

The voyage was speedy, the seas not over-rough. At the Kattegat the question was Copenhagen or Stockholm and Uppsala? The Earl Marischal and David recommended the latter. Young King Christian was studying at Uppsala University, famed throughout Europe, and it seemed probable that his mother and sister would still be with him there. Best to keep on sailing round the southern tip of Sweden than to divert into the Danish Sund.

Docking at Stockholm, David was sent on ahead to inform, as well as to ensure that the royal family were still at Uppsala. Lisa accompanied him.

They found all at the palace, as before, the queen mother expressing surprise at seeing them back so soon, and declaring that it gave her little time to prepare for the king's arrival, and his large company. Was James in fact coming to *marry* her daughter, or merely personally to inspect her as possible bride? Marriage indeed, David told her. He wondered whether to inform that the King of Scots was a somewhat odd-seeming character, very clever and learned and talented, but less than handsome, indistinct of speech, tending to slobber; but Lisa said to let their hosts discover all that for themselves.

Two days later the Scots party arrived in style, James, who normally cared nothing for his garb, dressed at his somewhat slovenly best, his entourage in finest array. James himself must have raised eyebrows, especially with handsome characters like the Master of Gray and the Earl Marischal with him, not to mention the good-looking Master David Lindsay, the king's much-favoured chaplain, whom he had brought with them to ensure that he was properly wed, in case the Lutheran ceremony was inadequate.

Reaching the palace, and bowing to Queen Sofia, ignoring young King Christian, he all but ran to the only young woman present, Anne, and held out arms to enfold her. She, in a sort of alarm and uncertainty, stepped back a little at this rather headlong approach, unused to such behaviour, which had her mother waving the sixteen-year-old forward. A somewhat fumbled embrace followed, James demanding what she thought of the poem he had sent her, she, not understanding, gabbling almost as incoherently as did he. It made a strange first encounter.

The queen mother took charge, which was as well, and with the Marischal's help more formal introductions were made, especially to the wondering Christian, who had been staring at it all, bewildered. James, now, as a fellow-monarch, patted him on the shoulder.

Presently they were all led off to their various chambers. David and Lisa, with so many visitors having to be accommodated, were given the option of sharing quarters with Lord and Lady Fleming, or rooming in a tiny attic in the stableyard. With nothing against the Flemings, they nevertheless chose the latter.

Rather oddly, at the spendid dinner thereafter, James, seeing them being seated at a lowly place in the huge hall, among strangers, went so far as to come himself and take them up to where one of the lengthwise tables joined the royal one, quite close to his own seat, insisting that they sat beside Johnnie Mar, and declaring that he was not having his friends left in what he called limbo, he having to displace a couple of Swedes to accomplish this, to David's embarrassment. There was no dais at the top end of the hall here, just a single long table, crosswise, for the principals present.

A most notable banquet followed, which grew the more noisy and boisterous as the evening progressed, as the aquavite or schnapps and beer flowed, strangely to be washed down with milk, James participating in the liquor, if not the milk, with evident appreciation. He had always, since boyhood, been a great drinker, but somehow never seeming the worse for it. David wondered what effect this schnapps would have on the royal behaviour, but observed nothing other than the usual curious royal comportment. The king was seated between the queen mother and her son Christian, with Anne at her brother's side. James much disconcerted the boy by frequently leaning over and passing titbits of the provender to the bride-to-be, with his recommendations, Anne equally disconcerted.

Lisa, eyeing it all, wagged her lovely head.

The eating over, the drinking far from so, the tables were cleared, save for the flagons of liquor, and pushed to one side of the hall, and dancing began, this of a very lively sort, with much swinging and grasping, stamping and laughter, some of it not unlike the Scots reels but rather less conforming to a recognisable pattern. The visitors did their best to join in, if less vigorously, and tried to adapt to it all after their own fashion. But the music was very different, with a loud, beating rhythm which did not lend itself to their accustomed footwork. James, not to be outdone, did stagger about with the bemused Anne, and even tried to teach her the Scots footsteps, with scant success, owing to his own knock-kneed gait and that pounding musical background. David and Lisa, like most of their colleagues, were content to shuffle in the sidelines, and beat time to the rhythm.

The revelry got the wilder as the evening progressed. Johnnie Mar observed that he understood now how the Viking invaders of Scotland had been the men they were.

It took some time for the Murrays, at least, to get over to sleep that night, after it all.

James, in leaving Ludovick of Lennox as his principal representative and viceroy meantime, had declared that he ought to be gone no more than three weeks; but they discovered that Queen Sofia had made arrangements for the anticipated wedding to be on 23rd November, that is a full month after leaving Leith. So clearly it was going to be a deal longer absence from Scotland than envisaged for the royal party. This concerned not only the king, at least at first; but their hosts, active and vehement in all things, organised so much and many all but hectic pastimes and diversions, day and night, that the weeks passed so swiftly as to be scarcely counted or a cause for calculation. They took part in hawking and hunting, boating and fishing, games and races, competitions in archery, spear-throwing, pole-jumping, wrestling, dog- and cock-fighting, feats of arms and the like, as well as evening festivities as the days shortened, with bonfires, torch-tossing, candle-racing and much else, in addition to the indoors amusements, these often quite extraordinary, with play-actings and pageantry, and of course the favoured dancing.

As well as all this, with the university and cathedral close by the castle, there was opportunity for more intellectual exercise for those who felt so inclined, young Christian coming into his own at length, with saga-telling; explaining mathematical advances including something called logarithms new-brought from the Netherlands, of which only King James had heard;

religious theories; even the study of iron-ore possibilities, a stone on which Sweden appeared to be built, this learned from the Chinese via Russia; rug and carpet design coming from the east also; and much else. Not all the visitors were greatly interested, but James Stewart was; he, incidentally, having been seeking to learn the Swedish–Danish language while he was here, with his aptitude for the like, claiming that he already could read or speak eleven tongues, including, as well as French, German, Netherlandish and Spanish, the Greek, Hebrew, Aramaic and, of course, Gaelic.

When Christian introduced him to the famous astronomer, Tycho Brahe, he was greatly pleased, and while most of the Scots were off at the hunting and other outdoor activities, he tended to be closeted with this Brahe, learning, ever learning. Davie and Johnnie Mar became the recipients of much rarefied information, for instance that the astronomer had founded an observatory at Uraniborg on Hven island, had compiled a catalogue of over one thousand stars, and had foretold a total eclipse of the sun back in 1560. And he was not only an intellectual but a practical man, and had invented a pressure system for flushing down wall-closets or garderobes with water to cleanse them, and a contrivance for binding parchments and papers together to form convenient books. James was much impressed, and urged him to visit Scotland, where he would be a most honoured guest.

So the November days passed, and the increasing cold became very much a preoccupation for the visitors, the lakes beginning to have ice at the edges, and would later freeze over entirely, with a dry cold such as they seldom experienced in Scotland with its Norse Sea and Atlantic winds. It seemed that it was going to be a chilly wedding.

That great day dawned at last, and they all trooped to the cathedral. This was packed. James was much concerned that his chaplain, David Lindsay, was to be sufficiently prominent beside the archbishop and all his Lutheran aides. The ceremony was rather different from such as the Scots were used to, either Episcopalian or Presbyterian, but fortunately not overlong. King Christian supported his sister, with Johnnie Mar and the Marischal flanking James, even David given his small part to play, bearing the sceptre of the Honours of Scotland, which the king had brought for the occasion, this being carried just behind the monarch. So its bearer had an excellent view of the proceedings, and was interested to see that James was more agitated throughout than was his bride who, obviously schooled for her part, went through the motions with calm correctness, whereas her groom shuffled and fumbled; that is, until Master Lindsay stepped forward and signed for them to kneel for *his* blessing, which had not been called for by the archbishop, and which occasioned some difficulties with Anne's fine and voluminous wedding gown as she rose, with James hoisting her up.

As the royal pair thereafter turned to head for the door, David handed over that sceptre, which his liege-lord held in one hand while the other gripped the new queen's arm, symbols of sovereignty and mastery, this as the choristers sang, drums beat and the congregation cheered.

Then it was back to the castle, with a flurry of snow in the air, for prolonged banqueting and celebrations.

When eventually all this was drawing to a close, and the time came for the presumably happy couple to depart, David and Lisa were interested to see, as no doubt were others, that while the king duly escorted his bride to the hall door, thereafter he came back and rejoined the company. Was this some arrangement between them? Or was it an indication of James's concern for maidenly modesty, maidenhood now over as it had to be? Or did it signify something deeper, a reluctance to indulge in mutual bed-going on the part of this hitherto non-woman-oriented male?

Whatever it was, James remained with the rest of the company, drinking and convivial, giving no impression of eagerness to join his new partner, even when Queen Sofia led the other women from the hall. Lisa, rising, whispered to David that he should perhaps suggest to James that it would look strange if the bridegroom delayed any longer in joining his new queen. He nodded.

But Johnnie Mar had thought the same way, and moved over to the king's side, gesturing discreetly. James rose, and together they left.

When presently David rejoined his wife, they wondered how the newly weds were faring. Lisa said that, fond in a way as she was of their monarch, she by no means envied Anne of Denmark, now Queen of Scotland, that night.

18

Snow as well as ice was becoming frequent, indeed all but continuous thereafter. Queen Sofia had little difficulty in persuading King James to delay his departure for his own land. Ludovick of Lennox kept sending messages, by the shipmen, that all was in order in Scotland, no serious problems arising; and its monarch was well content to linger on at Uppsala where he was being so well entertained and provided for, however questionable were his relations with his wife who, at only sixteen years, was seemingly not greatly concerned.

David and Lisa were somewhat worried about this long absence from their home and properties and duties, like others of the king's company; and Chancellor Maitland did depart for Scotland. But James urged, indeed commanded that Davie and Johnnie stayed with him. And their hosts were untiring in their hospitality and entertainment.

So Christmas was passed at Uppsala, in great festivity. And on the first day of 1590, the weather being very cold but still, a move by the Danish court was made to Copenhagen, to join in the New Year celebrations going on there.

This made a notable change for the Scots, and that great city's very special attractions were sampled and appreciated. James was apparently quite content to let his realm rule itself, looked after by his so reliable cousin, while he enjoyed new satisfactions. When he had left Leith, he had told Lennox and the others that he would be back in three weeks, God willing. It looked now like being six months.

At Copenhagen, James quickly became involved with

another famous philosopher, Hemingius, introduced to him by Tycho Brahe, and they held lengthy discussions on a variety of subjects, the three of them getting into an ongoing dispute on predestination, an unusual concern for a young man of twenty-three as against these elderly scholars, this involving him in his theory of the divine right of kings.

The other king, Christian, went back to Uppsala to continue with his studies there, but Queen Sofia remained as hostess to the Scots monarch, and giving necessary guidance to her confused daughter.

David became a quite expert skater on the frozen canals of the Danish capital, something he had never had experience of before; but James did not find it to his taste, with his knock-knees and shambling gait, and preferred careering out over the ice on sledges drawn by horses, the canal system so involved and interconnecting that he could go for miles thus.

It was April before the cautious monarch accepted advice that the Norse Sea would now be suitable for safe voyaging. He and his entourage prepared to sail. And entourage it was, for he and his Danish queen were to be escorted by no fewer than thirteen ships, under the command of the High Admiral of Denmark, the Baron Peter Munck.

The main part of the voyage was uneventful – whatever it was for the new queen, sharing a cabin with James. But the situation changed with the first sight of Scotland, an augury or otherwise. For as they skirted the fierce cliffs of the Berwickshire coast and passed St Abb's Head and Fast Castle, not exactly a storm blew up but the wind rose, and the seas with it; and by the time they reached the wide entrance to the Firth of Forth the ships were tossing and heaving, large as they were.

This was unfortunate, for with the prevailing westerly airstream, and over a score of miles still to sail to the port of Leith, their destination, it could make the unpleasant sailing which James was not alone in disliking. It so happened, as all Scots mariners knew well, the seas were anyway almost always disturbed there, caused by the underwater cliffs which represented the final extent of the land and the commencement of the considerably deeper seabed, a source of turbulence. So the king suggested that the flotilla should lie off the eastern cliffs of the mighty Bass Rock, which soared a mile offshore, these rising to a height of over three hundred feet, this to gain shelter and a smoother surface. It was evening anyway, and they did not want to arrive at Leith in darkness, as would be the case against these contrary winds.

So the thirteen vessels huddled close to each other in the lee of that extraordinary and isolated island, amid the screaming seafowl, a rather strange welcome to Scotland.

As most on the king's ship, including David and Lisa, were considering retiring to their bunks from an overcrowded saloon-cabin where they had partaken of their evening meal, such as had appetite therefor, the king came down from the deck where he had gone, for reasons of nature presumably, in much excitement and agitation.

"Witches!" he announced to Anne and the rest of them. "Evil witches! Aye, and in the guise o' hares! Rowing a boatie. Atween here and the Bass. A dozen o' them. Oot frae North Berwick. Hares, see you. It'll be yon ill limmer Bothwell – he's nae freend o' mine. And kenn't to be a witch-maister. Him frae Hailes, nearby. Hares, I tell you!"

They all stared at him, wondering whether they heard aright. The monarch did claim to see visions on occasion, but this was extraordinary, even for James Stewart. He had been drinking deeply, as they waited off that vast stack of rock, but he did not appear to be drunk, he never did. Anne gaped.

"I'll hae Bothwell for this!" they were told. That earl was another Stewart, indeed a far-out kinsman of the king's, son of one of James the Fifth's many bastards, who had married the sister of the previous Earl of Bothwell, Mary Queen of Scots' third husband. Handsome while James was not, they were unfriends.

None hearing him liked to declare that their liege-lord was talking nonsense, whatever his reputation for learning, but their expressions were eloquent enough.

"Why did he mak his witches into hares?" James demanded of them. "Right unchancy critturs! And oaring wi' their paws. Yon was an unco sight, an ill welcome hame!" He went over to console himself from a wine flagon.

Johnnie Mar decided that it was best to change the subject. He asked about their reception at Leith. This lying off the Bass overnight would upset the ceremonial which Maitland and Lennox would certainly have prepared for the royal landing and the welcoming of the new queen. Should they not send a boat ashore to North Berwick haven, so that messengers could ride to Edinburgh and Leith to inform them there?

James conceded that this could be done, but wondered whether those hare-witches might assail such boat? Tactfully, in view of the company, Johnnie said that their shipmaster's crewmen ought to be able to cope with anything such. He would order it.

Later that night, in their bunks, David and Lisa wondered about this fantastic delusion that James had experienced. Had marriage been too much for him? Had his discussions with those Danish pedagogues turned his head? He had been drinking deeply, yes, but that was nothing new, and never before had such as this resulted, so far as they were aware. Witchcraft he had always frowned upon, but hares! They reached no conclusion, save that they should seek to convince their royal friend that he had somehow suffered from an illusion.

In the morning, with the wind considerably lessened, the

ships left the shelter of the Bass and sailed on westwards for Leith, the port of Edinburgh. It was to be hoped that word of the king's curious vision did not reach the ears of their Danish friends. How much of it all had Anne understood, or at least apprehended, with her scanty English?

Approaching Leith, the fleet was greeted by a resounding and continuous cannonade from Edinburgh Castle, which Maitland no doubt judged would impress the Danes with their love of flourish. And when the vessels went through the lengthy process of docking at the quaysides, a great company of notables was lined up to receive them, headed by Duke Ludovick, Chancellor Maitland and an array of earls and lords and bishops – including, David noted, as no doubt the king did also, Bothwell himself – with the Lord Lyon King of Arms and the Lord Provost of Edinburgh and his bailies, and the Masters of the Trade Guilds of the capital. Pipers played, drums beat and the cannon continued to bang, this all rather tending to defeat the speech-makers in their welcome to the new queen.

James, eyeing Bothwell especially, mumbled a guarded reply, and Johnnie was given the task of introducing the Danish magnates. This over, to the skirl of the bagpipes they were all escorted to another and wider quayside where the churchmen took over, and they were treated to a Latin oration, and even a quite lengthy sermon by the Kirk leader, Master Patrick Galloway. This before the voyagers and their receivers could mount horses or enter carriages for the almost two miles of road up to Edinburgh and its Holyrood, the visitors exclaiming at the dramatic scenery, especially the towering mountain, as they called it, Arthur's Seat in the midst of the city, and the lesser hills of Calton, the Castle Rock, the Blackford, Braid and Corstorphine Hills and much else.

At Holyroodhouse, formerly the abbot's residence of the Abbey of the Holy Rood, named for the fragment of Christ's cross once treasured there, all was prepared for the accommodation of their foreign guests, even the Murrays' quarters being very fine. David noted that the Earl and Countess of Bothwell were installed nearby, and wondered how their situation would work out.

The duke and Maitland had prepared all with much care and forethought, and great were the celebrations of the king's marriage and return after so long an absence from his realm. Edinburgh would prove that it could outdo any festivities that those Scandinavians might have laid on, the new queen to be shown it. Day after day demonstrations were held, with pageantry, play-acting and speech-making throughout the city and around. At the Canongate Port, or gateway, where the separate community of the canons of Holyrood met the city proper, a marriage masque was enacted for her, and from a purple velvet canopy a silken cord was lowered bearing a velvet-covered casket decorated with the letter A, for Anne, in diamonds within a circle of rubies, this while choristers sang.

Cannon thundered from the castle on its rock as the royal cavalcade moved on up the High Street; and, at the Butter Tron, nine maidens in gold and silver, reputedly the Nine Muses, sang to the queen, while further on, at the Mercat Cross beside St Giles High Kirk, she was handed the keys of the city, in silver, by the Lord Provost, and a psalm was sung. Then the royal pair were led into the great church for a service and sermon, by Master Robert Bruce, little as young Anne would comprehend it all.

David, in his capacity of Cup Bearer to the King and Master of the Horse, had to accompany the royal couple in all this, and Lisa as lady-in-waiting, and they sought to play their parts as adequately as they might, feeling that it was all perhaps slightly overdone, especially the psalm-singing and sermonising.

There were further if slightly less solemn heavenly relations thereafter when, at the West Port, a globe was let down, to open and reveal a child, with wings, in the guise of an angel, bearing a parchment in Latin which a Presbyterian minister read out – but because this was situated directly under the Castle Rock, the noise of the cannon-fire deafened all.

What Anne thought of it all was anybody's guess.

Two days of this, and a sort of coronation service was held in the abbey church, Episcopalian this time, with Master Lindsay setting the golden circlet on the queen's head, while three bishops looked on. Probably that young woman could at last feel herself to be a queen indeed.

Thereafter David sought leave of absence from James's court for a spell. He and his wife had been away from their two baronies for all those months; and barons had their duties as well as privileges, baron courts to be held to deal with petty crime, disputes about land boundaries settled, common-grazing rights emphasised and markets to be permitted. So David was busy indeed. And as well as all this, their home life at Dunsinane they felt was to be maintained, as far as was possible, as important to both of them. Being friends of the monarch had its drawbacks for a couple who valued togetherness.

James had allotted them only three weeks away from his court. They got back, to become involved, however unwillingly, in echoes of that strange delusion of the monarch's, lying off the Bass Rock: witch-hunting. This, allied to James's enmity towards his kinsman, Francis, Earl of Bothwell. They were to go to North Berwick to deal with the matter.

So a move was made from Holyrood, where the royal pair were now making their favoured residence, instead of Stirling Castle, and where hunting and hawking were to be profitably pursued in the royal forest around Arthur's Seat and Duddingston Loch. They went to the Douglas Earl of

Angus's mighty cliff-top castle of Tantallon, just opposite the Bass Rock. From there James summoned Bothwell, whose main seat of Hailes was nearby, to join them at the old church near the quayside of North Berwick, for what he called an exercise on the subject of witchcraft. Wisely, Lisa elected not to accompany her husband on this particular mission.

The king had sent out his officers to arrest and bring to North Berwick all known or reputed females believed to be witches, as well as such men as might be called warlocks, for which this area was notorious, especially the village of Samuelston, west of Haddington, said to be the seat of a coven of which Bothwell was the alleged master. David did not look forward to this engagement, but James wanted him and Johnnie to be present. They knew quite well that it was a favoured method for some women to denigrate others they disliked with accusations of witchcraft.

There was quite a crowd, mainly females, waiting for them at the old church, with the guards, all looking apprehensive. They heard that there were ninety-four witches and six wizards. The officers had been busy.

James, glowering at them, had them all arraigned before him, but he delayed proceedings until Bothwell arrived, late. But he had to be present, as commanded. He seemed amused by it all rather than perturbed.

At the church door the king announced what he was now calling "his vision" of the boatful of hares, these seeking to stir up the seas off the Bass to endanger his ships, this leading to his determination to wipe out witchcraft from his realm. He declared that this great company had been culled from the area, through report, reputation and accusation; and he was going to discover how many of them were in fact guilty of practising witchcraft, obtain confessions, and exact due punishment.

First he would call upon Francis Stewart, Earl of Bothwell, reputed witch-master, to testify.

The earl waved a hand, laughing easily. "I am no wizard nor witch-favourer, cousin," he asserted. "I see all this as folly. Your Grace has been deluded by tale-bearers, slanderers and grudge-bearers. Ignorant and malicious."

"Nane sae ignorant, man!" James returned. "I hae here a woman o' some repute in these pairts, who tells a different story. Daughter o' a one-time Kirk minister, nae less. Bring forrard Agnes Sampson."

A quite comely, plump female of middle years was led out from the crowd, better dressed than most there. She dipped a curtsey to the monarch.

"Oot wi' it, woman," James ordered. "Anent Bothwell."

She glanced over at the earl, and shrugged. "My lord has been at me mair than once," she said. "I have the sight, mind, at times. To tell him how lang Your Grace was like to live. And whether I could seek a way to mak awa' wi' you, the king."

"Lies!" Bothwell exclaimed. "Complete untruths. She havers. Heed her not."

"Wheesht!" the monarch commanded. "Woman, did you, or did you no' mak a waxen image o' the young Laird o' Wardhouse, and roast it in the fire, promising doom? And nane sae lang after, he died. This to gain his lands for the earl here."

"We did, aye."

"Can you deny that?" James demanded of Bothwell. "Mind, *I* signed the lands ower to you, under the Great Seal, kenning naught o' this."

"He was a sick man, Sire. Dying. And he owed me much siller. This of plotting and witchery is a nonsense. A woman's spite."

"You'll no' deny that you had dealings wi' this witch?"

168

"Nothing of that sort. She came to me at Hailes over matters at Samuelston, which I own."

"I'ph'mm. Weel, she's confessed to ill demoniac practices, aye, demoniac! Sae she shall die! Awa' wi' her. She's to burn at the stake. That's my royal judgment. The stake!"

"No! No!" the woman cried. "Not that! I was promised if I confessed that I'd be spared. Promised."

"*I* made nae siclike promise!" the king said. "Awa' wi' her." He looked over at Bothwell. Earls, the lesser kings of the ancient realm, could not be tried and punished save by their peers or the Privy Council. But there was no doubt that James would have condemned him also if he could have done.

"Noo, the next witch," he ordered. "Gellis Duncan, is it no'? Hae her before me. The charge?"

This time a younger woman was pushed forward. One of the officers read from a paper.

"She renounced her baptismal vows, this before the altar of this kirk, with the Earl of Bothwell in the pulpit. She played on the Jew's-harp to him, and swore spells against his enemies. She sought some clothing of a miller, and pronounced doom on it. He fell from his horse, and broke his neck. She had the coven dancing naked round a fire, with my lord present, each bearing sticks burned black at both ends, these the devil's wands. She then—"

"Enough! Enough!" James cried. "Francis Stewart, how say you to that?"

"If women throw off their clothes to dance, and you come upon them, cousin, would you look away?"

"*I* ask the questions here, no' you, man! Do you deny this Duncan woman is a witch?"

"How should I know? I am no warlock."

"You maister them, do you no'? If you werena' an earl, I'd, I'd . . ." James turned back to the woman. "It is enough. Plenties. Hae her awa'. The stake for her, wi' yon other.

Next, then." He gazed at the crowd of other women, and the few men, then turned to those behind him, including David and Johnnie Mar. "A deal to be seen to yet, eh? A' these."

His two friends were not looking joyful nor approving. They had not welcomed these witch trials, nor wished to attend, but had been commanded to do so.

"Is more necessary, James?" Johnnie asked. "Enough, surely. The lesson taught, and learned. These all will be the wiser. You have made your will known."

"Need they die, those two?" David said. "Punish them otherwise. In this town's gaol? Or in the stocks. Not burned . . ."

"They serve the devil, man! And must pay the price. I am God's vassal here, in my realm, and must serve His cause. I hae vowed so to dae, and these others must be taught. I canna try them a', but some I can, and must. I learned frae yon Spanish envoy a ploy they hae in Spain. For getting the truth oot o' siclike folk, ill-bent women. They use a bit leather strap just. I've brought the like." He delved into a pocket and produced a sort of little belt, this for fixing spurs on to a riding-boot. "This roond their heads, and twist it. To win confessions o' guilt."

They gazed at him in disbelief.

"It's right effective. A dirk in it, and twist, see you." He turned. "Bring one o' them. Any one."

A stumbling, protesting woman was dragged over to the king by two of the guards.

"Kneel, woman," she was told.

Forced down, her hair had to be dealt with. James grasped it, pulling up the long locks, and telling one of the men to hold them there. He then took the strap and buckled it round the woman's brow. Then he ordered the guard to give him his dirk, adding, "Sheathed, mind!" He pushed the dagger up between the leather and the brow, tightening the strap, and started to twist.

The unfortunate victim screamed with the pain of it, and James, nodding his satisfaction, went on twisting. The leather did not yield, so the skin must, and as the screwing continued, the scalp rose from the skull. The struggling woman, held down, fainted.

The monarch tutted his disappointment. "Another," he commanded.

David and Johnnie protested, but were ignored.

A second female was propelled forward forcibly and pushed down on her knees.

"James, no." Johnnie cried. "This is . . . devilish!"

"Aye, that's the word, man. Devilish. To deal wi' the devil. In his ain fashion. These women are committed to Satan. Ask Bothwell! He kens. Sae they hae to learn what it costs. Aye, and confess." He stooped to detach the strap from the fallen female, and went through the same procedure with the new kneeler, she beseeching shrilly.

David would have darted forward physically to restrain the king, but Johnnie held him back. *Lese-majestie* was a dire crime in law, punishable by death. None must hold back the royal person.

The woman, at the first twistings of the leather, yelled that, yes, she would confess. Yes, in God's good name, she would confess. Anything! Witchery, spells, devil worship, sorcery. All. Anything.

James nodded, satisfied. "Sae, we hae the rights o' it." He extracted the dirk from the strap, and handed it to the guard. Then took off the leather and pocketed it. "She's confessed. Hae her awa' wi' the others. She can burn wi' them. And you a' ken noo how to deal wi' a' these others. Gain their confessions. Yon Spaniards ken what they're at. We'll get rid o' this witchcraft, I tell you." He looked over at Bothwell, still watching. "See you, Francis. Your coven's broken, man. See – and tak heed. Nae mair witchery."

That earl turned on his heel and strode off.

"Aye," James said, smiling now, and turned to his friends. "Has he learned his lesson, think you? God's will be done!"

Neither Johnnie nor David answered that royal question. Set-faced, they turned away, to the royal surprise.

Was this how the Almighty's will was to be done by the head of Church and state? Presumably James Stewart believed so.

19

The king did more than have witches burned, however. Much fearing Francis Stewart, Earl of Bothwell, who might just have aims to gain the throne – as a son of a bastard of James the Fifth, and had been legitimated, and James had as yet no heir-apparent – the monarch ordered Maitland to arrest him and confine him in Edinburgh Castle. Admittedly earls could not be tried and punished save by other earls; but James held this of being involved in witchcraft and satanism as allowing himself, as the Lord's Anointed, to make such decision.

So on 2nd June he was taken while in Edinburgh, and confined in the fortress-citadel by the Chancellor, something that raised eyebrows throughout the land, David's among others, doubting the wisdom and efficacy. This could alienate other earls.

However, Bothwell proved that he had other abilities than demoniac ones, for, whether he achieved it by bribery or threat or other persuasion, he engineered his escape from that formidable prison within some ten days, and disappeared to the Borders, there to summon his supporters to arms.

James promptly declared him forfeited of his position as Lord High Admiral, this a mere honorary style, since he possessed no ships, and of being Sheriff of Berwickshire, this last carrying more authority.

In answer Bothwell rode back to Edinburgh, this time with five hundred horsemen. He settled these in the royal parkland below Arthur's Seat, and thereafter got himself into the palace of Holyrood by night. He was making for the royal quarters, whatever his purpose, when he was seen by Chancellor Maitland, who straightway sent out to summons the citizens of Edinburgh to the king's aid. The good loyal folk came in large numbers, with whatever arms they could find, and the earl had to extricate himself and rejoin his Borderers. He could have had them attack the townsfolk, but his business was with the monarch, not the citizenry. He retired to Hailes.

All this convinced James that he had to take prompt and firm steps to halt the activities of this distant kinsman. Ignoring the customary forty days' notice, he called a parliament at Stirling, as only he could do.

David attended, and heard Maitland, presiding, declare that it was the royal wish, and indeed command, that the Earl of Bothwell, risen in treasonable rebellion, should be forfeited, in more than the admiralship and the sheriffdom, and put to the horn, that is outlawed. There were a sufficient number of fellow-earls present to endorse this. Although the Earl of Moray was Bothwell's brother-in-law, none spoke up for the awkward accused, not himself attending, and the sentence was passed.

So far, so good. But just how that sentence was to be enforced in the Borderland was another matter. The Border chiefs, the Homes, the Kerrs, the Scotts, the Elliots, Turnbulls and the rest, would have to be persuaded to act, and in no uncertain fashion.

But Bothwell acted first. From that parliament, the king had gone to Falkland for his favoured diversion, hunting, David and Johnnie Mar with him. And there messengers arrived hot-foot from David's barony-town of Auchtermuchty to announce that the Earl of Bothwell, with a force of moss-troopers, the like seldom seen thereabouts, was enquiring as to the best discreet approach to Falkland.

That was enough for James. Instead of riding after deer,

he and his company rode for Lochleven Castle, the nearest secure hold.

This of Bothwell was becoming just too much. Presumably the man was seeking to take over the kingdom. Could he possibly achieve it?

Johnnie and David offered to go to the Borders, and try to get those lords there to muster their full strength to challenge the rebel, in the king's name, promising royal rewards. Home and Kerr were the most powerful. Offer them positions at court.

So they rode for the Tweed. They would see Lord Home first. There were fully a score of Home lairds in the Merse. The chief's main seat of Home Castle stood high on an isolated ridge between Greenlaw and Kelso, a dominant position from which practically all the East March could be seen, and central for a line of beacons which, lit, could arouse the March from end to end in a matter of little more than minutes, from Berwick almost to Hawick.

There they found Alexander, sixth lord, whose mother had been an aunt of the Master of Gray. If he could be won to their cause, he was to be offered the sheriffdom of Berwickshire and the lands of Coldinghame Priory, presently held by Bothwell, so significant a figure was he on the borderline.

He did not take a deal of persuading, for he already had had disputes with that rogue earl, and, a strong Catholic, greatly condemned witchcraft and demon worship. He would have eight hundred men assembled in two days' time.

Well pleased, they went on south-by-west, to cross Tweed at Kelso, and proceed up the River Teviot, which here joined it, for some ten more miles until the Jed Water came in from the south and the borderline, Kerr country now. And, not far from Jedburgh town with its great abbey, they reached Ferniehirst Castle, the stronghold of Sir Andrew Kerr, whose father had been the famous Sir Thomas, whom Mary Queen of Scots had called her Protector, and who had died five years earlier. He also saw Bothwell as something of a menace, and promptly agreed to provide, with his Cessford kinsman, six hundred mounted mosstroopers.

This made an excellent start; with the Turnbulls, Elliots, Haliburtons, and Learmonths, not to mention the Scotts of Buccleuch, they could reckon on well over two thousand, surely enough to deal with Bothwell.

Back at Home Castle, leaving Johnnie with its lord to oversee the muster, David rode north to try to discover Bothwell's present whereabouts. There was no word of him at Melrose or Ersildoune or Lauder, this last Maitland country. So he headed, still northwards, up the Leader Water and into the higher hills, by the Kelphope and Hopes Waters, round lofty Lammer Law, and so by Gifford village, making for the Hailes area itself, a difficult and round-about route through the sheep-strewn hills, this in the growing dusk.

The failing light did not worry him, since it meant that he could approach Hailes more or less unseen, at the far side of the proud summit of Traprain Law, from whence all Lothian got its name, the one-time capital of the king of the Southern Picts, Loth. Hailes nestled in a deep valley on the far side of this.

David was able to ride to the castle vicinity without fear of challenge in the half-dark.

Dismounting some way short of the castle, he approached it cautiously on foot. Only a couple of lights gleamed from the central keep. That looked as though there would be few folk therein. Closer inspection seemed to confirm this, no sign of any large numbers of men or horses, one single lamp showing on the gatehouse. So Bothwell and his troopers were still absent, wherever they were. Had he gone further, seeking James? This was what David had come to discover.

He turned and headed due southwards now, not whence

he had come, through the hills, by night, but on that main road towards England. He did not mind riding all night, if need be, his mount a stout animal and he not forcing the pace. By Colbrandspath and the Pease Dean, where many an English invading force had been ambushed, he went, and so reached Reston village, all houses dark now, Home country, with Ayton, one of their strongholds, nearby. Here he was able to turn westwards, by Duns town and Polwarth and Greenlaw. Weary, but well pleased with the situation, and himself, he approached Home Castle with the dawn, sentinels brightening up the smouldering campfires of the still slumbering host.

He had no compunction in rousing the sleeping Johnnie, and with him went to Lord Home's chamber. What he had to tell them was such as to excuse this. However yawning, and at first protesting, these learned that Bothwell was still absent from his Hailes; and unless he arrived there this new day, that stronghold was ripe for assault.

This news had the rouser forgiven, the opportunity for prompt action apparent. So while David ate, drank and snatched a couple of hours' sleep, the camp was readied and all marshalled to move.

About three thousand strong now, the Border host rode north the way David had so recently come, he on a fresh horse.

Nearing the Hailes area, scouts were sent ahead, and these sent back word that there was still no sign of any large numbers of men about the castle. Well pleased, the intending attackers advanced.

That fortalice could not be encircled, perched as it was on the edge of the rushing river, and its landward-side defences were adequate enough. But a besieging array of thousands was not to be repelled nor readily defied by any small garrison, especially when taken unawares. When summoned to surrender in the king's name, by Lord Home and the Earl of Mar, or face trial and death for treason, the keeper and his few men, after a fairly short interval for consideration, announced that, if promised their liberty and no reprisals, they would yield.

This was agreed, and presently about a score of men came out, and were allowed to depart, but not with their horses. Thus easily Hailes Castle fell to the Borders host.

Now for the next step, which David had been considering throughout all his long riding. This deep trench of a valley under Traprain Law was just made for an ambush, part reason for the castle being there. Any force approaching, from either end, north or south, and there was more than two miles of it, would have to be strung out over a long distance, two or at most three abreast being as much as the twisting road would allow. Admittedly, attackers lying in wait could use only the one side to hide on because of the Tyne; but there was a sufficiency of bushes and scrub birch on the steep bank, and also loose stones and rock to roll down, to upset horses. Hiding and ambush could be effective.

So be it. They would wait. And for so long as was necessary.

Three thousand men, of course, could not all just camp in those narrows. The great majority would have to dispose themselves elsewhere. But hidden, not obvious, to give warning. Where? To be summoned promptly, when needed.

David suggested the other, southern side of Traprain Law. There was really little else possible, the river barring all to the north. There was fairly open ground beyond the sheer cliff-face on that flank, at Cairndinnes, and another farm beside a tall, ancient standing stone of Pictish days. Admittedly this was a good mile from the castle, but less far from the riverside further west. So they could make their ambush attempt there. Bothwell, coming as he would from north or west, would have to cross the river at Haddington, there being no other bridge or practical ford until Prestonkirk.

Scouts were sent out the four miles to the town's outskirts to keep watch, but the major numbers of their force moved out of the valley and round the law, to that southern open area.

How long would they have to wait? The leaders, David with them, went to examine and explore the steep banks flanking the roadway, seeking the best section to stage their ambush.

Without much dispute they found the favoured location about half a mile west of the castle, where the banking was sufficiently steep and lofty to serve but not so abrupt as to make descent by the attackers too difficult.

All was now prepared for. But where was Bothwell? King James had fled from Falkland to Lochleven Castle. Would he linger there, or make on westwards for the great citadel of Stirling, his true home? Probably the last. Lochleven would be quite difficult to take, standing on an islet near to Kinross; but it was small and could not withstand any long siege; indeed it had fallen to besiegers on three occasions in its history. So the king would not be likely to remain there for long, if he heard that Bothwell was still seeking him. He would have gone to safe Stirling. And that fortress, on the great rock above the town, Bothwell certainly would not seek to capture. None had ever managed to take it, save by negotiation.

So what would the rogue earl be doing? Waiting somewhere, hidden, in the hope that James would decide that danger was over, and emerge, as Ruthven had done? Something was delaying his return to Hailes.

The waiters there did not have overlong to tarry, however. Two afternoons later, scouts came hastening to announce that Bothwell's company was approaching Haddington from Edinburgh, across the Gleds' Muir. They ought to be at Hailes in just over the hour, unless they delayed in Haddington.

So it was all haste to have the Borders men come from beyond Traprain to man the stretch of river valley chosen. Most were to line the heights of the steep banks, leaving their horses behind. But some hundreds, mounted, were to head westwards to near Stevenston, halfway to Haddington, to get behind Bothwell's people in due course to carry out a hoped-for attack from the rear.

Home and the other leaders placed their men along almost a mile of the roadway, hidden by uneven ground, burn channels and bushes. There was to be no attack until horns sounded.

Home stationed himself about midway along the line, Sir Andrew Kerr all but above the castle, David and Johnnie near the further west end, all with their horns ready to blow. It made tense waiting.

Placed where he was, David was one of the first to see the foe coming along the road below, led by outriders, and then a banner-bearer flying the red shield with a white chevron and a rose between two lions combatant, of Hepburn. Presumably the rider just behind that proud flag was Bothwell himself.

Watching them ride down there, and not acting, was a testing experience, David hoping that none of the men under his command would move before the signal was given. Below, the horsemen were riding two abreast. Five hundred or so of them would take some time to pass.

Those minutes, probably no more than two or three, seemed to take long indeed to elapse, as David all but held his breath. Then, at last, the horn sounded, in high ululation, echoes from the hillsides behind. And his breath was needed now for his own horn to be blown. And, right and left, men acted, first hurling the rocks and stones that they had been collecting and loosening down on the riders below, then themselves, swords and dirks drawn, rising from hiding, to go leaping down that steep slope to the chaos on the road.

Chaos it was, for those tumbling missiles of boulders and rubble, raining down on them, had the horses rearing and plunging and bolting, some throwing their riders. Following the hail came the attacking men, and in far greater numbers than the distracted enemy in their pairs. This would be going on along all the mile line.

There was no question as to the result, defence all but impossible for the strung-out force. It became extended pandemonium and turmoil, but now less than chaos, for the attackers knew just what they were to do, and in overwhelming force; and in the circumstances, being on foot a positive advantage, the frightened and alarmed horses become a handicap, some indeed plunging off into the river.

Extended as the line was, the time taken to break up and destroy it was anything but extended. In only minutes the ambush was over, and the enemy vanquished, thrown from their mounts, wounded or slain, or managing to flee, some into the Tyne to try to swim across, others managing to scale the slopes down which their assailants had just come, others just lying flat in surrender.

The victorious leaders had to try to restore order along that now bloody roadway, which took some time. Their triumph was undoubted and complete – save in one respect. Where was Bothwell? No sign of the earl was to be found, among the dead or the wounded or the prisoners taken. Had he escaped by dashing on eastwards along the road? Some of Home's men, stationed there to prevent flight, declared than none had got past them. It was one of the captives, pleading for mercy, who eventually said that he had seen the earl diving into the rushing river and part-swimming, part being carried away downstream by the strong current.

So, had he survived and escaped? Or had he drowned?

Whatever the answer to that, Francis Stewart looked like being a finished man, that was for sure. His kinsman on the throne, when he heard, would sigh with relief from those slobbering lips.

20

In fact, Bothwell did survive, and was next heard of as a fugitive in Perth. From there word came that he had gone north, presumably seeking sanctuary in the Highland fastnesses.

But meantime the king and court were plunged into a different kind of upset, this concerning two other earls, Huntly, the Gordon chief, and Moray. The former, the sixth of his line, was the realm's foremost Catholic. And he held a grudge against the Stewart Earl of Moray, this, as it were, a grudge at two removes, but none the less smouldering for that. For his grandfather, the fourth earl, had died at the Battle of Corrichie, where Moray's grandfather had been the victor, Protestant against Catholic, and whereafter his son, Sir John Gordon, had been executed and disembowelled, he this Huntly's uncle. That was thirty years before; but memories could be long, especially in the north. At any rate, this present Moray was very good-looking and gallant; indeed he was known as the Bonnie Earl, and at court was much admired by the ladies, including Queen Anne, James all too well aware of it and tended to frown on him. This Moray was another Stewart, descended from another of James the Fifth's innumerable bastards. And the king was currently favouring Huntly, Catholic as he was, this because he had searched out the fugitive Bothwell, and hounded him off sufficiently to flee in a ship from Aberdeen for London.

Now learning from Anne that a fine gold and diamond bracelet she was displaying was a gift from Moray, James, annoyed, and probably jealous of that man's good looks, sought to have words with him. And having heard that the other was planning a great hunt at his Fife seat of Donibristle, to outdo Falkland, and which the king and queen were invited to attend, lodging at his castle, he decided to send Huntly there, to warn Moray that his attentions towards Queen Anne were unwelcome, at least to her husband.

Huntly rode off for Fife with a train of his Gordons.

The dire results of that mission resounded throughout Scotland. Huntly had worked out his grudge against the Morays in no gentle fashion, presumably assuming that the monarch would not be greatly distressed, and unlikely to punish him. He approached Donibristle Castle by night, and it being nowise readied for any defence, Moray only there to prepare for the proposed royal hunting-visit. The door, to be sure, had been locked and barred; but Huntly knew of a weakness, not looked upon as such, the other earl indeed apt to boast of it. Recently renewing much of the building which he had inherited from his mother with the earldom, he had installed a most unusual sanitary convenience, to improve the wall-closet garderobes on each floor, this by constructing a drainage shaft in the thickness of the stone walling, so that human waste and effluent could be washed down this, and so be dealt with outside, the great basin there to be emptied by servants, instead of carrying buckets down the stairs, this something he had heard of in French châteaux.

Now Huntly inspected the foot of this tower's walling, and soon discovered the outflow of the shaft. He set his men to gather brushwood, much of it, and to pile it up around the basin, and to set it alight, well aware that the flue-like vent would serve as a chimney, and the smoke pour up it and so to each floor of the tower. More and more brushwood and whin branches were brought, and piled on, and the result would be that the keep would become quite impossible to breathe in, filled with clouds of smoke. The Gordons surrounded the castle, watchful.

They did not have long to wait for results, men and women coming stumbling out of a postern door at the rear, some of them naked from their beds, coughing, eyes streaming. These the Gordons drove away, well away. And in due course out came the Earl of Moray, in his nightshirt, to face drawn daggers. The Gordons stabbed and stabbed. The earl, bleeding, fell to the ground, and gazing up in the flickering firelight, recognised Huntly bending over him, and cursed.

The other earl slashed with his own dirk across the victim's handsome features.

"Huntly! Huntly . . . you! You have spoiled . . . a better face . . . than your own!" he got out, the last words that Earl of Moray spoke.

All this the Gordons thereafter recounted with glee, even if Huntly himself scarcely did.

King James at first heard only Huntly's version of it. He averred that the earl had overdone it, that he had only commanded Moray to be brought before him, not slain. This was all unfortunate, and would arouse much ill-feeling. Huntly had better retire to his northern lands until the clamour had died down. He, James, was going to accept no responsibility.

So Huntly left court.

Scarcely was he gone before Sir Robert Bowes, Elizabeth's envoy to Scotland, came to James to announce an alarming development. A strong Catholic, George Kerr, brother of the Abbot of Newbattle and related to Kerr of Ferniehirst, a Gentleman of the Bedchamber, had been reported to the minister of Paisley, one Knox, as having come into his area of the Clyde coast, and was paying for a ship to take him to Spain, to pick him up at Little Cumbrae isle in the estuary. This destination struck the vigorous divine as highly significant; and with the assistance of Lord Ross, hereditary constable of the royal castle of Renfrew, he had gone in the hired ship to the Cumbraes, and had arrested this George Kerr. He had found him to be in possession of a number of sheets of paper, blank save for the signatures of sundry powerful Scots Catholics, these including the Earls of Huntly, Errol and Angus, and addressed to the King of Spain, to fill in his own terms. The Kerr, with the signed sheets, was taken to Edinburgh where, under torture, he confessed that the blank letters were to be filled in afterwards, as pleas to King Philip, for his requirements for a descent on the Scottish west coast with a fleet and army, where he would be joined by a host under the said signing earls and other Catholic supporters, this to re-establish Catholicism in Scotland by armed force.

Immediately reported to King James at Stirling, prompt action had to be taken. Angus was in Edinburgh, and arrested and confined in that fortress. Huntly and Errol were ordered to put themselves in ward at St Andrews Castle, or the monarch would personally lead an army to arrest them and their Catholic colleagues in the north. Word of this was given to Bowes to send to Queen Elizabeth, with the request that she should show her approval by either imprisoning Bothwell, now in London, returning him to Scotland for punishment, or at least banishing him to France or Spain, this on the advice and urgings of Johnnie Mar and David Murray.

So the feared Spanish pro-Catholic invasion of Scotland did not take place. Bothwell was duly expelled from England to the Continent. But Huntly and Errol and the other lords failed to deliver themselves up at St Andrews, and instead mustered their men in the north. And sympathisers allowed Angus to escape down the cliffs of Edinburgh Castle on a rope.

At Elizabeth's urgings, James rather reluctantly went in person with a modest armed force, despite difficult February weather, and got as far as Aberdeen, Johnnie and David with him, and there was joined by the strongly Protestant Earl of Atholl with nine hundred horse and twelve hundred foot. Huntly and Errol, in these circumstances, removed themselves up into the remote lands of Caithness. They were declared forfeit, but their great Catholic-populated properties were almost impossible to take over, and the king had no desire to attempt anything such. So he returned to Stirling, Atholl was appointed Lieutenant of the North, and Elizabeth informed, with suggestion that some financial help for the expense of it all would be appreciated by her heir.

This extraordinary and involved affair became known as the Spanish Blanks, and was the talk of the land. The Earl of Angus, a Douglas, was the only one of the Catholic lords based near enough at hand to be forced to pay the price. His lands at Tantallon, near North Berwick, and Bonkyl and Billie in the Merse given to the Lord Home, if he could take them, and Douglasdale seized by the Borderers in the crown's name. Thus the matter rested, the Protestant cause, for the meantime, reasonably secure.

The ministers of the Kirk demanded the utter destruction of the Catholic faith, its extirpation in Scotland; but this far James would not consent, even if he could have done so. There were thirteen powerful nobles of that persuasion, and most of his subjects in the north and the Highlands and Isles were Catholic. So a rift developed between the Kirk and the crown. Moreover, James had some personal fondness for Huntly.

Scotland was a difficult realm to reign over and rule.

James decided to hold a parliament, at Edinburgh, to seek to settle at least some of the problems that early summer of 1593. But even that was beset by difficulties. For instance Chancellor Maitland was a strong Episcopalian, and as such would be held to be prejudiced against both Presbyterian and Catholic members if he presided, some refusing to attend. So Sir Alexander Seton, chief judge, President of the Court of Session, was to conduct affairs, his religious leanings uncertain, little known.

Then the actual opening of the assembly was delayed for days on account of which magnates were to carry in the Honours of Scotland before the monarch, various claims put forward, however petty a matter this was. Eventually it was agreed that the Duke of Lennox would bear the crown on its cushion, the Earl of Argyll the sceptre, and the Earl of Morton the sword of state, this considered a fairly even distribution.

Despite his lofty court appointments of Cup Bearer and Master of the Horse, David Murray occupied a fairly modest seat among the barony-holders; but Johnnie of course sat on the earls' benches. Maitland, despite being Chancellor, on this occasion also sat near David, having the barony of Lauderdale. As usual, Lisa watched from the gallery, ever interested in the realm's affairs.

When James was seated on his throne, Seton, announcing that he was only *acting* Chancellor, opened by asserting that it was His Grace's wish that parliament, including necessarily all earls present, should declare Francis Stewart, Earl of

Bothwell, guilty of highest treason against the crown and the realm, and be condemned to death should he return to Scotland.

If Bothwell had any friends or supporters in that parliament, none contested this sentence. It was passed unanimously.

The next business was very much on the king's behalf. It was to point out that Queen Anne's jointure, as her dowery was referred to, was still not fully paid by the King of Denmark, and representations should be made. Needless to say, this met with no opposition.

Then, to try to keep the Kirk reasonably quiescent – none of the divines was present, save for two watchers in the gallery beside Lisa, for the Presbyterian Kirk held its own General Assembly and had no seats in parliament, although the Episcopalian bishops and mitred abbots had as Lords Spiritual – a motion was put forward that Kirk ministers' stipends should be exempt from taxation. James himself had been loth to agree to this, but had been persuaded, despite his chronically empty treasury, the more so because of his Anne's extravagance. Somehow the religious bickering must be reduced, if ended was scarcely possible. This motion was contested, but Seton, declaring that it had the royal approval, gained a slight majority vote.

While still on matters religious, it was proposed, because of the Spanish Blanks affair and the Popish machinations, that the mass, while not prohibited in this Protestant realm, should only be held in private. That produced some countermotions by the more extreme Presbyterian members.

A further proposal that all Catholic earls and lords should be prosecuted and forfeited as enemies of the state, in siding with the attempted Spanish invasion, this strongly urged by the Campbell Earl of Argyll and the Lords Lindsay, Forbes and others, was declared unlawful by Makgill, the

Lord Advocate, for parliament to pass. Whereupon it was shouted from that gallery beside Lisa, of all places, that this was a *black* parliament, by Master John Davidson, a leading minister, who added loudly that he prayed that the king, by some sanctified plague, might be turned again to God!

Pandemonium reigned in that hall. Seton, wisely, glancing at the monarch who nodded, deemed that it was time to adjourn the session, with tempers mounting motion by motion. James rose and shuffled out.

Thereafter this became known as the Black Parliament, Lisa much exercised by having been present, and indeed so close to it all.

If the king and Seton, as well as others, thought that the parliament and its adjournment might help to ease dissention in the realm, they were to be sadly disillusioned. For within only the July days thereafter the most unprecedented and bizarre series of events took place, and in James's very palace and presence. Robert Bowes, Queen Elizabeth's ambassador, brought north in disguise as an English courier, and into the royal quarters early one morning, none other than Francis, Earl of Bothwell himself. With the connivance of certain members of the court, and bribed servants, they got the intercommunicating door between the king's and queen's bedchambers locked – James preferred to sleep apart – and with the further aid of the Countess of Atholl, chief lady-in-waiting to Anne, and John Colville, former Scots envoy at the English court, they took the Duke of Lennox from his bed at dagger-point and marched him to the king's room. James, roused and still half asleep, wearing only the night-cap he always wore, and his shirt, did shout, "Treason! Treason!" But there was nobody, apart from the plotters and Lennox, to hear him.

There, of all things, Bothwell sank to his knees, yet with a drawn sword in his hand, and loudly disclaimed all disloyalty to his royal kinsman, the monarchy and the throne. Kissing the hilt of the sword, he took it by the point and held it out, offering it to James, bowed his head, parted his long hair to bare his neck, and called on the king to strike it off if he believed that he, Francis, had ever harboured a thought against the royal person, and calling on the others to witness.

The astonished king, recoiling from the proffered weapon, as always afraid of cold steel, cried that here was mischief, folly and farce, that Bothwell had come seeking his life and the crown, and that he was ready to die. Better to depart with honour, he declared, than to lie in shameful captivity. He called on Lennox and the others to witness his declaration against the witch-master.

But Bothwell, still on his knees, continued to assert his loyalty, and declared that he came with Queen Elizabeth's approval, Bowes substantiating this, also Colville.

With Anne now wakened, and hammering on her locked bedroom door, James looked from the kneeling man to Lennox, who spread his arms, shrugging in mystification over it all.

This of Elizabeth being presumably behind it had the king nonplussed. What could be her intention in the staging of it? Evidently she wished Bothwell to be reinstated, despite parliament having condemned him to death for treason. Why? He, James, was her heir. Did she prefer his wretched cousin? Or was it just some device to bring pressure to bear on himself, to act for England's benefit in some obscure fashion? Just roused from sleep, as he was, the monarch could only wonder at it all, and what to do about it. And what had the Countess of Atholl to do with it, Anne's friend?

In the circumstances, James, in his nightshirt, like Lennox, and highly embarrassed as well as at a loss, had to end this ridiculous charade, unseemly as it was, urged on by his wife's continued banging on her locked door. He told Bothwell, still kneeling, to get up and to hand that sword to the duke. Then, in God's good name, to be gone, *where* he did not specify, save that he was to leave the court. He told Bowes and Colville to go also with the earl if they wished; and directed Lady Atholl, who before her marriage had been Lady Mary Ruthven, daughter of the Earl of Gowrie, and to whom Anne had taken a fancy, to have that door unlocked, and to attend to her royal mistress.

Waving his hands, James dismissed them all, and retired to his bedside for his clothes, demanding of himself how anything such as this could have happened to the King of Scots.

Johnnie Mar, told of it, and likewise astonished, duly recounted it to David. Neither knew what to make of it. If it was at Elizabeth Tudor's bidding, she must have very odd notions as to suitable conduct for monarchs. Was she becoming deranged in her declining years? She would now be sixty years old, not yet ancient. Johnnie had spoken with Lennox, who likewise could not make head nor tail of it.

At any rate, Bothwell had disappeared again, presumably back to England and Elizabeth, what gained, who knew?

Lisa said that if James Stewart was odd, Elizabeth Tudor might be becoming odder. Was this the good Lord's retribution for executing their Queen Mary? Long lines of monarchy could deteriorate, of course, Plantagenets and Tudors as well as Stewarts.

Strangely, next time David saw the king, back at Stirling, he did not refer to the incident, and his Cup Bearer did not like to raise the grotesque and possibly embarrassing story.

Besides, James was much exercised, for Anne had declared that she was pregnant. She had apparently suspected it for some time, with interruption of her monthly functions. Now she was sure. An heir! Pray God that it would be a son!

22

At Dunsinane a month or so later, the Murrays had a visit from Lisa's younger brother, Robert. He was studying at St Andrew's University, and came to tell them, knowing of his brother-in-law's closeness to the king, of a great convention of the Kirk held in that town, not the General Assembly but an especial gathering held, among other matters, to denounce King James as a backslider and worthy of God's strictures, this not only for his support of the bishops and their tyrannies, but of his tolerance, indeed friendship, with Huntly and the other Popish emissaries of Satan. Condemnation was to be pronounced in every kirk of the kingdom, and prayers said for due punishment.

As well as this scandalous assault on the throne, it was resolved that all others who showed tolerance of and sympathies for the said Catholics were to be threatened with excommunication, in the name of Christ, and so delivered to the devil and eternal damnation, this in especial for those who saw good in Huntly, the murderer of the good Earl of Moray.

But what was worse than all this, and more dangerous, was the fact that the Earl of Bothwell had sent his greetings to the divines gathered there, declared that he supported them, and claimed *their* support for his own efforts to better the state of the realm – this from Doune Castle in Menteith. Which meant that he was still in Scotland, or had returned thereto from England. And the Kirk members had welcomed his declaration and adherence, and given him their blessing.

The king should be informed and warned, and this promptly.

So David, much concerned, rode to Stirling with this ill news. Poor James; he had not his troubles to seek.

He found his liege-lord already in new upset, and from two developments. One was word from Huntly that Queen Elizabeth had actually sent some envoy named Lock to him at his Aberdeenshire seat of Strathbogie, Catholic as he was, urging him to support Bothwell's efforts to gain the Scots crown, and to persuade his friends to do the same. This was scarcely believable. And the other news was that the Lady Arabella Stewart, hitherto all but an exile in some remote part of England, was now invited to attend court at Windsor, and hints conveyed to her that she might well become Elizabeth's successor on the throne of England, displacing James.

This, needless to say, had the king in anger and dismay. For the said young woman, aged nineteen, was in fact, after himself, the nearest in line to Elizabeth. She was the niece of the late Lord Darnley, Mary Queen of Scots' second husband and reputedly James's father (whatever was said about Davie Rizzio), Darnley's brother's daughter. Moreover she was the great-granddaughter of Margaret Tudor, Henry the Eighth's sister. Always her lofty royal background had been to her great disadvantage, she ever kept at a distance from Elizabeth. Now she was suddenly being shown the royal favour, whether seriously considered as a successor to the throne or merely a threat and warning to James was uncertain. But the danger was there and the king worried. What could and should he do?

David and Johnnie said that he could do nothing about Arabella Stewart, other than tell Sir Robert Bowes to inform Elizabeth that he, James, looked on this favouring of the young woman as unwise and unsuitable, and to declare that his own eventual succession to the English throne was firm and undoubted. But as regards Bothwell and the Kirk, active steps should be taken, his remaining in Scotland a menace. He should be ejected from this Doune of Menteith, and sent under guard out of the country – for clearly he would not leave on his own accord – back to Elizabeth, or wherever else.

But this Doune Castle was a quite formidable strength, and the fact that Bothwell was being entertained there, a Moray stronghold, linked with the condemnation of the Kirk on the death of the Bonnie Earl, had its significance. Some effective royal force should be gathered to dispossess Francis Stewart.

James agreed, and said that Huntly could supply the necessary men, no doubt. But both Johnnie and David declared that unwise. It could alienate many. David suggested Lord Home and the Borderers. These could be raised at short notice, and there was no doubting their loyalty. He offered to go and seek the said aid.

This was gladly accepted.

So next day David rode south for the Tweed and Home.

He found that lord perfectly willing to help the monarch against Bothwell, declaring that he would be at Stirling in three days' time with five hundred horsemen. Would that be sufficient?

Four days later, then, the quite impressive array of moss-troopers, with the royal guard in addition, rode to escort the monarch to Menteith, the Mounth of the River Teith, a former royal earldom, this hilly country on the skirts of the Highlands, James advised that he should go himself to challenge one who was seeking to take over the throne. James rode, as Johnnie had once described it, like a bag of potatoes, this to the amusement of all the Borderers, born horsemen, but effective enough, as was proved by his enjoyment of hunting.

Doune Castle occupied a strong site at the junction of the Ardoch Burn and the Teith, a short distance from the little town of Doune, and a dozen miles or so north by west of Stirling, so no long riding was involved. James the Fifth had granted it, part of his royal earldom, to one of his many Stewart offspring, who had been created Lord Doune, and whose grandson had been the Bonnie Earl of Moray, who had gained that title by marrying the heiress of the previous earl, another Stewart, and by her had a twelve-year-old son, now Earl of Moray. His grandmother, however, the Lady Doune, still lived, and was a dominant woman, who presumably favoured Bothwell if she was giving him refuge here; she had never forgiven James for his forbearance with Huntly over the murder of her son. It was necessary that the king came in person with this company, so that any refusal to surrender the castle, and Bothwell, could be labelled high treason, with its dire consequences.

They found the stronghold to be a large courtyard-type fortalice within forty-feet-high curtain walls, eight feet in thickness, these topped by parapet and wall-walk, and within, two great keeps linked by a lower building. It had been erected largely by Robert, Duke of Albany, brother of the weak Robert the Third, who had married the Countess of Menteith, and had starved to death at Falkland the young heir to the throne, the Duke of Rothesay, seeking the crown for himself. So the place had a grim background, apt for the present situation. Certainly it seemed notably hostile in the eyes of the present visitors, drawbridge up and portcullis down.

James, with his over-large tongue, was not good at shouting, so Johnnie Mar had to hail the gatehouse guards.

"Here is His Grace, King James in person, come to demand the delivering up of Francis, Earl of Bothwell, known to be hiding from justice here," he cried. "Yield him up, or all be guilty of highest treason, with its due penalties. This to be obeyed, and promptly, by the Lady Doune and her grandson the young Earl of Moray, John. See to it."

There was no response from above the portcullis.

David raised voice. "His Grace has sufficient men here to isolate this hold and starve you all out, if his commands are not swiftly obeyed. Bothwell to be handed over. Lord Home's followers will show no mercy."

They waited.

It was a woman's higher-pitched voice that eventually came to them.

"The Earl of Bothwell is my guest. I do not deliver him into the hands of a friend of my son's murderer!"

James spluttered.

"It is a royal command, lady. Refusal is treason. For you and your grandson," Johnnie said. "Mar speaks."

"King James wars against women and children?"

"Only if they reject the orders of the monarch."

No reply forthcoming, they waited further. And still waited.

It was no vocal reaction that eventually reached them there, unless shouting was to be so called, this from some way off. Home's mosstroopers had sought to encircle the castle, and although this actually was impossible on these steep drops to the Teith and Ardoch Burn, they could overlook these. And it was from the latter that the shouts came. David went hurrying round to discover the cause.

And there he found great excitement. A man had been seen slipping out of a small postern door in the curtain walling above the burn, and making down for it. Some of the Borderers had given chase, and caught him where he was hastily prospecting a crossing of the rushing waters. It proved to be none other than Bothwell himself, making an escape. He had besought them not to give him up into the king's hands, instructing them not to lay hands on an earl, and offering bribes. But they held on to him. Thus David came face to face with him.

They eyed each other warily.

"Murray!" the earl all but snarled.

"None other, my lord," he admitted. "Come with me."

The mosstroopers gripped the earl's arms, and marched him back with David.

So James and his company had what they wanted. Johnnie, called to the gatehouse, declared that the king would take it that Lady Doune had expelled the rebel earl from her house, and so would not condemn her and her grandson for treason. Let them be grateful.

Bothwell, arms bound, earl or none, was mounted behind one of the Borderers, and the party turned and proceeded back for Stirling. There the prisoner was deposited in one of the fortress's very secure dungeons.

What to do with him? He had been condemned to death by parliament for treason. But to execute him would much displease Elizabeth. James held a conference with his friends, and Lennox, that night. The decision was that the English queen should be informed of his capture, and of parliament's sentence of death – which she must have known of – and to declare that James would only use his royal prerogative, where treason was concerned, to remit execution if she, Elizabeth, renounced all favour and interest in the captive, and banished him for ever from her realm, sending him to France, Spain, Italy or elsewhere as a fugitive, in poverty, his lands sequestered. Otherwise, he died.

This seemed the best course. Bothwell would be driven from both realms.

But there was also his family to consider, little as he had seen or shown any interest in them for years. As a young man he had married the Lady Margaret Douglas, elder daughter of his neighbour the Earl of Angus at Tantallon, and widow

198

of Sir Walter Scott of Buccleuch. She had produced three sons and three daughters. These were all now married, in their turn, and into prominent families, and had distanced themselves from their uncaring and awkward father. To visit any sort of retribution upon these would be unfair, and provoke much animosity undoubtedly. Yet the royal displeasure must be demonstrated, to warn any Bothwell supporters, and to ensure that there were no attempts to bring back the errant father from exile. His earldom had been officially forfeited, of course, with his lands at Hailes and elsewhere.

It was decided that since his family had seemed to wash hands of the earl, they should not suffer unduly. James could make and unmake earls, so he might pronounce Bothwell no longer that but allow his elder son, another Francis, to inherit the title, without the forfeited lands, much of which had gone to Home. His brother John could continue to call himself commendator of the priory lands of Coldinghame, with some portion of the revenues therefrom still coming to him. The third son, Henry, having married a rich wife, was comfortably settled. And the daughters were married to the loyal enough Lords Cathcart and Cranstoun and Macfarlane of that Ilk. These would undergo no hurt.

This all seemed satisfactory and wise. And hopefully the long-ongoing Bothwell trouble would now be at an end, Scotland the more fortunate therefor, England also possibly.

It could well be a trouble-free year to come.

23

It started well with, in February, the birth of a son, to great rejoicing, James a proud father, and all at court hailing the heir, the new Duke of Rothesay. It was announced, at the Mercat Cross of Edinburgh, that the nobility and gentry of the realm were to entertain all foreign ambassadors and envoys, to celebrate – thus saving the empty royal treasury from the costs, emptier than ever owing to Anne's fondness for gold ornaments and jewellery. The new mother was pleased with herself also, and acclaimed the fact by buying ever more adornments from the Edinburgh goldsmith, George Heriot, Jingling Geordie as he was known, thanks to his well-filled pockets, this to her husband's alarm.

But the queen's joy did not last long. For James decided that the baby prince should be put in the care of Johnnie Mar and his Countess Anne at Stirling Castle, his own childhood home, and that of most of his predecessors, rather than reared by what he looked upon as a flighty and somewhat irresponsible young female. This might be well enough when the royal couple were in residence there. But more and more the king was judging that he had to be in his capital, Edinburgh, at Holyroodhouse, which was much more convenient for state affairs than the rock-top fortress thirty-five miles to the north-west. So, in fact, neither Anne nor James saw much of the child in those first months, to her vehement remonstrances. Even Johnnie Mar, who had thus become all but guardian of the tiny prince, thought this unsuitable. But James insisted. There were quarrels amany.

And there were exasperations over the important matter of baptism and christening. The king felt that this must be made a highly impressive and dramatic event, an heir to what he claimed was the most ancient throne in all Christendom. Not only that but eventually to the English one as well. So invitations must go out to innumerable great ones, far and wide, and time given for them to appear. And it was hoped that Queen Elizabeth would come, and possibly bear part of the cost, since she was to be godmother to the one-time successor to her throne. Other monarchs, the Kings of Denmark, France and Spain, and sundry princes, grand-dukes, dukes and governors, were to be invited to attend.

However, mainly because of worsening relations between the infant's parents, largely over his separation from the mother, the baptism was delayed and delayed. Another dispute was as to what was to be the prince's name. James wanted him christened Henry, after his own assumed father, Henry, Lord Darnley. Anne demanded Frederick after her own father. Neither would give way. This contest went on, and it was not until August that the six-month-old was finally christened at the Chapel Royal at Stirling, the Bishop of Aberdeen having to name the infant both Henry Frederick and Frederick Henry, surely a unique arrangement.

This delay resulted in the non-arrival of most of the lofty invitees to the occasion, although Anne's grandfather, the Duke Ulric of Mecklenberg, and her brother-in-law the Duke of Brunswick, did appear. Queen Elizabeth was represented only by the young Earl of Sussex. He, in his monarch's name, was given the honour of carrying the new Duke of Rothesay. Lord Home bore the ducal coronet, Lord Livingstone the towel, Lord Seton the basin and Lord Sempill the ewer, these the symbols of royal baptism.

David, unsure whether he, as Cup Bearer and Master of

the Horse, had any duties in the proceedings, found himself, with Johnnie, merely expected to support the monarch; and Lisa, with the Countess of Atholl, the queen.

The curious naming over, the bishop thereafter preached a long sermon, which most there could have done without. Eventually the Lord Lyon King of Arms hailed, "God save Henry Frederick, Frederick Henry, by the grace of God Baron of Renfrew, Lord of the Isles, Earl of Carrick, Duke of Rothesay, Prince and Great Steward of Scotland!" which seemed more than enough for the six-month-old.

Adjourning to the great hall of Stirling's fortress, the baby was actually knighted by his father, gingerly with the sword. Johnnie Mar touched his small chest with a spur, and David placed the ducal coronet over the tiny head, without making contact.

Gifts to mark the occasion were then presented, this to the proud mother rather than the father. Elizabeth sent a silver coffer and gold cups. King Christian a gold chain for his sister and a smaller one for his little nephew. The Dutch ambassador surprised all, especially James, by offering a gold box containing a parchment promising an annual pension of five thousand guilders for the child. What was the reason behind this more than princely and ongoing donation? David and Lisa imagined that James would not fail to act the trustee of this unexpected windfall from, next to Spain, the wealthiest nation in Christendom.

After all this there was, of course, a banquet for guests and courtiers, during which the doors of the hall were flung open and in came a white-painted chariot drawn by Anne's special and muscular negro page-attendant, making heavy pulling, for in it were young women representing Ceres, Fecundity, Concord, Liberality and Perseverance. These descended to hand round sweetmeats and fruit to the assembled company.

Nor was this all, for the replica of a ship, fully eighteen feet long, was propelled in by men hidden beneath blue curtains representing the sea, steered by a helmswoman in cloth of gold, Neptune holding his trident at her side. James's tame lion was brought in from its cage. And lastly ten deerhounds were led in on golden chains, to be sent as a return present for King Christian.

Anne's notorious extravagance was thus demonstrated to all. Small wonder that James maintained a frown during most of it.

So ended a truly memorable and remarkable day, such it had to be believed this Scotland had never before experienced. What of the chronically empty royal coffers now? the Murrays wondered at their bed-going.

In the morning David learned something of the answer to that question, and of the consequences. For Lisa was told by her royal mistress to bring her husband to her, and privately, unusual as this summons might be. And in the queen's quarters he was bidden to go to Edinburgh, with an escort and with highly valuable burdens for pack-horses – namely most of the gold and silver gifts presented to the queen for her child's christening. These were to be taken to that well-known usurer and goldsmith, George Heriot, in the capital's High Street, this seemingly in part payment for Anne's enormous debt to Jingling Geordie. He was renowned as an honest man, and would allot full value to the various precious items.

Astonished at this odd errand, David could not refuse, Lisa urging him on. He was told not to mention it to the king.

This last somewhat worried him. What if James saw him leaving, with escort and pack-horses? He was told to say, in that case, that he had goods to sell to help fill his own depleted coffers. The king would understand that. But he should set out early in the morning, the monarch a late riser save when hunting.

So with three men and six pack-animals he rode off two mornings later on the thirty-five-mile ride to the capital, the gold and silver wrapped in sacking, heavy loads which the men were told was kitchenware and the like for the palace of Holyroodhouse.

It made a full day's journey. At the long High Street of Edinburgh they found the full mile of cobbled thoroughfare packed with stalls and shops as well as very tall houses, the lower flats of these the town-houses of the nobility and gentry and senior burgesses, the upper ones the homes of the citizenry. The old city was built on a fairly narrow ridge running from Holyrood right up to the castle, and this had steep banks on both sides, which allowed the shops and tenements to have back premises for stabling, stores, sheds and the like, a great convenience.

Questioned, passers-by indicated Jingling Geordie's gold-smith's shop for David readily enough, he being obviously well known. Judging it wise, in the circumstances, not to draw overmuch attention to their unusual and bulky burdens, they led their horses down the alleyway next to the premises, steep as it was. Learning that Heriot was reputedly the wealthiest burgess of Edinburgh, David was somewhat daunted, in view of his own errand.

For a goldsmith, he was quite well connected, coming of an old landed family of Haddingtonshire lairds, the Heriots of Trabroun, and his aunt the mother of Sir Thomas Hamilton of Binning, the Lord Advocate, known as Tam of the Cowgate, whose town-house was down at the foot of the opposite slope, quite a large landowner as well as so prominent lawyer.

David found Heriot to be a cheerful, well-built man in his early thirties, busy with papers.

When he heard that the visitor came on behalf of Queen

Anne, Jingling Geordie raised his eyebrows. But when it was declared that he had brought much gold and silver and jewellery from Stirling, the other looked all but sceptical, declaring that this was unexpected, unusual. Normally it was . . . otherwise!

"Her Highness sends much of value, presented to her as christening gifts for the young prince," David declared. "She deems it all may be acceptable in reducing her debt to yourself, sir."

The other smiled. "Then it must be a proud load indeed, Sir David! Her Grace has expensive tastes!"

"No doubt. But she now offers recompense. My men have it, out there."

"Then have them bring it in, and we shall see. You are, if I am not mistaken, Cup Bearer to His Grace, Sir David?"

"You are well informed, sir. But I came not on His Grace's behalf today."

"Ah! And christening gifts, you say? Then . . . the queen's share? Not her royal spouse's?"

David hesitated. "As to that, I am not informed. But Her Highness sent these as from herself. Her debt to you."

"Let us see them, then. Such as myself, see you, has to be careful over the like. Where husbands and wives, royal or otherwise, have separate reckonings."

David did not have to be told that he was treading on difficult ground here. The gifts were presumably intended by the donors for the child. But the queen was sending them in repayment of *her* debt. If that was the way of it, then could not James claim at least half of it all? And he, David, was James's man. Was he in any way failing his liege-lord here? Should he declare that the value of what he had brought should be shared between the couple's seeming debts to this goldsmith?

He shrugged. "You, sir, know what will be the rightful

placing of these moneys. I but bring the gifts." Was that weak, placing the responsibility on Heriot's shoulders? "I will have them all brought in."

He went to order his men to carry in the heavy sackloads.

Emptying those bags, and setting out the great array of goblets, platters, cups, brooches, chains, some of them engraved with the arms of kings and dukes, was an odd experience. David felt as though he were handing over stolen goods. Had Anne the right to part with all this?

George Heriot picked up and examined closely every piece with an expert eye, glancing over at David now and then.

"Here is much worth, indeed," he observed. "Enough, I judge, to reduce their indebtedness much. Yes, by much."

"Reduce?"

"Lessen the amounts. Both such are substantial."

"Mmm. You will know best how to allot this payment, then." That was the best he could do. It seemed very strange that both the King of Scots and his queen should be deeply in debt to a goldsmith.

"I judge the value of all this to be, shall we say, £2,500 Scots. A fair price. Will that serve?"

"*I* know not, sir. It sounds much, but . . ."

"Very well. So be it. Shall I put half against each of the royal debts?"

"Will that end them?"

"Oh, no, I fear not. Both are large. Her Grace's the larger."

David was not a poor man, but this sort of money was quite outwith his purse. Heriot asked if he wanted a paper to record the transaction. And if so, one or two papers? For king and queen.

He hesitated again. "One, I would say. Which I can give to Her Grace. Since she it was who sent me here. How she makes it all out with King James is her concern." The last thing that David wanted was to become involved in a dispute over moneys between the royal pair.

He took the receipt paper, thanked Heriot, and departed.

He would talk this over with Lisa, and hoped that she would approve of his efforts at handling it all. Having a wife as lady-in-waiting to an extravagant queen and himself Cup Bearer to an impecunious king had its problems.

Actually this of the money and indebtedness was not what worried Lisa most, she told David. It was that Anne was conspiring with Chancellor Maitland, who was for some reason inimical to the Earl of Mar, to win the little Prince Henry out of the care of Johnnie at Stirling Castle, this against the king's will. Lisa well understood the mother's desire to have her child in her own care, but realised that this plot, if successful, must worsen relations between the royal couple. Anne had been beseeching James to allow it for months, but the king was adamant. It was all awkward. David was a friend to both James and Johnnie; but Lisa was attendant and in the confidence of Anne. What were they to do? Anne's plan was to wait until next time James went off to hunt at Falkland, and took Mar with him as was usual, then she would have Maitland and herself demand of the deputy keeper the delivery of her son. This Sir James Melville, however loyal to Johnnie and to the king, would be in no position to refuse the command of the queen and the realm's Chancellor. She would take young Henry to her dower-house of Linlithgow, and barricade her loch-side strength against any attempt at reprisal.

David was nonplussed. Where lay his duty? And Lisa's? This of bickering between king and queen was disconcerting, testing for them. Indeed both wondered whether it might be possible for them to resign from their court appointments and retire to domestic bliss at Dunsinane. Would James permit that? Possibly not.

While sympathising with Anne over her enfored separation from her small son, both recognised that if this Linlithgow plan was to succeed it would lead to still greater upset, all but anarchy, for Henry was heir to the throne, and his abduction, as it would be named, would be looked upon as all but high treason, and the royal pair's position become almost impossible. It must not happen.

To warn James would be as good as, or as bad as, to provoke outright war between husband and wife; and folk almost certainly taking sides, much of the realm in a state of controversy.

David decided that he should tell Johnnie Mar, and urge him to take the child to the king when they next went to Falkland. To say that there were rumours of a plot, not mentioning the queen, to take and hold the royal heir, this to bring pressure to bear on James to remit some serious punishment or forfeiture. This would not cause James to suspect Anne, but would balk her efforts, and so avoid any outright clash. Lisa agreed with this.

So David went and informed Mar, at Stirling. He learned that the king was intending to set off for Falkland in a few days' time. Johnnie recognised the need for some such contrivance, and said that he would so advise their royal friend, not mentioning the queen's involvement. Nor Maitland's. In fact the Chancellor had become a very sick man, and need not be brought into it all.

So Johnnie had a word with James, and, much to the surprise of all at court, the monarch announced that he was going to take his little son with him on this occasion, only eighteen months old as he was, somewhat early to introduce to the sport of stag-hunting. Anne was not to be included in the company, however. James suggested that David's Lisa should come with the child, as attendant, she quite happy to do so.

It made an odd expedition for her, riding with the infant, she confessing to her husband how much she would have preferred it to have been their own child that she was transporting.

Anne was furious, indeed in hysterics, when she heard, but could do nothing about it, the king's royal command as it was. She departed to Linlithgow with her favourite "confessor", as she called him, Alexander Seton, Commendator Prior of Pluscarden, of whom James was suspicious.

That hunting-venture was quite prolonged, the king in no hurry to return to Stirling. Let national affairs come to him, he said, not him to them! So Lisa had to settle in at the hunting-palace with the young Henry and the Countess Anne of Mar. At least she could see a lot of her husband.

It was into weeks before the word came from Linlithgow. Anne, pregnant again, in her vexation over her plans gone awry, her child taken from her, and the loss of her supporter, Maitland, who had died suddenly, in a paroxysm of rage had had a miscarriage. She was declaring that she had a mind to return to Denmark, and for good.

This news did have James worried. He had been hoping for another son, for little Henry was somewhat weakly, apt to suffer from bouts of sickness, and a second heir would be welcome. And this of Anne possibly returning to Denmark had to be countered at all costs. However at odds the royal pair were, she was James's queen and the producer of hoped-for offspring. He would take the unusual step of actually going to see her at Linlithgow.

A major move was therefore made for all the court, first back to Stirling and then the score or so of miles southeastwards, David and Lisa with the little prince included, an impressive cavalcade indeed, almost one hundred strong.

Linlithgow Palace, the traditional dowery-seat of Scotland's queens, occupied a picturesque site above its own loch at the western extremity of Lothian, near the borders of Stirlingshire, a handsome square red-stone building containing a large courtyard and ample accommodation. Nearby rose the famous church of St Michael, where much of significance had taken place in the nation's story, including the near-spectral warning to James the Fourth that he should not proceed with his intended expedition into England, at the behest of the Queen of France who sent him her scented glove as token of esteem, to offer the threat of invasion while Henry the Eighth was attacking France; a warning that that romantic monarch ignored, and suffered disaster and death at Flodden-field in consequence. And here his son, the ailing James the Fifth, had learned the news that his wife, Marie de Guise, had had a daughter, not the son he had wished for, to be heir to Scotland – Mary Queen of Scots, in fact – he sighing that "It came wi' a lass and it will gang wi' a lass!" referring to the crown coming to the Stewarts through the eventual heiress of the Bruce, who had married the High Steward. All this, and much else.

At the palace they found the queen in a state of deep depression, sad to see in a young woman only verging on twenty-two years. She was clearly not glad to see them, save for the infant which she all but swooned over. Prior Seton, seemingly her only companion other than servitors, had to act host to the monarch and his large company, a strange situation indeed, of which James clearly disapproved.

The court found itself having to settle in at Linlithgow for no mere fleeting visit, little as Anne appeared to welcome it, despite the child's presence. Johnnie confided in David that the delay was because James was doing much bedding of his queen, determined if possible to produce further progeny, this despite his lack of enjoyment of the process. The town of Linlithgow had to put up with an idling multitude seeking diversion meanwhile. David and

Lisa, however, were well enough content, so long as they could be together.

During this period of waiting, intrigues were going on, in especial various factions seeking to gain the appointment of a new Chancellor to succeed Maitland, this probably the most important office in the realm. Johnnie confided to David that Anne, on being so assiduously bedded by James, was seeking to get her friend Seton appointed to the vacant and so vital position, the king far from acceding. But a parliament was overdue, and such required a Chancellor to conduct it, under the king's presidency. And James was favouring John Graham, Earl of Montrose, unusual as it would be for an earl to fill such position. Montrose was the High Treasurer, competent and able, and doing his best for the so-empty royal purse. It was not in the monarch's appointment but that of the Privy Council, to be approved by parliament; but it was judged that Montrose would be acceptable.

Early December was fixed upon for the assembly, however unsuitable the weather conditions apt to be for travel. It would be held in Edinburgh.

24

On the Eve of the Conception of the Blessed Virgin Mary, 7th December, after the Lord Lyon King of Arms had ushered in the monarch at Edinburgh Castle, he announced that His Grace's Privy Council had recommended the appointment of John, third Earl of Montrose, to be Chancellor of the realm. His Lordship would now take charge. He was David's cousin.

Montrose, a man in his later forties, a judge as a Lord of Session as well as High Treasurer, made a quite popular choice, a non-controversial figure, an Episcopalian but not an over-fervent one – which was as well, for this parliament would be much concerned with matters of religion, or at least with the advocates thereof. James often complained that his reign coincided with great upheavals in the different forms of worship, in the post-Reformation period, between those who held to the old faith, the fervid Presbyterians of the Kirk, and the mid-way Episcopalians. The majority of his people were probably for the Kirk, but the aristocracy and gentry were divided. The king, of course, was Episcopalian, and the bishops had seats in parliament, the Kirk divines protesting about this. They were urging that the "prelatic incomers" as they called them should form their own assembly, as the Kirk had done, and not speak and vote in parliament. And the Catholic position was still very much in the national consciousness, with Spanish gold known to be coming in to aid their cause, and the Highland chiefs being aggressive in their support, or the majority of them. Also, it was being whispered that Queen Anne was turning in that direction, led by Prior Seton, however much of a commendator as he was styled. Huntly, Erroll and Atholl were as powerful as ever in the north, the king's Episcopalian regime failing to deal effectively with them.

So Montrose's first role as Chancellor was an uneasy one. David sympathised with him.

As usual, sundry appointments fell to be announced and agreed, such as justiciarships and sheriffdoms, Lieutenancy of the North to be confirmed for the Duke of Lennox, and a new warden for the West March nominated. It was this last which produced clamour and some hilarity. For Montrose had to report that Queen Elizabeth had instructed her envoy, Sir Robert Bowes, to protest vehemently and demand compensation, this on account of a recent incident on that March. It seemed that a certain and somewhat notorious border reiver, William Armstrong of Kinmont in Liddesdale, known as Kinmont Willie, had himself been captured while raiding and ravishing in the Debateable Land, this by quite a large English party, and taken and confined in Carlisle Castle. This had greatly upset the Scots Borderers and mosstroopers. Led by Scott of Buccleuch, nominal keeper of Liddesdale, and other chieftains, a night-time raid had been made on Carlisle, in a storm of rain, the castle entered by a postern gate and Kinmont Willie freed, partly, it was said, with the connivance of some of the garrison, Debateable Land Borderers themselves. Unfortunately two of the less amenable guards had been slain in the process. Elizabeth was angry, an English castle assailed, two of her subjects killed, and a prisoner freed.

Few at that parliament were greatly troubled by all this, some actually cheering, even with Bowes himself watching from the gallery, near Lisa. And as it happened, the Bold Buccleuch, as he was known, was present, sitting on the barons' benches not far from David; he rose to declare that Kinmont Willie had been attacked and captured by Englishmen returning from a meeting of deputy wardens in what was accepted as a day of truce. So this, contrary to all Borders laws, had had to be put right. No apologies and compensation over the Carlisle raid were called for.

On his throne, James looked somewhat worried about it all, even if no others did, his relations with Elizabeth always to be considered, in the hope of eventual succession to her throne. And she was now in her sixty-fourth year.

At least this lively incident's telling produced a fairly good-humoured atmosphere to start that parliament.

Which was as well, for controversy over religious affairs came thereafter. There were no divines there able to speak, although a few were in the gallery, but there were many champions of the Kirk present, including young Campbell, Earl of Argyll, an enthusiast, new come of age, the Earl of Rothes, the Lord Forbes and others. These demanded that the king should himself lead a large force northwards, to defeat the wretched and treasonable Catholics, who were known to be in constant receipt of Spanish gold to impose their perverted and shameful faith on the nation.

The Earls of Huntly, Erroll and Angus, with the Highland chieftains, had elected not to attend this parliament, the December weather, with snow in the high passes, providing sufficient excuse. But the Lord Home was there, Captain of the King's Guard now, and the most powerful figure in the Borderland; also the Master of Glamis, both strong Catholics. These now rose to denounce Argyll and Rothes as mere Kirk puppets, they having gained great Holy Church lands at the so-called Reformation, and now holding on to them by becoming tools of the divines who were claiming Church lands.

Uproar erupted, and Montrose's beating of his gavel on the

clerks' table could not still it. The Duke of Lennox, along with other Episcopalians, sought to quell it but to none effect.

At length King James rose from his throne and left the hall, that parliament consequently over. Were such assemblies useless in these days? So many had been thus ineffective, fruitless.

The repercussions from the Kirk were prompt and violent. At a hastily called General Assembly, one of the leading ministers, Master David Black, of St Andrews, delivered a blistering attack which was loudly cheered by his colleagues. He declared that the king was supporting the Papist lords, and was himself therefore guilty of manifest treason to his realm. Also that the Queen of England was known to be an atheist, and her alleged Protestant religion but an empty show. Were not all monarchs in fact but the devil's bairns? And Satan guiding their courts; their judges and Lords of Session miscreants and bribers; the nobility cormorants; and Queen Anne a female disaster.

Needless to say, this outburst, acclaimed in Kirk circles, was reported by Bowes to Elizabeth. In fury she demanded that the man Black be summoned before the Scots Privy Council and duly punished for high treason. James was well prepared to comply with this, but the divine refused to appear. Backed by his colleagues, he issued what he called a Declinator, a lengthy paper, calling himself the ambassador of the Lord Jesus, and demanding that these earthly monarchs submit forthwith to Christ's Kirk's heavenly authority. Copies of this document were to be sent to every parish church in the land.

This, of course, had James in a spluttering rage, and he issued his own public proclamation condemning the assembly members and forbidding them to hold any further meeting until he gave them permission. Also each and all of the parish ministers to leave Edinburgh, where the assembly was held, within twenty-four hours and to return to their flocks.

So it was war between monarch and the Kirk. James sent word of what he had ordered to London.

The Catholics rejoiced.

David and many another did not. He approached Johnnie Mar, and together with the moderate Duke of Lennox they held a private meeting with the king at Holyrood, to seek to persuade him to take a more lenient line, more tolerant with the divines, who had the ear of the people in their parishes, for the sake of peace in the realm. The king declared that Black must pay for his Declinator, and face trial before the Privy Council; nothing else would do. Then he would modify his anger against the Kirk at large, he agreed.

But Black again refused to appear before the council, asserting that he was only subject to Christ's word. He in fact disappeared. It was presumed that he was being preserved in hiding in the city by well-wishers. But despite much questioning, none would discover his whereabouts nor betray him. So James held a brief meeting of the council, in which the rebellious minister was tried in his absence and condemned, to just what punishment was not announced.

The refusal of the citizenry to yield up the hiding man, plus rioting in the streets, persuaded the monarch to leave his capital, with queen and court, commanding all judges, officials and leal men to do so also, the Lyon King of Arms declaring at the Mercat Cross that the former capital was no longer fit to live in, and all nobility and gentry to retire to their country seats, and all merchants and traders and shopkeepers to move out to surrounding suburbs and villages.

The court moved off for Linlithgow, David and Lisa like-wise, unhappily.

In the event, however, this ordered exodus of all magnates and great ones from their town-houses, with their servants, had a major effect on the citizenry, the merchants in especial protesting, trade and services the poorer. The Lord Provost and magistrates came to Linlithgow to plead with the king to come back and restore his favour to the unhappy capital, for the man Black had left, none knew where. They asserted the utmost loyalty and goodwill.

James was persuaded by his advisers, including David and Mar, so to do, especially when none other than George Heriot arrived at Linlithgow, seeking Sir David Murray. He declared that he had no thought of approaching the King's Grace himself, but believed that his Cup Bearer might well have some influence on the monarch. The present situation, in shunning the city, was exceedingly bad for all trade and prosperity, not only in Edinburgh itself but for the nation at large, since this was the capital, and its port of Leith the principal import and export location of the realm. If this denunciation was continued for any length of time all Scotland would suffer, with many dire consequences; and raising his eyebrows, the king's and queen's banker included the need to raise interest rates on lending. David took the hint, and promised to do what he could. He spoke with James to this effect.

Whether or not it was the deciding factor, the monarch decided to lift his anathema, and to assert that the city was now to be fully reinstated in the royal esteem, and all must return to normal therein. And to emphasise this, he would make a resounding royal re-entry, with his entire court, and ride from Holyrood up to the castle and back, to the sound of trumpets and cannon-fire, the folk to be out on the streets to celebrate.

This was done, in great style, Queen Anne in especial enjoying it all, waving and throwing kisses left and right, to cheers.

So the crisis was over, the royal authority accepted and established, and David Black all but a forbidden name. The Kirk had suffered a defeat.

Queen Elizabeth was duly informed. Christmas could be celebrated joyfully.

David sought leave to spend Yuletide at Dunsinane, and to attend to his duties as baron, especially at the town of Auchtermuchty, presiding over his baron's court there. Petty crime had to be mastered, Lisa accompanying him and advising. It all made a notable change from participating in the various crises in affairs of state.

David could not escape some involvement in national concerns, however. For as well as having his court duties, with his visits to Falkland for hunting with the king – who enjoyed the chase whatever the season and the weather – he and Lisa saw a lot of the new Chancellor, his cousin John of Montrose. Although Graham lands extended to the north, especially in Kincardineshire, most of the properties were in Perthshire, none so far off, at Braco, just across the Ochil Hills, at Cowgask in Strathearn, at Invermay and Muckersie in Forteviot. So it was convenient for the earl and his wife, Jean, elder daughter of the Lord Drummond, also from Perthshire, with their young sons, to visit Dunsinane, and vice versa; and it was inevitable that matters of the kingdom were discussed and debated, sometimes such demanding royal attention.

What would the next year bring forth?

25

David found himself summoned to court at Edinburgh for an unusual development. James wanted himself and Johnnie Mar to be the first to be shown a venture, no less than a finished book which he had personally written, to be entitled the *Basilicon Doron*, however strange and foreign-sounding a title this might be. He had, apparently, been working on it for long, in secret, together with a treatise on demonology. The book was dedicated to little Prince Henry, and was an exhaustive expounding on royal government and the divine right of kings, which presumably would be applicable to the youngster one day. He had written it largely to counter the pretensions and diatribes of the Kirk's divines, who so insolently abrogated to themselves the privileges and right of monarchs. It was to be reproduced, printed and issued in large numbers – but not revealed as written by himself, in order that it should have the greater impact, copies to be sent to every parish in the land, so that royal authority should be known and understood by all, it written in clear and explicit language, that none who could read might mistake.

His two hearers were astonished, as so often by James's oddities. The volume shown to them was bulky, wordy to a degree, and they thought scarcely the kind of writing that would commend itself for popular reading. The assertion that it was set out with clarity for ease of reading was hardly borne out by the title, *Basilicon Doron*. What did that mean? Neither of his friends knew; so, would any? Save some scholars, perhaps. Scornfully James told them it meant kingly endurance. They were ignorant, he said. The divines would know it well enough, and learn from it all. He would have it printed by the hundred, the thousand, and distributed far and wide.

It occurred to David to wonder whether Geordie Heriot would have to be approached for loan of the wherewithal to pay for this extraordinary production and its dissemination throughout the land.

The king showed them the other book, on demonology, which he declared was necessary with the ongoing spread of witchcraft, in this as in other lands. He had heard that the wretched Bothwell was now in Paris and practising it there. This increasing and devilish cult must be halted.

They learned of another monarchial activity, with which they were in better accord. James had been told of two renowned comic actors who had been entertaining the English court and London citizens, these named Fletcher and Martin, their cantrips and humorous chatter proving very popular. He had sent for them to come to Scotland. Could they not all do with some such entertainment? This was far from denied.

In due course, James's issue of his strangely named book, at such cost, had its effect, if not always to the author's gratification. Distributed as it was throughout the land, the Kirk ministers were not long in becoming acquainted with it. And, whether they guessed who had written it or not, their disapproval was immediate and forceful. It was proclaimed a work of Satan from almost every pulpit; and at a specially called assembly, Master Andrew Melville, the leading presbyter, announced that there should be a fast instituted nationwide, for two days, to pray for divine judgment to fall upon whoever had written it, and upon all apostate monarchs; there was no doubt as to who were included in that term, Elizabeth Tudor also considered to be in need of heavenly chastisement. She was indeed reported to be suffering from bouts of some sickness, so perhaps the Almighty was taking matters into His own hands without Holy Kirk's prompting. James himself, waiting impatiently for his succession to the English throne, for once could say Amen to the Kirk's verdict, in this respect at least.

But presently he was again subjected to the Kirk's anathema. This followed the arrival in Scotland of the two comedians, Fletcher and Martin, and their playing before the king and queen and court at Holyrood. It was disgraceful, it was declared, profane and licentious mummery by English buffoons, almost as detestable as the mass itself. They called for all such to be banned.

James admitted to his friends that, as well as the advantages to be gained by his uniting of the two kingdoms, he would be the happier man to get away from the sway of the Scottish Kirk. There was no such folly in England. Why should religion breed these animosities? Was it not supposed to be the celebration of God's love, not hate? He ordered the Lord Provost of Edinburgh and the magistrates to condemn the Kirk's prohibitions, and to continue with the performances in the city.

This admittedly made a strange royal activity, but that made nothing new for Jacobus Rex, as he often called himself.

In early March word reached court of a new arrival in London, and a Scot. This was John Ruthven, the young Earl of Gowrie who, having fled the country at the execution of his father, had grown to manhood on the Continent and become quite famous for his learning, studying for five years at the University of Padua, and eventually becoming its rector. Now he had come to Elizabeth's court and, handsome as well as talented, had commended himself to that queen. She wrote to James that he should welcome the young man back to

Scotland, where he would be an ornament to the court. The king was doubtful about this, not only because of his father, the first earl, executed, but because that man, while he had been High Treasurer of Scotland, had lent James £85,000, some of it believed to be his own money, and the monarch was concerned that the son might be anxious to win at least some of it back. The earl's younger brother, Alexander, Master of Ruthven and Gowrie, often joined the royal hunting-parties at Falkland.

It was in August, and at a hunt, Gowrie recently returned to Scotland, that there occurred a notable development. The chase had led the royal party westwards into the Ochils, to none so far from Balvaird, at Strathmiglo, when, as a fine stag was being gralloched, the young man, Alexander Ruthven, rode up from still further west. He told the king that he had been coming to join His Grace's hunt, but had learned some highly interesting news. It seemed that a strange man, a foreigner, had been found wandering around the town of Perth, seeking just who knew what, with of all things a pot, carried in a bag, full of gold pieces. He had refused to say what he was intending to do with all this wealth, but it was reported to Alexander's brother, the Earl of Gowrie, who was hereditary provost of Perth, and he had taken the individual and his gold to Gowrie House, the town residence of the earl. It proved to be all Spanish coin, and presumably had come in a ship to the Tay, no doubt intended for the rebellious Catholic lords. Gowrie thought that the monarch ought to be told about this, and had sent his brother with the news. His Grace should perhaps come to question this man, presumably a Spaniard, knowledgeable as to languages as he was.

David and Johnnie, with Lennox, were somewhat doubtful about this odd story. But James, ever interested where money was concerned, was eager to learn the facts. Strange, if it was destined for Huntly and the Catholic lords, that it should have come to Perth, on the Tay, and not to Aberdeen. James was intrigued. They would ride on the few further miles to Perth to discover the situation. The gold might be better in the royal coffers than in Huntly's.

So they proceeded to Perth, eight or nine miles, a small group, leaving most of the hunt to continue with the sport, David, Johnnie, Lennox and a few others, with a new young favourite of the king's, John Ramsay, his page as he was calling him.

At Gowrie House, on the western outskirts of the town, they were greeted by the earl, a handsome young man whom James had never before actually met, and who said that he had sent his brother to invite the monarch as surely was suitable over this of Spanish gold. James agreed. The presumably Spanish bearer of it was being held upstairs in a garret chamber. Would His Grace come up and question him, for none of them could speak Spanish? Perhaps take over the gold?

James was only too glad so to do. Gowrie mentioned that it was only a tiny chamber but secure, with no room for many therein. He suggested that his brother Alexander took the king up, while he conducted the other visitors through the orchard to the cookhouse, where a meal was being prepared, of which all were invited to partake.

James agreed to join them all there presently after he had seen this stranger. He went off with the master up the main, twisting turnpike stair, the earl leading the others off. They would all be glad enough of some nourishment, for the hunt had started early, after only a hurried breakfast, and it was now early afternoon.

Presently, eating and drinking, they were beginning to wonder at the royal delay in rejoining them with the page Ramsay, when one of Gowrie's men came to announce that the king had gone off, with the master and Ramsay, down a back stair he called the Black Turnpike, to ride off across the parkland called the South Inch, this to visit the vessel that had apparently brought the stranger with the gold at the Tay dockside.

This seemed rather odd. David, looking back to where he could see their horses tethered, perceived the monarch's favourite white mare still among the others. They would surely not have gone afoot to the riverside, half a mile away?

He and Johnnie went round to the back of the house, to find the rear door where presumably the Black Turnpike descended, and found it locked. Something appeared to be very much amiss there.

That surmise was swiftly confirmed, for they had barely got back to the others when all eyes were turned upwards. There, from an opened window of the upper chamber, was the king's head thrust out, a hand at his throat, further muffling his always thick voice, whether his own hand or another's.

"Treason! Treason!" he was crying – at least that was what he sounded like saying. "Help! Vicky! Johnnie! Davie! Help! I am murdered!"

In horror and haste they all rushed for the doorway and the main stair, and up the winding steps, jostling each other in their urgency.

At the top there was only the one door. They found it bolted and barred. Hammering on it, they heard cries and shouts within, but no unlocking. Something to batter it open! But what? A single chair they found broke at the first smash. The duke found a ladder, for access to the roof loft. Using this as a sort of battering-ram, they combined to assail the timbers. But it was a strong door, with boarding both horizontal and vertical, the wood pinned by iron pegs. The din inside was dying down.

At last the timbers yielded and the wielders rushed within.

James was there, standing with blood on his sleeve, babbling. John Ramsay, the page, a burly young man, sword in hand, dirk in the other, was bending over a twitching body on the floor. Even as they all entered, he stabbed again and again. For so youthful a character, he appeared to be the epitome of bloodshed and aggression. The fallen figure he was assailing was Alexander, Master of Gowrie. The other, lying motionless, was his elder brother, the earl. No one else was in the room.

So much for the stranger with the pot of gold! And for the House of Ruthven!

The door-smashers led the incoherent monarch down to his horse, a man beyond all words.

It was back to Falkland, but no more hunting meantime.

It took the king a considerable time to get over that grim day's doings. Ever in horror of naked steel, he was now the more so, even the grateful knighting of young Ramsay having to be performed with Lennox holding the sword. But at least there was satisfaction for the monarch shortly thereafter when the pregnant Anne was brought to bed to produce a brother for Henry. They named him Charles, amid great rejoicing. This, curiously enough, was the king's own first Christian name, although never used, called after his uncle, Darnley's younger brother. David was sent to George Heriot to obtain a gift for the mother, a jewel costing £1,333 Scots – on loan, to be sure.

The succession, surely, would now be secure.

26

A parliament was called for that November. Elizabeth, or more accurately Sir Robert Cecil, son of the late Lord Burghley, who was now in turn Secretary of State and in effect ruling England, with the queen increasingly incapacitated, was urging that Scotland should send an armed contingent over to Ireland to assist the Lord Mountjoy in subduing what he called the rebellious Irish under the Earl of Tyrone. James was reluctant, and believed that a parliament would refuse this. Also Elizabeth's deteriorating health was making the question of the succession to her throne the more urgent, with James's position made the more vital, and some assurance called for.

As anticipated, the request for Scots aid in Ireland was unanimously rejected, vehement opposition being led by the Highland lords and chiefs, Argyll being particularly vocal. Were the Irish not their friends and cousins, fellow Celts? Why aid the ancient enemies of them both, the Angles and Saxons?

So that issue was disposed of with a minimum of debate.

But the matter of Elizabeth and succession to England's throne was quite another question. Not all present, by any means, judged James's strong ambition therefor to be advantageous for Scotland. If their king sat on the English throne, would not the affairs of the larger nation outrank those of the smaller? After all, the Scots numbered under one-tenth of the English population. Would not the great and powerful English lords tend to dominate, the Scots parliament be looked upon as of little import? And the religious question came up inevitably. The English were predominantly Episcopalian, as was His Grace. Almost certainly Scottish Presbyterian interests would suffer. The King of Scots, after over one thousand years, would be apt to become a mere empty title, and His Grace would become His Majesty, King of England.

James had to intervene, for practically none spoke up for the union, although Montrose, the Chancellor, asked for the alternative point of view. None there declared that it would be of any real advantage to the northern realm. The king had to point out that there would be real benefits: an end to all threats of invasion; trade would greatly increase; no more attacks on Scots shipping by English pirates; no bickering on the borderline. The Scottish parliament would remain entirely independent, yet Scots needs would have to be taken into account by the English one.

These assertions did not still all dissent, by any means. And there was the question of whether, in fact, His Grace would become Elizabeth's successor. Had he any proof of it? She was a strange woman, and had never loved Scotland, like all her predecessors. She had never visited it. Aye, and she had slain Scotland's Queen Mary, His Grace's mother. And what about the Lady Arabella Stewart? She was of the same line of descent as was King James, stemming from Margaret Tudor, the wife of James the Fourth, and legitimate. Elizabeth and her advisers might well select her, as less likely to complicate matters than bringing in the Scots monarch.

James very much saw the point of this. He announced that he had made enquiries, and learned that the Lady Arabella had no desire to ascend the English throne, a quiet and retiring woman. But he would indeed send special envoys to London to try to gain the firm promise of his assignment. He asserted that Scotland would be the gainer, certainly not the loser, in this so important matter.

Another issue before the parliament was the request, all but a demand, that the Kirk should be represented in parliament, since the bishops were, as they would speak for the greater numbers of the realm's worshippers. Six divines were proposed, these to act as the voice of the General Assembly, and to be appointed for only one year each, so that ongoing policy was maintained.

Parliament agreed to this, even though the bishops looked doubtful.

Later, Johnnie Mar and David were told by the king that they were to be his envoys to the English court, as entirely trustworthy. An Episcopalian churchman had better go with them, in case issues of religion came up, and he intended to send Edward Bruce, Commendator-Abbot of Kinross, an experienced negotiator, who had already been on missions to London.

The friends decided that it would be best, and probably quickest, to go south by sea, especially as Master Bruce was elderly for lengthy horse-riding. But there was always the problem of English pirates, this plague ever to be reckoned with, something that James's hoped-for attaining of the Elizabethan throne ought to put an end to. They would call in at Berwick on their way, gain the Lord Willoughby's aid in this. He was governor of Berwick Castle, and if he gave them a large English banner to fly from their masthead, that ought to gain them protection.

They sailed from Leith in a vessel bound for the Low Countries, the shipmaster much impressed by having an earl, a commendator-abbot and a knight as passengers. At Berwick-upon-Tweed they had no difficulty in getting Lord Willoughby to lend them an English royal flag to proclaim their immunity from assault, he agreeing that this long-standing piracy, although traditional, ought to be put down. The trouble was that some of the offending vessels were in fact owned by English noblemen, who profited from "the trade" as it was called.

They did encounter ships, off Flamborough Head and the Wash, which they assumed might be pirates, some sailing quite close, but which, seeing the English monarchial banner prominently displayed, sheered off.

They reached the mouth of the Thames, and commenced the long sail westwards, this among great waterborne traffic such as they never saw in Scotland. This great river had a lengthy estuary.

They sailed by Shoeburyness and Southend, Tilbury and Woolwich, and came to London at last, over fifty miles on. They docked near the Tower's dominant mass, where they enquired whether it was known if the queen was presently at Whitehall Palace or up-river further, at Windsor. They were informed that she had not been to Windsor for long, being now too frail for the upset of being carried down to a carriage, transported to the riverside, transferred to a boat, then ferried up Thames, and all the disembarking thereafter. This sounded as though Elizabeth Tudor was indeed in a poor state.

At Whitehall they announced their identity and mission, and were conducted by handsome corridors and hallways to a magnificent chamber, where they were told to wait. An official presently arrived, enquired their business, and said that he would inform Sir Robert Cecil.

They had a long wait, but were served with wine.

Eventually the Secretary of State did arrive. He greeted them with cautious affability, a shrewd-eyed man of middle years, richly clad. He, of course, could be speaking with the representatives of his future monarch. He asked after King James politely, but his manner was guarded.

Johnnie Mar explained that they had come to gain for their liege-lord the assurance that he, and he alone, was to succeed to the English throne. And that, as such, in due course, he would be accorded the fullest co-operation and aid from the court and government in London.

Cecil smoothed his chin and small pointed beard. "Is it not somewhat early to be seeking such pronouncement?" he asked. "Her Majesty Elizabeth is presently less than well, yes. But she is entirely capable, and in control of herself and her realm. Talk of succession is, shall we say, premature?"

"His Grace is concerned for Her Majesty's health and wellbeing," Johnnie declared. "But this of eventual succession is important, and should be addressed without delay. If your queen was to die suddenly, King James would presumably have to make many arrangements, changes in his affairs in Scotland, before he could come south. Better that he knows of the position in advance. The Scottish parliament must be informed also, since *our* government is the King-in-Parliament, and any change in the royal position affects it."

"No doubt. But, may I say, Her Majesty is none so ill that she may not live for years. Surely haste is scarcely called for?"

Abbot Bruce spoke. "Monarchies, Sir Robert, needs must plan their concerns and futures well in advance, as you undoubtedly know. Our King James has had to do so over *his* successor, the young Prince Henry, Duke of Rothesay, or mayhap of Prince Charles. We all could die suddenly. Surely your Queen Elizabeth, unwed, childless and elderly as she is, should do the same?"

"Perhaps . . ."

"We would wish to see the queen," Johnnie said. "King James sent us so to do."

"Her Majesty may not be in a state to grant you audience. Nor wish to. Not . . . at present."

"We can wait."

"Mmm. I will go seek Her Highness's wishes in the matter."

Eyeing each other, the trio waited.

It was some time before Cecil returned. "Her Majesty is resting. But she graciously says that she will see you, as representing her good brother the King of Scotland. But only for a brief audience, you understand. She grieves over the death of the Earl of Essex."

"Did she not order his execution?" Johnnie wondered.

"That was necessary. He rebelled. But she had a kindness for him."

They were led upstairs and by highly decorated passage-ways to a great chamber, its door guarded by two scarlet-clad Yeomen of the Guard, these bowing to the Secretary of State and opening the door. He went within, but waved to the visitors to remain outside. The door closed behind him.

More waiting.

At length Cecil returned, and ushered them into the presence.

A huge canopied bed held the queen, two ladies-in-waiting standing near.

The Scots bowed.

"His Majesty of Scotland's emissaries, Highness," Cecil announced. "The Earl of Mar. And . . . others."

Elizabeth was sitting up, propped by pillows, even in bed much bejewelled, her somewhat scanty and tinted hair decked with pearls. She had a long thin face and a pointed chin, her sixty-eight years very evident, but her eyes were keen, searching and far from smiling. She raised a ringed finger and pointed at them, a curious gesture.

They bowed again.

"What brings you?" she asked, her voice authoritative however shaky. "Not more gold sought? As so often!"

"No, Majesty," Johnnie answered. "His Grace the King of Scots sends us with warm greetings and good wishes for Your

Highness's health and wellbeing. And with a small gift." He produced from a pocket a brooch of diamonds and rubies, which had come from Geordie Heriot, and which he handed to Cecil to pass on to the queen.

She took it, eyed it expertly, holding it up close to her face, which seemed to indicate failing vision, nodded, and placed it on the bedcover beside her. She offered no thanks.

"I am Mar," Johnnie went on. "And here is Sir David Murray, Cup Bearer and Master of the Horse to His Grace. And the Abbot of Kinross, Master Edward Bruce."

"A Papist?" That was sharp.

"No, Highness. A commendator. A mitred abbot of our Protestant Church."

"And your errand?"

"His Grace seeks Your Highness's assurance that *he* is the rightful, recognised and accepted heir to the English throne, as, apart from the Lady Arabella Stewart, who offers no claim to it, the only other legitimate descendant of Queen Mary Tudor, wife of our King James the Fourth, from that marriage. This assurance he seeks is very necessary for the ultimate succession of his sons the Princes Henry and Charles, this as against possible claims being made by the descendants of the Plantagenets, whom Your Majesty's ancestor defeated in the Wars of the Roses, and are still enduring." This threat had been concocted by James as bound to be on Elizabeth's mind as she lay sick. There were still Plantagenets among the English nobility.

That certainly had the queen tightening her already tight mouth. She glanced at Cecil. The descendants of Henry the Sixth, deposed a century ago, were still very much in evidence, and inimical to the incoming Tudors.

"They shall not succeed!" she jerked.

"His Grace agrees. So, there is no other claimant than himself?"

"Is he not being over-expectant? Somewhat previous, for James Stewart!"

"Your Highness knows well how it is with the orderly destination of a crown. That there be no wrongful inroads. As you followed your sister, Queen Mary, and she her, and your, father, King Henry. Now His Grace seeks the same assurance." Diplomatically Johnnie Mar added, "However distant the prospect, Majesty."

Silence.

"We shall inform the king that Your Majesty does not contemplate seeing another than he on the English throne?" Abbot Edward summed it up.

"I find this talk of my presumed death distasteful!" Elizabeth declared, and waved that hand, with one of the many rings actually embedded in the flesh from continued wearing.

They took that as dismissal, as clearly did the Secretary of State. All backed out.

Had it been a purely negative interview, not worth coming all this way for? Not entirely, perhaps. For Cecil, as he led them off, observed that James's annual pension was to be somewhat augmented if and when he forbade all traffic with Spain, financially and otherwise.

The king had told them, to test out the reaction of the authorities while they were in London to the Scots monarch's eventual arrival, in the hope that all should be favourable and welcoming, seeing the Lord Mayor and the Masters of the Guilds, the Lieutenant of the Tower, senior members of the English parliament and the citizenry in general. So this they sought to do. They found no great enthusiasm but no real animosity either. Elizabeth still was most clearly popular, and her state of health much worrying her people; but the attitude seemed to be that King James would be as good a successor as any, and certainly no competition was to be sought.

They saw no more of the queen, but spent an interesting few days in London and nearby, and were adequately entertained, Cecil seeing to this. And when they felt that it was time to leave for home, the said political figure demonstrated his astute recognition of facts in a notably dramatic fashion, this no doubt to ensure his continued prominence under the new dispensation in due course. He handed over to them no less than £10,000, allegedly his own money, to be presented to James "to help defray the costs of his and his court's journey south" – an extraordinary gesture. There could be no doubt that he intended to remain Secretary of State and the leading figure in James's new administration. Presumably it was a sufficiently wealth-producing office.

He arranged for a ship to take the visitors back to Scotland.

27

James, needless to say, was delighted to receive Cecil's £10,000. And it transpired that the far-seeing Secretary of State had already taken his own precautions to ensure his continued mastery of the English political scene by sending an emissary to the Scottish court, the Lord Henry Howard, this to warn James of what he called a dangerous opposition faction, which he asserted had other plans for Elizabeth's successor, this under the Earl of Northumberland, Sir Walter Raleigh and the Lord Cobham, pro-Catholics, with a plot to support the Lady Arabella Stewart. She had recently turned Papist and become a Jesuit, and was reportedly going to marry the Cardinal Farnese, who presumably would give up his cardinalship. He was a descendant of the Plantagenet John of Gaunt; and so they could claim succession to the English throne jointly on Elizabeth Tudor's death.

James was much concerned over this. He decided to send his cousin, Ludovick, Duke of Lennox, to London to be his personal representative at Elizabeth's court, and to co-operate with Cecil, keeping him informed of all developments.

Meanwhile he was determined that no bickering among his nobility should seem to damage his reputation as a strong monarch and his ability to rule two nations. The worry over religious strife particularly concerned him. He decided to demonstrate this notably. He told his friends that he would have Argyll's daughter marry Huntly's son, and thus unite the two leading families of the Presbyterian and Catholic faiths, for the realm's benefit. When David wondered how this could possibly be arranged, he was told to wait and see.

The two earls were summoned to the presence, and informed of the royal will. If they agreed, it would be to the great advantage of both of them. If not, then they would be in considerable disfavour, and lose such offices as were in the royal grant.

As the pair, who had fought each other at the Battle of Glenlivet, eyed each other, the king went on.

"You, Huntly, could be the first marquis in Scotland. How say you to that?" Marquis was an English title, these ranking above earls and below dukes.

The Gordon blinked, and looked impressed.

"And you, Argyll, could be the second!"

The Campbell frowned, and shook his head. "I would remain earl, Sire," he said. "I want no English style. Earls were the lesser kings of this ancient kingdom, the *ri*, who elected the Ard Righ, the High King. I am content with that." And he looked haughtily at Huntly.

"As you will. What if I make you lieutenant-general of my realm? And give you the county of Kintyre?" The great Kintyre peninsula, seventy miles of it, adjoining Lorn, the southern portion of Argyll but a separate entity, had ever been coveted by the Campbells, a former MacDougall inheritance.

Argyll drew a deep breath. "So be it, Your Grace."

"Very well. You both agree to this marriage? The young Master of Huntly to the Lady Anne Campbell, a very worthy match. See to it, my lords."

Thus James Stewart saw himself as playing father to his people, that Yuletide of 1602.

The word sent by Lennox from London was of Elizabeth's continued deterioration of health. She spent most of her time in bed, but therefrom still sought to rule the land, her councillors having to meet in her bedchamber. She had contracted a severe cold to add to her sickly state, and her physicians declared that it was caused by the draughts of old Whitehall Palace, and that she would be wise to move to the palace of Sheen, at Richmond, eight miles down-Thames, where the air would be kinder to her health than the smoky city. This she had done, to the inconvenience of her courtiers and advisers. Lennox himself had had to go there.

James did not pray for Elizabeth's recovery. Still she did not name him as her successor.

He did, presently, obtain a letter from her, however, which he showed to David and Johnnie, written in so wavering a hand as to be almost indecipherable. It commenced "My Very Good Brother" and dwelt on the duties of a sovereign, odd to be sending to the writer of the *Basilicon Doron*, warning him against the intrigues and blandishments of Spain, and adding that she had been informed of his favour being shown to the Catholic Huntly, and making him Scotland's first marquis; indication that she was still well versed in Scotland's affairs. She bade him be done with all such. And she ended by signing herself "With Sure Affection from your Loving and Friendly Sister".

Admittedly this was not any assurance of his succession, but he took it as a hopeful sign.

David and Lisa, like many another, frequently discussed this preoccupation of their liege-lord with gaining the English throne. Why? Was not his own Scotland good enough for him? They were none so eager for such to happen, for they neither of them wished to go and live in London and become part of the court there, Johnnie Mar equally disinclined. Could James force them to do so, by royal command? They would be much happier dwelling peacefully at Dunsinane.

Lennox's next report was that Elizabeth was definitely sinking fast. She was unable to sleep, would take no nourishment, refused the medicaments her physicians prescribed. She sighed incessantly. Yet she clung to life, and had Archbishop Whitgift of Canterbury and the Bishop of London permanently at Richmond praying for her immortal soul. Had she become all but an imbecile as well as an invalid?

It was now March 1603.

On the 27th night of that month, as David and Lisa learned later from Johnnie Mar, for they were at Dunsinane, an exhausted horseman on a still more exhausted horse, which actually collapsed and died in the yard of Holyroodhouse, arrived in the early hours of the morning, the man demanding to see the king. The night-duty guards objected; but the newcomer, announcing that he was Sir Robert Carey, son of the Lord Hunsdon, Queen Elizabeth's cousin, come from Richmond Palace after three days and two nights in the saddle. He must see King James immediately. Informed that the monarch was abed and asleep, he said that he must be wakened, and forthwith, so important was the news for him.

Doubtfully, Carey had been conducted to the royal quarters, where he was handed over to the Master of Gray, that day's lord-in-waiting, who roused Johnnie and together they escorted the Englishman, staggering with weariness, to the king's bedchamber. James, wakened, sat up in bed and gabbled. Draping a blanket round his shoulders, blinking at the intruders, nothing would do but that he must remove his night cap and don a tall hat at the bedside, looking quite ridiculous; he always insisted on keeping his head covered of a night, this for fear of bat-droppings, he said, as had been a problem in his childhood at Stirling Castle.

"Hech, hech, what's this?" he demanded. "It's no' . . . ? It's no' . . . ?"

"Sir Robert Carey, from Richmond, with tidings for Your Grace," Gray declared.

"Eh? Carey? Wha's he? And I'm asleep!"

The courier, unsteady as he was, sank down on his knees at the bedside and reached to clutch the alarmed monarch's hand. "Sire!" he cried. "Sire! Twice! Thrice the king. Humbly I acclaim and greet you. Hail to the king! King James of England! Of Scotland. Of France. Of Ireland. God save the King!" That was almost as much of a gabble as had been the monarch's.

"Guidsakes!" James got out, jaw sagging, dribbles running.

Gray demanded, "This is certain, sir?"

"You have a writing?" Johnnie asked.

Carey, delving into a pocket of his wet doublet, drew out not a letter but a ring, diamond-studded. This he held out to James.

The king took it in a trembling hand. "This I ken!" he asserted. "Aye, fine I do. It was my mother's ring. I sent it to Elizabeth, one time. My mother, Mary Queen of Scots. She slew her, Elizabeth did. I sent it to mind her o' the slaying. Aye. Hoo cam ye by this, man?"

Still kneeling, Carey launched forth. "My sister, the Lady Scrope. A lady of the bedchamber. When Her Majesty's last breath was drawn, she drew the ring from the royal finger. We had known that she was dying for hours. She had me waiting outside, below, all that night. It was a compact between us that I might have this proud task of bringing it to Your Majesty. She threw it to me from a window. I have ridden, night and day!"

There was a long bubbling sigh from the monarch. "Aye, weel, so she's awa'? At last! She's awa'! God be praised for a' His Mercies!"

The master dropped on one knee beside Carey, and took James's shaking hand and kissed it. "Your most royal Majesty's humble, devoted and right joyful servant!" he declared.

Johnnie Mar patted the royal shoulder, wordless.

"May Her Majesty rest in peace perpetual," Gray, rising, added piously.

"Ooh, aye. To be sure. Indeed aye. Our beloved sister and cousin!" James found the words to say, "When, man? When was this?"

"The night of Wednesday, Your Majesty. No, it was Thursday morning. At three of the clock."

"Thursday? And this is but Saturday night!" Gray exclaimed. "Four hundred miles! In three days and two nights!"

"I killed four horses. Or five. I have not stopped. Save once, when I fell. I must have slept awhile, where I lay, then. Near to Alnwick, it was. In Northumberland."

"Expeditious!" the king commended sagely. "Maist expeditious. Aye, and proper."

"I . . . my sister and I esteemed that Your Majesty should know. Be informed at the earliest moment. I sought the honour to be Your Majesty's first subject to greet you. First *English* subject, Sire."

"A worthy ambition, man. Carey, is it? I'ph'mm. Meretricious. You'll no' suffer for it, we'll see to that."

"I thank you, Sire."

"Sir Robert – the succession?" the Master of Gray demanded. "The queen's death, yes. But was aught said as to the succession to her throne? If not, we must work on it, and fast!"

"Waesucks, aye!" James's voice quavered again. "What o' that, man? Was it decided?"

"Yes, Sire. The royal decision is assured. The queen decided it, in the end. Before she sank. Earlier in the night. I was there, then, with other kin in the bedchamber. They questioned her – the secretary, the archbishop, the Lord Admiral – to name her due successor. She said, 'My seat has been the seat of kings. And none but a king must succeed me.' The last understandable words she spoke."

A great sigh of relief from James. "Aye. Maist fitting. And due."

"Is that all?" Mar asked. "No more specific word? She spoke no actual name?"

"After she said it, they put the names to her. The King of Spain? The King of France? She made no move. But when they said the King of Scots, she heaved herself up, and shaking, held her hands clasped above her head. In the manner of a crown. Then she fell back. She did not speak again."

James nodded, beaming now. "Explicit, full explicit," he declared. "The auld woman had some glisks, some glimmerings o' sense to her, after a'! Aye, though she was a fell time in showing it! So, a's by-with. England's mine! England's mine! D'ye hear? I'm rich, Johnnie – rich!"

Gray turned to Carey. "What of Cecil? And the council? What of a proclamation?"

"Cecil said to the archbishop that the succession of King James would be put to the council just so soon as it could be called. In the morning. The proclamation issued thereafter. The same morning."

James beat on his bed. "So I've been King o' England for twa days, nae less! And didna ken it! Guidsakes, you wouldna think it possible! It's a right notable thought. I could indite a poem on it – aye, a poem. An ode. I'll dae that. Here's an occasion for notable rhyming."

Carey stared.

Gray bowed. "Yes, Your Grace. But, at this hour?"

"To be sure. What has the hour to dae wi' the divine creation? Paper, man. And hae the bells to ring. The kirk bells. In a' the city. To be rung until I command that they cease. Aye, and hae bonfires lit."

The master spoke again. "Majesty, might I suggest slight delay? Until the English council's word arrives. Sir Robert's tidings are joyful and welcome. But they are those of only a private subject, however excellent a one. It would be seemly, would it not, to await the proper messengers of your Privy Council in England? And to inform your Scots council before the public rejoicings?"

The monarch's face fell. Then he shrugged. "Aye, maybe," he conceded shortly.

"Do you wish Her Grace to be informed, Sire? Queen Anne?"

"Annie? Na, na, nae hurry for that. She'll but haver ower it. Soon enough for her the morn."

"Very well."

Johnnie asked if he should call a meeting of the council for that day.

"Aye, dae that. And see to Carey, here. Sir Robert. We'll hae to reward him. I'll mak him a bit lord. Noo, paper! Paper and pens, man . . ."

28

Great was the stir and excitement, and not only for James. The entire nation was affected, agog. The Auld Enemy was conquered! Scotland's king become King of England. The notion of a united kingdom had not begun to occur to most. It was the thought of no more war and bickering with England. And *they* had won! King Jamie would see to that!

James was all eagerness to be gone. But a council meeting had to be held first; no need to wait the forty days' notice for a parliament. There were fine royal clothes to be ordered – no arrival in London looking poverty-stricken. And Geordie Heriot would get paid out of the *English* treasury.

This preoccupation applied in some measure to the entire court, for almost all were expected to accompany the monarch, at least for the initial enthronement, David included, of course. Anne could come on later, with the royal children, which meant that Lisa would have to wait with her, and go by carriage rather than on horseback.

It took a week for all to be prepared, and it was 5th April when the great day dawned, and the company of over one thousand assembled in the royal park of Holyrood to ride the fifty-seven miles to Berwick-upon-Tweed. James was clad in an extraordinary yardage of velvet and cloth of gold, ribbons, jewelled chains and decorations, not to mention ostrich plumes. If he did not outshine all his entourage, it was not for lack of ornaments. He rode between Sir Charles Percy, brother of the Earl of Northumberland, and Sir Thomas Seymour, son of the Earl of Worcester, the

English envoys who had brought north the official news of Elizabeth's death and the call to her throne from the English Privy Council, three days after Carey's spectacular dash. That man himself, promised a peerage, rode just behind, with Johnnie and David and the Master of Gray, and more English nobles. The Duke of Lennox, who should have been at his monarch's and cousin's side, was being left behind to act viceroy of Scotland.

The king, although he rode like a sack of grain, was good on a horse and could cover great distances. Nevertheless, a thousand men must travel at the speed of the slowest, and some of the clerics present were scarcely speedy horsemen. These would not be able to keep up, and get the length of Berwick in one day. So the king and a small group pushed on ahead for Berwick Castle, leaving the rest to halt for the night at Coldinghame Priory.

They would all quite enjoy being the guests of Lord Willoughby, the governor of that castle and of Berwick town, he who had hitherto been the symbol of English hostility. Now he would have to be all respect and deference towards the new monarch. Outriders had been sent on ahead to warn him.

The royal party, reaching Tweed, proceeded on down to the town first. Berwick was in a peculiar position politically. It had originally been one of Scotland's foremost ports, at the mouth of its great river. But it had been taken over by English invasion, and was now claimed to be part of Northumberland. Yet it gave name to the Scottish county of Berwickshire, otherwise called the Merse, or March. Most Berwickers still looked upon themselves as Scots – apart from the large numbers of Flemish and Baltic traders who based themselves therein. And still the bulk of the goods exported and imported there were from or to Scots destinations.

So James was concerned to show, not exactly that it was

back in Scotland but that it paid allegiance to the Scots monarchy again. He had the mayor and magistrates and guild-masters arrayed before him, declared that their leader should now speak of himself as provost, not mayor, and otherwise lectured them on their new position.

Then it was back up to the castle, which rose on a high point north of the town. There Lord Willoughby was left in no doubt as to his situation and fealty. That man was suitably dutiful. He had prepared a banquet to welcome his new liege-lord. It was a long time since a King of Scots had sat in Berwick Castle, much less been lauded and bowed before therein. The six Wardens of the Marches, Scots and English, were there to tender their respects to the king; and to wonder whether, in fact, their offices and styles were any longer to be maintained and necessary, now that the borderline was more or less redundant. James assured them that they were still to keep their titles, for although there would now be a united kingdom, yet Scotland and England would remain separate distinct nations. He was still King of Scots as well as King of England.

It was mid-forenoon next day before the bulk of the Scots contingent arrived at Berwick from Coldinghame, and the historic move across Tweed and into England could be made, an occasion to be marked and remarked on indeed. There had been cheering folk in towns and villages thus far. It remained to be seen whether the like would greet the king hereafter.

James had ordered a cannonade of blank shot to thunder out from Willoughby's artillery to mark the crossing, and to its din he proudly led the way on to the timbers. And, ever easily alarmed, he became aware of the effect of all these horse hooves on the lengthy wooden structure, for the river-mouth was fully a quarter-mile wide, and the timbers, patched and mended after floods and storms, shook somewhat.

He cried out that it was a shoogly brig. It would have to

be improved and strengthened, if not altogether replaced: the first charge on his English treasury!

He and the other leaders were nearing the southern end of it when a single horseman came cantering out to meet them from the community of Spittal, this referring to the former monkish hospice there, a young man handsomely and fashionably clad. He reined up before James, jumped down, and knelt before the king's horse, holding out a large iron key.

"Your most gracious Majesty, serene exemplar of learning, humanity and piety, the heart's desire of all true Englishmen!" he exclaimed. "I am John Peyton, son to the Lieutenant of the Tower of London, and the most humble of all your servants. Here is the key to that dread Tower, Majesty, England's citadel, which I have ridden post-haste to present to you ere you set foot on England's devoted soil."

Such magniloquent and flowery language had David, among others, somewhat embarrassed. But not the king. Dismounting, he took the key, and even patted the kneeling young man's head. Then, on impulse, he turned to Johnnie Mar, demanding his sword, and grasping it with his usual clumsiness where cold steel was concerned, especially with that large key in his hand, he brought it down heavily on the kneeling man's shoulder.

"Arise, good Sir, Sir John . . . John . . . eh, what's the laddie's name?" he demanded, peering round.

"Peyton, Sire – Peyton," Somerset said.

"Aye, weel – arise, Sir John Peyton. Johnnie, here tak this key, man. It's ower heavy. Come, Sir Percy. Come, Somerset man. Aye, and you Johnnie and Davie. See me across this unchancy brig. It's gey rickmatick by the looks o' it. I dinna like the feel o' it."

"It is quite safe, Sire, I assure you," Percy asserted. "I have crossed it many times. Heavy cannon cross it."

"Aye, maybe. But you go ahead, just the same. It shauchles . . ."

It was perhaps inevitable, possibly essential, that so long a bridge should sway somewhat, constructed of wood, and with a bend in it two-thirds of the way across to counter the swift currents of the tidal river. Still afoot and clutching Sir Charles Percy's arm with one hand and the parapet rail with the other, the monarch left David to lead the two horses and, almost on tiptoe, stumbled on, lips moving in what was probably prayer.

Thus James Stewart entered his long-desired inheritance. Reaching solid ground, he sank to his velvet-clad knees and symbolically kissed the soil of his new kingdom – to the astonishment of his followers, none of whom knew whether to emulate him, or otherwise suitably mark the occasion.

Everyone stared, and eyed their neighbours.

The Earl of Northumberland and the Prince-Bishop of Durham, there to welcome the monarch, looked doubtful, and after a whispered consultation decided to get down on their own knees beside James, who, eyes shut, seemed to be thanking his Maker and damning Satan in the same breath. When he opened his eyes and found the two others kneeling beside him, he tut-tutted his displeasure, but used their shoulders to help himself up to his feet.

They rose, and were launching into an address of greeting when he cut them short, and instead denounced them for expecting their new prince to risk his life in coming to them across that death trap of a bridge.

"It's no' right and proper, I tell you!" he declared, wagging a finger at them. "I . . . we are much displeasured. Yon's a disgrace. We might a' hae been submerged in the cruel waters; aye, submerged. It wobbles, sirs, it quakes. It'll nae dae, I say. It is our command – aye, our first royal command on our English ground, that you build a new brig. A guid stout brig o' stane, see you. That'll no' wobble. Forthwith. See to it. Our treasury in London will pay for it."

"It shall be done, Majesty. A start shall be made at once," the bishop said. "And now, Sire, here is my lord of Northumberland. He craves permission to present an address of welcome."

A very flowery speech followed, James becoming impatient. Before it was finished, he turned to eye those behind him.

"Here's whaur we hae the severance, aye, severance," he announced, interrupting the earl. "Some come wi' me to London-town. But maist o' you return hame. You'll ken which." Then he pointed. "Aye, you, Maister o' Gray, here's whaur we part. Mysel' and you, Maister o' the Wardrobe. You, back. Aye, back."

Gray stared. "I . . . I do not understand, Your Grace," he got out.

"D'you no', Maister Patrick? Is it no' simple? *I* go on. You go back whence you came."

"Your Grace means that you wish me to return to Edinburgh meantime? To complete some business there? Before coming on to London?"

"My Grace doesna' mean any such thing! We left a' things weel arranged in Edinburgh, you'll mind."

"Then, Sire, I repeat, I do not understand you."

"It's no' like you, man, to be sae dull in the uptak! Maist times you're quick enough! Aye, ower quick, by far! What's come ower you, man?"

"I think, Sire, that I must ask that of your royal self!"

"Oho, testy, eh? Vaunty! To me, the king! Aweel, Patrick, I must needs discover you the matter. Now, as guid a time as any. You are a rogue, Maister o' Gray. I've aye kenned you were a rogue, but betimes I needed a rogue to berogue the lesser rogues around me! I had them in plenties! Ooh, aye, Scotland's a great place for rogues! But I leave the like

here, see you. And if they hae rogues in London-town –
waesucks, I'll find one o' their ain breed to berogue them.
Sae I'll no' need the likes o' you, Patrick, Maister o' Gray.
You understand me?"

There was silence from all around, and drawn breaths.

Patrick Gray, the handsomest man in Europe and the so-
called Machiavelli of Scottish politics, who had been influential in ensuring the succession as frequent envoy to Elizabeth's
court, said nothing. He looked the monarch in the eye. Then
he bowed low, but with a thin smile and an elaborate flourish
of sheerest mockery, and turned his back on the king.

"My horse," he called out. "And quickly. I mislike the stink
of this place!"

"Maister o' Gray," James cried, his voice quavering with
anger. "I've no' finished wi' you yet. Wait you. You're
deprived o' your offices, man. You're nae mair a Privy Councillor. Nor are you Maister o' my Wardrobe. Nor yet a Lord o'
Session. Nor Sheriff o' Forfar. And, and . . . d'you hear?"

But Patrick Gray was not waiting. He strode over to his
horse, mounted, and jerked the beast's head round towards
the bridge, and dug in his spurs.

The king plucked at his lower lip. Then his frown faded,
and he actually chuckled. "*Alea jacta est!*" he said, and dug
the Bishop of Durham in the ribs with his elbow. "Or, mair
properly, *jacta est alea*? Is that no' apt, man? Apt. Hech,
aye. Caesar crosses the Rubicon, and I cross Tweed. *Aut,
Caesar aut nullus!*" He glanced round to discover how many
recognised his learning and wit. Disappointed in what he saw,
he sniffed. "Aye, weel, come. To horse. Johnnie. Davie. And
you Englishmen. To horse wi' us."

Mounting, some two hundred followed the monarch into
England, the greater number turning back after the Master
of Gray.

*   *   *

David, for one, was glad to be moving, having had enough of cross-talk and formalities. James was surrounded by English notables, so Johnnie and he found themselves riding a little way behind, with George Heriot, who had been commanded to accompany the monarch to London. That man was dryly amused. He showed them a note of hand signed by the new Sir John Peyton, for £1,000 sterling. This, it seemed, was the price that James was charging for making him a knight. And according to Heriot, he was going to charge others the like, many others.

"He is *selling* knighthoods?" Mar exclaimed. "This is shameful. Knighthood is an honorable estate. Chivalric. A token of royal esteem. Not to be bought for money."

"His Grace thinks otherwise, my lord. I have learned, and informed him, that the English treasury is empty, indeed in debt. During Queen Elizabeth's long sickness, and her government lacking her efficient guidance, taxation, import duties, feudal dues and the like had been neglected and used to fill private purses. His Grace is direly disappointed. He has been awaiting his accession to riches. Now he finds his coffers no fuller. So he says that he will have to make the English pay. And this of knighthood at £1,000 each is something that he, and he only, can do. Can you blame him? He has his own great debts to make up."

"And to *you*, my friend!" David observed.

"To me, yes. And no doubt to others."

"How much?" Johnnie asked. "A large sum?"

"His Grace owes me £60,000 Scots. And his queen, £75,000."

"Whe-e-ew! I see why he sells what he can."

As they rode down through Northumberland, it was not long before they saw the royal money-making at work. Squires and landed gentry came to pay their respects to their new monarch as he passed through or near their properties, and, to their surprise, were promptly knighted, and thereafter, as promptly, referred back to George Heriot to pay their £1,000, to still greater surprise, the latter building up a collection of notes of hand, which he knew well how to turn into cash. And by their first halt for the night in England, at Fenwick Tower, the king was £28,000 the richer, and in sterling, not pounds Scots.

Johnnie noted the fine land they were passing and the large herds of fat cattle, and observed that this terrain looked well capable of paying the price James was charging. The king conceded to his friends, that night, that if he could get £1,000 for each knighthood, what might be raised by creating lords, peerages as the English called them?

The journey southwards took a month and a day, no haste now, so great were the celebrations on the way, so eager the English magnates and clerics to demonstrate their loyalty and welcome to their new monarch. Pageants, revels, masques, gift presentations, even hunting-parties laid on, so that some days no actual progress was made, and on few were more than a dozen miles covered. James and his Scots supporters were made ever more aware of the wealth of the English nobility; and the king not infrequently wondered how it could be that the London treasury was reputedly empty, and he vowed that it would not be allowed to remain that way for long.

David appreciated it all, with almost wonderment, but wished often that it would not take quite so long, for he greatly missed Lisa's company, and, however impressed, was counting the days until he could get back to her and their own fulfilling life at Dunsinane. He would remain in London for just as short a stay as was allowed.

The Prince-Bishop of Durham, Doctor Tobie Mathew, gave them perhaps the most princely hospitality, with one hundred gentlemen in special liveries; and at the same time discussed theology and scholarship with James, to such effect that he was promised a London town-house, so that such talk might continue, and indeed be recommended to become the next Archbishop of York, the present incumbent being an old man and failing. Even the landlord of an inn at Doncaster was given the lease of a royal manor as reward for a single night's entertainment. At Hitchin the flourish was highly unusual but effective, with no fewer than seventy teams of ploughmen and horses drawn up to demonstrate the value of the good use of land.

At length they reached the outskirts of the City of London, and there were met by Cecil, the Secretary of State, Privy Councillors and the Lord Mayor, the last with no fewer than five hundred mounted citizens. Vast crowds thronged the streets, with long tables set in the squares and market-places laden with wines and provender, minstrels played their instruments, acrobats performed, guild banners were flown, and triumphal arches had to be negotiated. It was almost as though the boasted glorious days of Elizabeth were forgotten.

David wondered why the arrival of Scotland's odd monarch should be so especially celebrated. Was it all not rather strange? James himself, however, seemed to take it all as his due.

The visitors learned just how vital this London was to the English polity, infinitely more than was Edinburgh to the Scots. It seemed that there were no fewer than seventy-five thousand citizens dwelling within the walling behind the gates, Aldgate, Bishopgate, Cripplegate, Ludgate, Newgate and the rest; and another one hundred and fifty thousand outside these. There were no fewer than thirty-two boroughs in all, with their own local councils, the Lord Mayor and his magistrates being merely the pinnacle of the extended municipality.

James, of course, was particularly interested in the royal palaces, there apparently being many. They were led to the Tower of London first, it the major representative of them all, and the most ancient. Here the lieutenant thereof welcomed them, he the father of the recently knighted Sir John Peyton. James was shown the Royal Mint, which much pleased him, the arsenal, the menagerie and much else, before their overloaded stomachs were further burdened.

It seemed that the new king was expected to spend his first nights in the capital in this rather grim stronghold, before moving to more comfortable premises in Whitehall, St James's Palace or Hampton Court. But it transpired that there was insufficient accommodation there for all his ever-growing entourage, and David and Johnnie found themselves transferred to Whitehall.

And there they more or less roosted. James, they gathered, was being conducted by his new councillors and advisers in an endless succession of tours of inspection, events and introductions, and their participation not required, or at least not sought.

Four days of this, and David decided that His new Majesty was no longer concerned with his own whereabouts. He could surely go home. Johnnie Mar felt that he must remain on call meantime, whatever the king's present preoccupations; but saw no reason why David should remain there in the circumstances. If James did need him back, he would no doubt summon him. Whether he ought to seek leave of absence was a moot point; but there did not appear to be any real need for his presence.

He said farewell to Johnnie, and commenced the long ride back to Scotland.

29

When, at Dunfermline Castle – which Queen Anne was now preferring to Linlithgow Palace as her Scots residence – Lisa learned that her husband more or less saw his duties as Cup Bearer and Master of the Horse to the King of Scots as no longer relevant, and was looking forward to a quieter life at Dunsinane as Baron of Collace and of Auchtermuchty, she applauded. She hoped that the queen might release her from some of *her* duties as lady-in-waiting; after all, she had five others, and now the English Countess of Bedford and the Ladies Hartington and Kildare. She was indeed allowed to call herself the Extra Lady, but apparently her services were to be still required. But at least she was permitted to absent herself meantime, and the couple were able to head off for their home. Bliss!

There were tasks for David at Dunsinane, of course, particularly those related to his barony of Auchtermuchty, Collace demanding little baronial jurisdiction. But the royal burgh did; and one of its difficult problems for him ever was that it lay so near to the Lomond Hills, which were part of the royal hunting-forest of Falkland, and he the keeper thereof. Deer-poaching from the town still went on. A little of it could be winked at, but . . .

Then there was the matter of squabblings over the bleach-fields, these in theory part of the town's common land and grazings, but necessary also for the linen millers, who were the principal employers of the burgh. These were always in competition and dispute over their use, the baron court having to make judgments. The malt kilns and the distillery were apt to be at cross-purposes also, their interests clashing. David sometimes wished that he had never been given this barony.

It was however Lisa's responsibilities that mainly interrupted the couple's hoped-for quiet summer, this despite her now being an Extra Lady. It seemed that in the queen's estimation extra stood for extended services. Anne decided that it was time that she rejoined her husband in London; and although she did not require Lisa to accompany her there, she had various tasks for her in the run-up to the journey, this mainly in connection with her children, now three in number since the birth of her daughter. She was still resentful over the guardianship by Johnnie Mar over young Prince Henry, now aged nine, and being well aware of David's friendship with that earl, besought Lisa's aid in getting the boy back into her own care. Mar was still in London, and a royal command to David to fetch the prince from Stirling Castle could not be ignored. Also little Charles was delicate and the queen felt that he could not be taken on the long ride to London; so he was to be left there at Dunfermline. Moreover the Princess Elizabeth had fallen sick, and was in the care of Lady Fyvie, another of the ladies-in-waiting. Lisa was to oversee all this.

And not only that, for the ever-extravagant queen chose to mark her departure by distributing to the ladies she was leaving behind – as distinct from her new English attendants – much of her clothing and jewellery, such as they might choose, this also a responsibility thrust upon Lisa.

On the last day of May, Anne drove, with Prince Henry, in her fine new coach drawn by six horses, accompanied by her Scots and English ladies in other coaches or on horseback, to Edinburgh, David ordered to go with them. She commanded that the citizenry lined the streets to greet her and the heir to the throne, the cannon of Edinburgh Castle to welcome them with continuous bombardment, even sending £90 of Geordie

Heriot's money to pay for eight stones weight of gunpowder for the occasion. Anne was like that.

At St Giles Cathedral – it was no longer being called the High Kirk, on royal orders – she was met by the Duke of Lennox, in his capacity as viceroy, who was to accompany her to London. Much was made of the occasion, although the cannon-fire from the nearby citadel drowned out much of the speeches, including the provost's and magistrates' farewells.

This proved to be a little premature, for the queen then went on down to Holyroodhouse, where there was a scene, with the little Princess Elizabeth, unwell, dissolving into tears and beating small fists on Anne's person when she learned that she was going to be parted from her beloved governess, the Lady Livingstone, of whom she was much more fond than of her mother.

They all had to linger there until the physicians declared that the child was fit to travel, although certainly not on horseback. Prince Henry was impatient, for his mother had presented him with a fine new French horse, and provided him with two pages of honour. He was eager to be off.

David and Lisa were required only to stay with the queen as far as Berwick-upon-Tweed, they were thankful to learn. Then, it was hoped, they would both be free from their court obligations.

They got on well with young Henry, who was anxious to try out his new horse, and doubtful as to these pages of honour. He asked the Murrays to take him round this mighty hill of Arthur's Seat to see the two lochs he had been told about, one low-lying, at the far side, the other high up on a sort of terrace. This they were happy enough to do while they waited, although they could not find a hawk for him to fly, this for ducks over the lochs, as the boy wanted.

So they explored Duddingston and Dunsappie Lochs, recognised that these were excellent locations for hawking, and agreed with the prince that there ought to be a falconry at Holyroodhouse.

In a couple of days little Elizabeth was considered to be well enough to set off for London with her mother and brother. So the royal cavalcade, of hundreds, could move. Lady Livingstone agreed to go with Elizabeth as far as Berwick.

As ever, a halt would have to be made for the night, not at Coldinghame this time, as over-far for the children, but at Dunbar Castle where in the adjoining town there would be ample accommodation for all.

At the Tweed next day, the Earls of Sussex and Lincoln were awaiting them, with Lord Willoughby, sent north by James to act escort. So Lisa and David were able to bid the queen God-speed, with her children, and to promise frequently to visit little Charles at Dunfermline. They could now turn back, with Lady Livingstone, although to more tears from Elizabeth.

Was this an end to their monarchial responsibilities?

In all this of association with the royal children, which they enjoyed, they did not fail to grieve over their own apparent inability to produce offspring, a constant source of disappointment. Which of them was to blame? It was not for lack of trying!

They rode home by way of Dunfermline, crossing Forth at Queen Margaret's Ferry, and were able to see Prince Henry's little brother, Charles, a great-eyed grave child, who was looked after by Lilias, Lady Fyvie, a daughter of the Lord Drummond married to the Seton lord, another of the ladies-in-waiting, her husband being presently with the king in London, like so many of the Scots nobles.

The little boy was now three years old. He had been so

weakly at birth that he was baptised the same day, as none thought that he would live. But he had survived, and James was so pleased that he gave the midwife £26 Scots.

Did this indicate that James was interested in children? He never appeared to be so, any more than he seemed so in women, a strange son himself for the quite amorous Mary Queen of Scots. Yet he had produced three progeny, four others having died in infancy. So he was seemingly more potent than his late Cup Bearer.

Back at Dunsinane they learned from a message sent by Johnnie Mar that there had been a dire and treasonable plot to oust James and place Arabella Stewart on the throne, she now married to William Seymour, son of Lord Beauchamp. Actually there had been two plots, being referred to as the Bye Plot and the Main Plot, one the precursor of the other. Cecil blamed them mainly on Lord Cobham, his own arch-enemy, with Lord George Brooke and Sir Walter Raleigh involved. The plotters had been waiting for the king to set out for a day's hunting at Theobalds, booted and spurred. But Cecil had got wind of it and had Raleigh arrested, and the second part of the conspiracy, the elevation of Arabella, could not go ahead. Raleigh and Cobham had been sent to the Tower. It was not believed that Arabella herself was behind it, her name and background merely being used by the Catholic faction, with Spanish support. Johnnie declared that it was being suspected that Cecil himself had largely manufactured it all as a means of ridding himself of his enemies whom he implicated, eight of them, and to consolidate his position as the most powerful figure in the southern kingdom. This had rather been substantiated by Raleigh being released shortly thereafter, for that successful admiral had been Cecil's friend and associate for long, sharing in the wealth gained from the attacks on Spanish vessels bringing gold from the new world across the Atlantic, he known to have helped

Raleigh in the amassing of a fleet. It was all very murky and involved.

Poor Arabella, now aged twenty-eight, was being used as a pawn in the games of others, she a quiet and modest woman with no least ambition to be other.

Johnnie sent other and more personal news. He had been appointed to the English Privy Council, so that he and Lennox were the only members of both such bodies. And he had been created a Knight of the Garter, the supreme order of English knighthood, and given the manor of Charlton in Kent to support it. Another honour for him was to be Bailie and Admiral of the Firth of Forth, something that David had never heard of. He did not know just what this represented, but James had discovered that it was a position of some profit established by James the Second. So he was to share its revenues with the monarch, who was ever on the look-out for such sources of money. He, Mar, was too much involved in affairs in the south these days – James was largely making him responsible for foreign affairs – but David was to enquire into and act in his name in this matter, which might well have considerable advantages. He could call himself bailie and admiral depute, and could deduct some proportion of the financial gains therefrom, say a quarter, the remainder to be divided between James and himself, Mar.

Here, then, was something that David could usefully and profitably do, and this none so far from his own doorstep, the Forth being little more than an hour's ride away.

He was going to require a ship for his new duties, no great vessel but no mere fishing-boat either. He would make that a charge on such revenues as were to be gained.

What were those revenues likely to amount to? Who could inform him on this? Leith was the greatest port on the firth, with its own provost, magistrates and trade guilds. He would make a visit there.

He did, and judging that in this capacity he could lodge at Holyroodhouse, Lisa could accompany him.

He learned much, even though the senior citizens of Leith tended to look on this new bailie and admiral depute with some suspicion and wariness at first. What did he demand of them?

This was what David himself wanted to know, for no one had told him what his duties and privileges were. The ports and havens along both sides of Forth would produce import and export dues from trading-vessels, which in theory went to the national treasury. There was the licensing of pilots, for which it seemed Leith had the monopoly for all the southern shores of the firth. There proved to be something of which David had never heard termed "prime gilt", the legal right to levy moneys for poor and invalid sailors. There were the rents for shipbuilding and repairing yards, and for rope-making and sailcloth mills, and cask and barrel yards for the export of whisky and ale, also glass-making works, all sources of revenue. But from the proceeds had to be deducted, apparently, the ever-recurring costs of deepening and protecting the tidal harbour along the banks of the Water of Leith.

Much calculation of expenses to set against income were going to be necessary here.

David asked about the possibilities of hiring or buying a smallish ship for his own use. Doubts were expressed about this, but the harbour-master said that there was still a chance that one or two of the collection of English pirate vessels captured by the late Sir Andrew Wood might be available at Dysart, in Fife, where he had deposited them. Most of the fair-sized craft had undoubtedly gone by now, but smaller ones were less useful, and one or two might remain. Here was something to be considered.

David was quite impressed with Leith altogether, a community that he had never had occasion to consider. It tended to be dominated by Edinburgh, some two miles off, for which it was of course the port; but it proved to have its own character and assets, a fine town hall, and many quite handsome houses, including the one that Mary de Guise, when regent of Scotland for her daughter Queen Mary, had chosen to live in rather than at Holyrood, for some reason. It had its wide links, or common parkland, much favoured for the playing of golf – David had heard that King James had played here, a game he himself had never tried. And he learned that he would have to be careful of his use of the term admiral depute, for the provost here also claimed the title of Admiral of Leith.

There were other lesser ports on the south side of Forth: Musselburgh, very proud of its independence from Leith although no great distance off, Cockenzie and North Berwick on the east – Dunbar could scarcely be styled as on the firth – and Queen Margaret's ferry-port and Boroughstoneness, Airth and Grangemouth on the west. He would inspect all these before he visited those on the Fife shoreline.

He had a busy time of it, but very interesting, Lisa joining him on some of his trips. They found Boroughstoneness, or Bo'ness as its locals called it, very much to their taste, it being the port for Linlithgow, the Scots queens' dower-house palace, and therefore apt to be much used by foreign vessels bringing goods from the Continent, wines in especial, fine cloths, perfumes and other female requirements. North Berwick, dominated by the Bass Rock and its conical tall hill, was the most picturesque. Altogether the consideration of it all was rewarding. David decided that his new duties of admiral depute were to his taste.

When it came to visiting the Fife shore it all proved remarkably different, considering that this was only an average of eight to ten miles across from the southern one, with the islands of Inchmickery, Inchcolm and Inchkeith in between. Especially the eastern part of it was quite distinctive, all very scenic little fishing-havens, with their smokehouses and salteries, with the larger communities of Leven, Dysart, Kirkcaldy, Burntisland and Aberdour further west, and Inverkeithing, the port for royal Dunfermline. And, of course, renowned Culross, where so much of Scotland's story had been enacted.

At Dysart David found what he was looking for. Of the English ships deposited here by Sir Andrew Wood only two remained, these left probably because they were small, not what traders and merchants wanted, two-masted, high-pooped craft, this last feature suitable for carrying a couple of horses, important for his purposes. He chose the larger of the two, named the *Raven*, not over-English-sounding. He went to the harbour-master to discover from whom it might be bought. This that worthy did not know. These captured ships had lain moored here for long, before *he* had come to Dysart, and he would be glad to see them gone. He suggested asking the provost. He, a saddler in the main street, had no idea either. So far as he was aware they had merely been left here by Wood of Largo all those years ago, and presumably had belonged to *him*. He had left no heirs in these parts. There they lay, nobody's property. David said that, in that case, they were probably crown property, and as such he would take them over and have them overhauled.

So now he had two ships instead of one. He would have the *Raven* taken up to Culross, handiest for Dunsinane, and leave the other at Dysart meantime. He would have to find a crew for his vessel: four or five men ought to be enough. Culross surely could provide such. He was unsure as to what his duties as admiral depute would amount to. This of being in the royal service did lead him into strange paths.

Lisa said that she would enjoy the occasional sail in the

Raven, and further off than just in the Forth estuary. David would have to invent excuses for longer and interesting voyages. Perhaps he could have Johnnie Mar gain for him some other position, in name at least, which would permit him sailing far and wide around Scotland, even on occasion down to London? No point in being an admiral and not making full use of its benefits.

He declared that of all the offices he had had thrust upon him, this of admiral depute was the oddest.

However, it had its interests as well as its responsibilities. He discovered that he was now very much involved in the royal burgh of Culross. He had not realised how busy a port this was, assuming that Leith, Dysart and Boroughstoneness were the important ones. But collecting a crew for his *Raven* there, he had been astonished to see no fewer than forty vessels lying off; there was room for only six or seven at a time at the quayside. And he was told that as many as one hundred and fifty sea-going merchanters could cast anchor offshore on occasion, this because of the great trade of the town and its environs.

This was mainly in coal, in which it seemed the area was rich. The mines had been developed by the monks of the Cistercian abbey here, which at the Reformation had been gained by the Bruce family, and now was making of Sir George Bruce a very rich man. David took due note, for the crown's dues. These mines apparently stretched far out from the shore, under the waters of the Forth estuary. There was iron-stone to be quarried also, in plenty; and this, smashed up by the hammermen, as they were called, and heated on great fires so that the iron melted out, was thereafter beaten into pots and tools and nails and the like, especially the round and handled girdles for which Culross was famous. These hammermen constituted the second-largest force of workers in the burgh after the coal-miners. All this, and the trade guilds that resulted, fell to be considered by the admiral depute.

Lisa especially was interested to learn that Dunimarle Castle, just to the east, had been where it was alleged Queen Gruach, MacBeth's wife, had been murdered.

Culross was evidently going to feature quite largely in David's life, he basing his *Raven* there, even though it was quite often moored at Perth on the Tay, closer to Dunsinane.

Lisa wondered whether there was anyone busier than her husband in all Scotland. At least she could, and did, share frequently in his many activities, this to his satisfaction.

30

That next year the news from London was grievous. The plague, being termed the Black Death, was raging there, and folk were dying by the hundreds, the thousands. Johnnie wrote that James was terrified, declaring that it was the rats of the London streets and sewers that were causing it, their fleas carrying the infection. He was moving the court from palace to palace every week or ten days, convinced that the drains harboured the rats, and that was as long as it was safe to remain in any one establishment. So it was from Whitehall to Hampton Court, from St James's to Nonsuch, from Greenwich to Windsor, in constant upheaval and alarm. Meanwhile the common folk perished. How Johnnie wished that he was back in Scotland. He was urging James to return, even if only temporarily. Surely he would recognise that the cleaner air of his native land's hills and coasts would keep such epidemics away, so different from London's crowded, windless streets and alleys. But the king was loth to leave his richer realm for the poorer.

One of David's many responsibilities was to call frequently at Dunfermline Palace to keep an eye on young Prince Charles, still there, in the care of Lady Fyvie, who had now become a countess, her husband in London having been favoured and become Earl of Dunfermline. The boy was now four years old, shy, silent and reserved, and with a slight stammer, still delicate but, the countess said, with a streak of obstinacy in him. She wondered when his father would send for him to be taken south, and she then could rejoin her husband?

He was having a fine new house built for them at Pinkie, beside Musselburgh, east of Edinburgh, so he must be finding working with the monarch profitable. David took note of this, for Musselburgh was one of the lesser Forth ports under his jurisdiction.

Those first busy six months of his new activities resulted in a major increase in revenues for the crown – if scarcely in his popularity with many of the payers – and he was able to transmit to London a statement to that effect, and to ask what was to be the destination of these moneys, presently being deposited in the care of the Scots Privy Council, and amounting to many thousands of pounds. The answer that came back was one of praise and gratitude from the monarch, and instructions for the said so useful funds to be sent south forthwith, as David had rather anticipated would be their ultimate destination. But the royal esteem over it all was emphasised in practical and all but dramatic fashion – this allegedly to give the admiral depute still greater authority for his admirable labours. He was, as from 7th April, 1605, invested with the barony of Ruthven and the lands of Scone, the crowning-place of the Scots monarchy, and created Lord Scone.

Here was not only a feather in his bonnet indeed but a notable advance in his powers and credit, which ought greatly to aid in the carrying out of his various duties. So henceforth Lisa became Lady Scone, instead of merely Lady Murray. More satisfying for both of them, however, was that it equalised the friendly rivalry between the cousins, for Sir John Murray of Tullibardine had been created lord thereof, for some undefined reason, the previous April. And Scone, of course, was the more renowned name and style, with all its royal associations and its links with the famed Stone of Destiny.

With the word of this advance in status came news of

interesting developments in national affairs. Something being called the Articles of Union had been drawn up, making quite sweeping changes in the relationships of the two realms. First of all, any laws that could be construed as inimical towards one or the other of the nations were to be cancelled, for instance the *Leges Marchiarum*, the notorious and elaborate special Borders provisions of the Debateable Land, this and the wardens' courts. A total of ten English and fourteen Scots edicts were to be abrogated. Free trade was to be established, imports and exports to carry the same duties on either side. Offices of the crown were to be available to subjects of both nations. Persons born after 1603 were to have all rights of nationality in either, and to be able to possess and inherit property without distinction. And to emphasise and celebrate this happy state of affairs, a suitable national flag or banner was to be created, conjoining the different crosses of St Andrew and St George, this to be named the Union Jack. And a new coinage, relative to both kingdoms, minted, to be called a Unity, a gold piece worth twenty shillings sterling, having the crowned thistle on the one side and the crowned rose on the other. The only issue that apparently had aroused some controversy in the English parliament was the provision that fishing restrictions were to remain as before, to prevent English boats netting in the better salmon-waters of the Tweed and northwards. On the other hand, no Scots linen and leather goods were to be allowed to pass into England.

To emphasise the efficacy of all this, a child born in Edinburgh in 1603 was taken to London, where ten out of the twelve Exchequer judges ruled that his nationality was a joint one.

Some of these edicts had a distinct effect on David's activities, especially that of the import and export duties, for much calculation had to go on in the ports of both nations to distinguish United Kingdom and foreign traffic. But at least now as Lord Scone he found his authority enhanced.

A pleasant surprise in the spring was a visit, not any permanent return to Scotland, from Johnnie Mar. He came to make a delayed inspection of his many properties. He brought the documentary confirmation of David's peerage, as lordships were now being termed after the English fashion. He said that efforts to get James to come with him remained unsuccessful. But he brought a royal reminder that David could now sit in the House of Lords under the new Articles of Union. The new peer had no desire so to do, with a sufficiency of duties nearer at hand.

Johnnie, as full Admiral of the Forth, was interested to learn of all the tasks and responsibilities of the office that he had delegated to his friend, and sympathised over the problems created by the said articles. He himself had no wish to take on any of these, he assured. In fact, he offered to seek James's permission to demit this office of admiral and have David take on the full office and style, since he had all the burdens and tasks of it. But this proposal was promptly rejected. Indeed, it would be preferable to be relieved of the deputyship altogether, despite the emoluments that went with it. Johnnie demurred.

David took his friend to Culross, which Mar had never visited; and for a sail in the *Raven*, Lisa with them. The earl now proposed that, if David would accept the promotion, then *she*, a practical and effective woman if ever there was one, could make a worthy depute, now that her duties as a lady-in-waiting were done with. She laughingly rejected anything such, saying that she had sufficient involvements in her husband's problems, in this as in other matters, without making it official. But she did enjoy the sailings.

Johnnie had many estates in the north – after all, the earldom of Mar was his – so he gladly accepted the offer to be taken up to Aberdeenshire in the *Raven*. They could hire horses at the various havens on the Dee, the Don, the Ythan, the Cruden and the two Ugies, and save much climbing over mountain passes with the winter snows not yet melted.

So they made something of a holiday of the inspection of farms and mills and common lands, as well as laird's houses and manors. David was able to enjoy seeing someone else acting the lord and presiding over barony courts, ever prepared to learn.

They much enjoyed and admired Kildrummy Castle, the main Mar seat, up near the head of Don, on the verge of the Highlands, an ancient stronghold dating from the early thirteenth century, and one of the largest in all Scotland. It consisted of a great courtyard within high curtain walls, with lofty round towers at the angles and a free-standing hallhouse block and separate chapel within. The fortalice had been built by Gilbert de Moravia, Bishop of Caithness, and the said chapel was larger than most parish churches, handsome with magnificent lancet windows, and a strange subterranean passage reached therefrom leading out beneath the castle walls to one of the flanking stream ravines – the reason for this a matter of conjecture. Kildrummy had inevitably seen much of warfare and strife, one dramatic happening among many – for the Earls of Mar had been a stormy lot – being the siege by Edward, Hammer of the Scots, when the Bruce's brother Nigel was captured therein.

The earldom covered many areas of Aberdeenshire, one of the largest counties of the land; but also of Forfarshire to the south. Strathdee and Strathdon and the Garioch were Johnnie's, by themselves a rich inheritance. But his lands went far to the north and east, to border the Gordon territories of Strathbogie and Huntly. And in the opposite direction, south to Brechin and Navar and Lethnot and parts of Forfar itself. So the little party had a quite lengthy and highly interesting survey before Johnnie declared that he had no time for more, and that London and the monarch's affairs beckoned. They returned to their ship.

Before David and Lisa parted from their friend, Mar advised them to go and do their own survey of their newly acquired lordship of Scone. David had been there, of course, on many an occasion, but, it having been Ruthven property, had never examined it in detail. Now, clearly, he ought to do so.

He explained to Lisa the ancient significance of the area, long before it became the coronation-seat, even before Christianity came to Alba. For here, in the very centre of what was now Scotland, the fresh waters of the Tay, that great river, overcame the salt water of the firth; and the ancients looked upon this as the symbol of fertility, where bounteous land triumphed over hungry sea, this why nearby Perth was so important in the nation's story.

Crossing the Derders Ford, where the Roman invaders had constructed a causeway, they went to examine the abbey, deserted now, derilict. Lisa said, since this was now *their* property apparently, they ought to do something about it. Could they not use the abbot's house as a residence, an alternative to Dunsinane? The abbots of Scone had cut a wide swathe in the past, always assisting in the crowning of the realm's monarchs. Had not one of them, knowing of Edward Plantagenet's resolve to take away the precious Stone of Destiny as a trophy to London, hidden it, some said on their own Dunsinane Hill, and substituted a lump of the local sandstone, the which worthless block was still beneath the coronation chair at Westminster, having been sat upon by all the subsequent English monarchs, the MacDonalds believed to have the real Lia Fail hidden in their Hebridean isles. David was now the custodian of this hallowed spot. What could they do suitably to cherish it?

They moved over to view and climb the Moot Hill nearby,

where the actual crowning had taken place. How many Kings of Scots had sat on top of it and received the fealty of their earls and lords, this symbolised by the pocketfuls of earth brought by each from their properties for the royal foot to rest upon as they swore the oath of allegiance, as indication that all the land was the king's and they each held some part of it of his favour and so owed him their duty. Where was that ancient throne-chair now? And would ever another King of Scots ascend this hillock, now that they were to be also Kings of England?

David, created Lord Scone by the present monarch, recognised his responsibility to maintain the traditions here enshrined. At least, thanks to his admiral's duties, he now had the moneys to pay for the restoration of the abbey, and the abbot's house as a second home. The pity that they were producing no children to inherit it all.

While they were in the vicinity, they paid a visit to Stormont, the community for this area, there being no village at the abbey itself. The name was a corruption of the Gaelic *starr monadh*, meaning the crooked hill, which of the many local eminences that was being uncertain. What proved to be little more than a hamlet seemed to be known locally as Stormontfield, for the Stormont itself referred to apparently was a great spread of country including the districts of Blairgowrie, Clunie, Caputh, Lethendy, Kinloch, relating to the head of Loch Drumellie, the largest of a number of lochs in the area, even so far north as famed Dunkeld. David found himself in the extraordinary position of not knowing just how much of all this land in fact belonged to himself and the lordship of Scone; presumably all that had been originally part of the abbey's territory. He would have to discover this.

At any rate, what with this and his earlier possessions, and the revenues accruing from his Forth admiralship, he appeared to have become a rich man, thanks to King James, and Johnnie Mar's influence.

So they would get busy restoring Scone's abbot's house, to start with.

It seemed that James was not having any smooth ride in his acquired southern kingdom. For scarcely was the alarm of the plague and all its casualties over than there was another and very different sort of challenge, in the shape of a treasonable Catholic endeavour to bring down king, court and government, and replace them by the now keenly Popish Arabella Stewart and her supporters, however little she herself was involved in it all. It was being called the Gunpowder Plot, and although it had failed, it had been sufficiently dangerous. A group of extremists, headed by Sir Thomas Percy, Robert Catesby, Guy Fawkes and three others, set out to destroy the opening of a parliament, on 5th November. They managed to gain entry to a cellar beneath the House of Lords, and filled this with no fewer than thirty-six barrels of gunpowder, along with much of timber and faggots, this to be blown up as the monarch presided over the ceremonial occasion above. Fortunately, one of the conspirators, Tresham by name, warned his brother-in-law, the Lord Mounteagle, not to attend the opening, and that peer, thus alerted, discovered the details of it all, and had the man Fawkes, evidently the leader, arrested. Under torture he revealed the names of the other schemers, five of them, and they were dragged through London's streets at horses' tails, and thereafter executed. James himself examined the arrested Fawkes, and demanded whether he did not repent of so foul and heinous a treason, to be told that "dangerous diseases require desperate remedies".

Parliament thereafter, in January, was able to sit securely, and established 5th November as a public holiday, to be celebrated with bonfires and fireworks and the carrying and burning of effigies, called guys, after Fawkes's Christian name.

Whether or not this threat to himself in parliament was the cause of it, James thereafter began to consider doing away with such assemblies, declaring that he was perfectly capable of ruling his kingdom without them.

However, this attitude did not apply to Scotland at least. There parliaments continued normally. One at Perth which David attended in July 1606 emphasised Episcopacy's triumph in the northern kingdom over the Presbyterian divines, with the eight bishops and two archbishops entering with the lords and earls, clad in peerage robes. And Archbishop Spottiswood of Glasgow declared that all preachers throughout the land were to pray for Christ's Holy Catholic and Apostolic Church throughout the world, and especially for the Churches in Scotland, England and Ireland, the king being supreme governor of these his realms and all his other dominions, and over all persons in all causes, as well ecclesiastical as temporal.

Episcopalian as he was, David felt that this was going too far, as did many another present, and the resolution was left undecided and not put to the vote, the Presbyterian faction disparaging.

The next parliament, held early in 1607, was less controversial however, sufficiently so for James, hearing of it, to declare that "Here I sit and govern Scotland by my pen. I write and it is done, and by a Clerk of Council I govern Scotland now, which others could not do by the sword."

David found himself busier than ever, with this of superintending, with Lisa, the Scone abbot's house rebuilding, the oversight of the many Stormont properties, the continuing baronial duties at Auchtermuchty, and the Firth of Forth visitations. And to add to it all, there came another command from London. Henry, Prince of Wales, now in his thirteenth year, was also Duke of Rothesay, the title of the Scottish heir to the throne, and had that dukedom's taxation and the revenues of the Isle of Bute, at least in theory. These, it seemed, were not being sent south regularly and in full, and the king was concerned. David, with his ship, was in a position to go to Rothesay and see to this matter.

So here was to be a quite lengthy voyage, right round Scotland. Needless to say, Lisa saw it as an attractive journey to make. So they set sail together for new waters for the *Raven*.

It did indeed make a very scenic trip, especially once they had rounded the far northern coasts of the Pentland Firth, and sailed down through the sounds and kyles of the Western Isles, ever eye-catching, but quite demanding on David's skipper, with the tidal currents and overfalls, the down-draughts from the hills, the skerries and reefs to avoid, all making exciting voyaging. Eventually they had to enter the great Firth of Clyde and make their way up past Arran with its spectacular mountains, to the Kyles of Bute, and so reach Rothesay, eight days' sailing, for the Hebridean seas were not such as to be navigated in darkness, and they had to lie up overnight in sheltered anchorages.

Rothesay was quite a major town, with its great castle in the midst, and certainly ought to be productive of quite substantial revenues for its duke. David had his interviews with the provost and magistrates, the trade and merchant guilds masters and the important fishing community leaders. They all, to be sure, had their excuses for inadequacies of their various payments to the royal exchequer; but David, used by now to the like from all the Forth authorities, was well able to counter most of the explanations and protestations, and succeeded in extracting back-payments owing, and promises for further better accounting. Indeed he found himself loading his ship with moneys and payments in kind, salt fish and meat, hides and leather goods, casks of whisky and other goods in lieu of silver and gold. It all made a rewarding visit for the young duke's emissary, although almost certainly most of it was destined for the boy's father's coffers.

Lisa liked Rothesay, and helped, with her friendly attitudes and smiles, to smooth the way for her husband's demands.

Finally, the couple decided that, instead of sailing all the way back round the northern shores, and then eventually down to London with all the proceeds, they might as well steer *Raven* southwards from the Clyde, past the Isle of Man into the Irish Sea to the English Channel, and so eastwards to the Thames, considerably the shorter route almost certainly. This of voyaging pleased them both, even rough seas not upsetting them.

So they progressed by this alternative course, with much tacking required against a southerly breeze, but this was changed to a quite speedy passage up the Channel.

At Whitehall the pair received a warm welcome from Johnnie and his countess; also from Lennox, now spending most of his time at London. James, while admitting that their arrival was acceptable, made it clear that he thought that Rothesay could have produced greater wealth than they had brought. However, he announced that he had further tasks for David. To emphasise his command that the border should now be seen to be merely a historic line on the map, with an end to all the centuries-old mosstrooping strife and raiding, new decrees were to be enforced. No Borderers on either side, save noblemen and lairds, were to be allowed to carry weapons. David was to arrange for the most powerful chiefs, such as Home, now made an earl, Sir Andrew Kerr of Ferniehirst, now created Lord Jedburgh, Walter, now

Lord Scott of Buccleuch, Johnstone of Johnstone, and the Lord Herries, even the doubtful Armstrong of Mangerton, on the Scots side, and the heads of the Fenwicks, Scropes, Ridleys and Metcalfes on the English, to be involved. The office of Lieutenant of the Border was now cancelled, and its Hermitage Castle become merely a private house, as was Bewcastle of the Croziers, these hitherto so-called keepers of Liddesdale and Tynedale. To help in maintaining some sort of discipline among the unruly Marchmen, the new office of justice of the peace was to be introduced, and not only on the Borders. Lists of suitable candidates were to be sent south.

All but dizzy with the implications of all this, David also learned of the proposed establishment of a new category of officials in every city, town, county and district, this to improve the collection of dues and taxes for the royal treasury, these to be known as revenue procurators, James's decision, but Johnnie had called them tax-farmers. The Scots Privy Council was to appoint these. The king was determined that Scotland should produce its full share of finance to improve the situation which had for so long beggared him, as he put it. He had written a new Book of Rates to aid in this.

This preoccupation with money was nothing new for James, admittedly, but something of the sort was clearly going to be necessary, when it was pointed out that the monarch was demanding a permanent annual grant from the Exchequer of £200,000. He was starting to make his new hereditary knighthoods, or baronets, £3,400 each; debts of some of his court favourites were cancelled at a cost of £4,400; and even the celebration of the creation of the young Prince Charles as Duke of York reached £3,000. Queen Anne's extravagances continued, and she was said to be in debt to George Heriot for no less than £94,000.

All this of money, money, money sent David and Lisa sailing back home thankful that their own situation in this respect was so satisfactory and uncomplicated. They did not have expensive tastes, the *Raven* was being paid for out of the Forth revenues, and the Scone abbot's house not costing them seriously. They had decided that they would make this their winter home, Dunsinane on its heights somewhat chilly in those months.

That year of 1608 David celebrated his forty-third birthday, and in great style, for King James, delighted with all the moneys he was receiving at David's sending, appointed him to be Comptroller of the Royal Revenues of Scotland, an office which made him more or less paymaster of the northern kingdom, and so in a position to influence largely much of what went on in the land. Ludovick of Lennox might still be President of the Council, or viceroy, but he spent most of his time in London, and David in effect ran Scotland. He was still, in name, Cup Bearer and Master of the Horse, keeper of Falkland Palace and Forest, Ranger of the Lomonds, Baron of Collace, Auchtermuchty, Ruthven, Seggie and Balinbrae, Admiral Depute of the Forth, a Privy Councillor, and held the lordship of Stormont as Lord Scone. What more could be looked for? He certainly desired no more. Above all, he had Lisa, his beloved, his partner, his devoted other half. If he was not the happiest man in the realm, he ought to be.

Grace and Majesty James Stewart might be, but David Murray was more than that, a man content, the good God be praised!

EPILOGUE

David Murray lived until 1631. He retained all his positions and titles, indeed was created Viscount Stormont in 1621, indicating his continued value to King James, who died in 1625; and thereafter to Charles the First, who succeeded, his elder brother Henry, Prince of Wales, having died in 1612, aged eighteen. David's wife Lisa long outlived him, dying in 1658.

Leaving no offspring, he bequeathed his many properties, on Lisa's eventual demise, to the children of his brother Dand, who had in turn become Sir Andrew Murray of Arngask and Balvaird, and to sundry other kinsfolk. By special remainder, agreed by King Charles, his eldest nephew, son of his sister Anne, who had married the fourth son of Murray of Tullibardine, became second Viscount Stormont, Mungo of Drumcairn. From him have descended the Murrays, Earls of Mansfield, still in possession of Scone Palace.

NIGEL TRANTER

The Islesman

This is the story of Angus Og MacDonald, Lord of the Isles. The semi-independent prince of the Hebrides and much of the West Highland mainland, he was a worthy representative of a notable line, living in dramatic and exciting times for Scotland and England, for Ulster, Man and Ireland. He took his part in it all, an active supporter of Robert the Bruce, chief of chiefs. He was a man who sought peace and prosperity for his so scattered people, encouraging trade, seeking to heal the feuding propensities of the clans, allying the Isles with Orkney and Shetland and Norway; travelling as far as the Baltic. He was also a man of humble mind, and a proud husband and father.

'One of Scotland's most prolific and respected writers'
The Times

CORONET BOOKS
Hodder & Stoughton

NIGEL TRANTER

Triple Alliance

Following his victory at the Battle of Dunbar in 1650, Oliver Cromwell made Colonel James Stanfield 'governor' of Haddingtonshire. When Cromwell died and King Charles II was restored to the throne, Colonel Stanfield made the highly unusual decision to stay in Scotland. Together with two Haddingtonshire lairds – Patrick, Lord Elibank and George Hepburn of Monkrigg – he established woollen mills in Haddington. But as the enterprise grew and achieved nation-wide importance, it was to bring dramatic consequences and unforeseen developments for the trio.

'A magnificent teller of tales' *Glasgow Herald*

CORONET BOOKS
Hodder & Stoughton

NIGEL TRANTER

The Admiral

The incredible 15th century story of how Andrew Wood, a humble laird from Largoshire, rose to become Lord High Admiral of Scotland, the nation's most famous sailor and one of King James III's most valued officers-of-state. He was a daring pirate-slayer and a skilled negotiator, who greatly aided his nation's cause at a time of international unrest.

'Through his imaginative dialogue, he provides a voice for Scotland's heroes'
Scotland on Sunday

CORONET BOOKS
Hodder & Stoughton